With best wishes,

Richard

State of Emergency

State of Emergency

Richard Drysdale

Published in 2016 by Richard Drysdale

With assistance from Lumphanan Press
9 Anderson Terrace, Tarland,
Aberdeenshire, AB34 4YH
www.lumphananpress.co.uk

Cover design by Mode
www.modedesign.tv
Image Copyright Semmick Photo

Printed and bound by Imprint Digital,
Upton Pyne, Devon, UK

ISBN: 978-0-9935971-4-5

CALEDONIA

O my people, my beloved sons and daughters,
I know of your love of me
While I am a witness to your quarrels
Over my body and its future
I do not doubt that each and every one loves me
No matter the disagreement about our future together
For I shall be here still, whatever it holds –
Whichever side wins the argument
For you are a quarrelsome bunch
But my towering peaks, my deep lochs,
My fractured coastline will always be here
Until the ends of time
And one day may peace prevail amongst you,
May you each and everyone turn to the other
And look them firmly in the eye
And shake hands and embrace
For you are all my sons and daughters
And you are brothers and sisters to each other.

(Anon)

Thanks

There are many people who gave me inspiration and support as I was writing this. Thanks go especially to Jean and Nick but also Jeremy, Richard, Peter, and Martin for their comments and support. Thanks too must go to Gale, my copy-editor, for her eagle eye and helpful criticism of the original draft. It is a greatly improved book as a result of her comments. Doug's help with the graphics was utterly invaluable and to him I owe a major debt. Ian's help with the website was vital and he has my gratitude. Duncan at Lumphanan Press has been exceptional in the help and advice he has given me. His patience, humour and support have been superb - thanks.

In Scotland support and inspiration have come from Eddie, Vance, Willie and Carol, David and Helen and all those with whom I trod many a mile in good spirits and hope.

Also very much in my mind as I wrote this have been Ray and Judith.

'To those who in spite of fear, suffering, or loss,
betrayal or disappointment go on for Scotland'
– Agnes Mure MacKenzie (1940)

To Chloe, Eloise and Olive.

Prologue

Just after 10pm, on Wednesday, 15th September, Murdo received the text he was expecting: 'Red Alert'. Such a simple message and yet one with consequences that would be shattering for the UK and Scotland in particular.

The sleeper and security units would be taking up their places the breadth of the land to swoop and make their arrests of key activists and the party leadership, scheduled for 6am on the day of the referendum. Nothing was to be left to chance. Giles Sutton, the Prime Minster, was to go on nationwide television at 6am and declare the State of Emergency. Direct Rule was to be imposed on Scotland. Internment was Westminster's reluctant weapon of choice.

Chapter One

IT WAS A SHARP APRIL morning seventeen months before the crisis erupted that David Manningtree was to remember for years. The Prime Minister had summoned him to Chequers for what was billed as a working lunch. It was one of these quiet, behind the scenes talks at which he sounded out his closest advisers before moving forward on policy.

David wondered who else would be there as he drove to Chequers on a crystal clear spring day with the daffodils in bloom. It was his favourite time of year. Judith was not amused that he had been summoned to Chequers at the weekend but she had grown to expect chronic disruption of family life since he had accepted the position of DG of the service. In a curious way she was proud of him and realised that for a few years their lives together would need to take second place. The pressures were immense particularly with Islamic extremism still rampant in the Middle East. At home a worrying number of young Muslims continued to make their way to Syria.

David speculated what the summons from the PM might be about. He expected it would be related to extremism and new measures that the Government was about to put before Parliament. His relationship with the PM was a cordial one and the two men liked each other. Their educational backgrounds were similar and they understood each other with little difficulty. The PM's relationship with the Security Services was close given that the nature of the threat to the UK had been steadily growing over the last few years.

Several hours later David was back on the M25 heading home, his mind grinding through the conversation with the PM and his advisors. He had been caught completely by surprise by the main topic of discussion: Scotland. It was not even on David's list of top priorities. Yes, of course, the Scots were chuntering but that is what they did. They would be doing that until the end of time.

The meeting was well attended: Neil Simpson, the somewhat pompous Scottish Secretary, Dame Juliet Cummings the quintessential unruffled Brit, Director General of MI6, Alison Empingham the hectic Home Secretary, Walter Goldsmith, veteran number cruncher with razor sharp intellect and DG of GCHQ. Added to these was the PM's Chief of Staff, Peter Finch, a man David had always found toxic. There were times when he wondered who was pulling the strings: the PM or Finch.

David re-played the conversation with the PM and the initial pleasantries between them.

'Florence good? Family well? West Ham not doing too well this season. Coffee? Yes, Spring Conference went better than anticipated. Of course, Major's bastards will always be with us – that's the Tory Party!' he guffawed.

He then quickly moved onto more serious ground.

'As you all know, we were lucky to win the 2014 referendum in

Scotland. There is little doubt there will be another as soon as Fraser feels they can win. At the moment I have no idea of the time scale of that but it is clear that since 2014 and the aftermath of the General Election in 2015 the independence issue is far from settled for a generation. We were lucky, too, that Fraser's party didn't obtain an overall majority in the Scottish Parliament election.

'The whole point about the Holyrood electoral system was that it was designed specifically to prevent the bloody separatists from gaining control. Unbelievable isn't it? And ironically Labour thought they had the whole thing stitched up. What utter idiots! I suppose it is yet another of those unintended consequences that seem to come round with alarming regularity.

'Worryingly, too, the polls have slowly been moving in the direction of independence. I am far from certain we would win another referendum even if we put the frighteners on the Jocks again. I think those tactics could only work once and, of course, they failed horrendously in the EU referendum. That's not to say that we won't deploy them again but this time we need to promote a more positive case for the Union. The last campaign we fought was negative in the extreme. My gut feeling is that Rodric Fraser will wait until the polls are moving more firmly in favour of independence and then call another referendum. For this reason we need to re-double all our efforts in Scotland.

'Under no circumstances can we be seen to allow the break-up of the UK. We would lose international credibility and our place at the top table. You know my views on our exit from the EU. I suspect Fraser will call a referendum in about 18 months. I want as many assets as we can spare on this – even if the immediate threats we face are coming from a different direction. That includes GCHQ, Special Branch and, of course, your people David. I want the group working within MI5 on Scotland to have a higher profile with a Scottish DG appointed as soon as possible. We need to know as much as possible about Fraser and the separatists in the coming months. All this is to be done on an informal basis for the foreseeable future.

'We must not stand by and watch Scotland go independent due to the irresponsibility of its people. The issues are much too important for the Scottish voters to be left to themselves to decide,' the PM said with a firmness that surprised David.

Each in turn was then asked for their perspective and comments. There was general agreement with the PM's analysis.

Neil Simpson's views were listened to with particular interest as he had the reputation for being an astute and perceptive Scot, fully aware of the currents and eddies of politics with all their nuances. Few people were better informed than he was about Scotland. His range of contacts in all walks of Scottish life was unrivalled. The pity was that he was the only Tory MP in Scotland and his seat with only an 800 vote majority was in the Borders.

When David was asked what resources MI5 had deployed in Scotland his reply was simple and straight to the point.

'Suffice it to say Prime Minister we have highly placed assets in Rodric Fraser's Party who keep us informed. GCHQ keeps us informed too. I would say that we know more about what is going on in Fraser's Party than he does himself.' The remark provoked laughter.

'Good,' the PM purred, 'Excellent. I want a section set up devoted exclusively to Scotland to co-ordinate our efforts and keep me informed,' said the PM. He then digressed on Fraser.

'You know I have to confess to detesting Fraser and I can't say that about many politicians whether they are in my Party or in Opposition. I really struggle to know if the man is one of the most outstanding politicians in the UK – never mind Scotland – or an absolute charlatan out for his own self-aggrandisement and nothing else.'

David was not unfamiliar with the PM's occasional rant. More often than not it was directed against a group of his wayward back-benchers. The thought that a high percentage of politicians could have been described in the same way and perhaps even the PM himself made David smile.

'Doesn't the man have any peccadilloes that we could tip the wink to the *Mail* or Bruce's *Sun*? They would both love to get their teeth into Fraser. Somehow we need to destroy the man's reputation. Surely, we have something on him David?'

'I am afraid he is whiter than white by Parliamentary standards, Prime Minister. There is nothing in the closet. No colourful life.' He was tempted to add 'unlike an alarming percentage of your Party and the Opposition' but kept his mouth firmly shut.

'Neil, what's your take on all this?'

Simpson was a man puffed up by his own sense of self-importance, despite being regarded as an irrelevancy by most Scots.

'Well, Prime Minister, I honestly don't think we have anything to fear on this one. The Scots are not mad. They rejected the uncertainties that independence would bring in 2014 and I am confident that they will do the same thing again.'

David noticed that Simpson referred to the Scots as though he wasn't one of them. It amused him.

'You must remember, Prime Minister, the Scots have an amazing capacity to fight amongst themselves and snatch defeat from the jaws of victory.' Simpson couldn't help himself smiling at his own humour. He was met by blank gazes.

'We have a substantial unionist Fifth Column inside the country, Prime Minister. This is our greatest asset. They are not going to let Fraser lead the lower social orders in some sort of mis-placed *Braveheart* sense of grievance and patriotic zeal to destroy the Union. The 'No' voters have too much of an economic stake in the Union to allow that to happen.'

'God, the Scots and that chronic sense of grievance. Where on earth did it come from?' It was a difficult concept for a man who had been born into the ruling elite and had economic security.

David had been reading more than his share of contemporary Scottish History recently. He could have said Thatcher's poll tax experiment or perhaps her speech to the General Assembly of the Church of Scotland, the so-called Sermon on the Mound when she pronounced there was no such thing as society. Then again, perhaps it was the decimation of swathes of industry. But, in truth, he knew that too many Scots were born with a permanent sense of grievance and its target was Westminster and the political elite.

'I refuse to be the Prime Minister when the Union disintegrates. I am just not going to let that happen. It would seriously dent my – I mean our – prestige abroad. It would be a national humiliation. God only knows how Washington would react. Then where would we park those Trident subs? The south coast? That would cost us a few Parliamentary seats.'

The meeting ended shortly later.

The traffic on the M25 was crawling slowly as usual for late Sunday afternoon as people made their ways home. David had been at Chequers for just under three hours and was ready to enjoy what was left of the day at home.

Several ploys flitted through his mind in response to the PM's general policy thrust on Scotland. Of course, he read the press thoroughly each day and had a general sense of what was going on in Scotland but there were too many other higher priorities for him to feel that he was in command of this particular brief. That would need to be rectified in the coming days.

The following week David called in Roger Bourne, the director of HR, and Tom Gunn, the Deputy DG. The usual pleasantries were quickly dispensed with.

'I was summoned to Chequers last weekend by the PM who wants us to keep a closer eye on events North of the border. He is concerned that it is only a matter of time before there's another referendum and the outcome is less assured as support for independence seems to be growing after the EU negotiations debacle. Basically, he wants better intelligence from the inside of the Party. I told him we have several useful assets but none at the highest level – yet. We aren't sure of the timescale, perhaps as little as eighteen months.

'Now I know our friends in Cheltenham have Rodric Fraser's every move as well as his contacts and phonecalls monitored but we need more than this, much more. We need to try and insert one of our own people into Fraser's inner team. I'll tell you exactly what I have in mind: Fraser's constituency is North East Fife. St. Andrews University is in that constituency. This may be a long shot but it is one I believe that it might be worth trying. If we second one of our own people, obviously a Scot, to do a post-grad degree who then joins the Party and makes himself indispensable to Fraser we could get what we want: access to that inner circle and his thought processes. Electronic surveillance docs have its limitations as I keep telling Walter at GCHQ,' David couldn't resist a small laugh.

'I think we should run this past Sir John at the Met. Technically, this is his jurisdiction with the National Police Intelligence Unit and Special Branch' Gunn said.

David sighed. Of course Gunn was right.

'Frankly, I am not sure how much confidence I have in the National Public Order Intelligence Unit or the Met come to that. They seem endlessly firefighting scandals and paying out vast sums of taxpayers money in compensation. I would very much rather we kept this operation in house but I suppose I should see John and at least discuss it with him.'

'Is this viable, Tom, and do we have anyone who fits the job description?'

After some discussion they were in agreement that the proposal had merit and was worth trying.

'Ideally we need someone fairly new but who already has a proven track record and, of course, the necessary background which means that he has to be a reliable Scot. The last thing we want is someone who goes native,'

'Could you please send up the HR files of any possible contenders in the next day or two?' David asked.

'I think I can safely say we are only talking about two or three people. The files will be with you tomorrow morning.'

'Good. We will need to meet Friday at some point to discuss this further once I have had a chance to read the files. I shall meet Evans as soon as possible to discuss the issue with him.'

David and Sir John Evans met five days later.

The two men had a good working relationship despite Evans' blunt no-nonsense Yorkshireman approach. The Home Office had not found Evans easy to deal with for that reason. Speaking one's mind bluntly tended to ruffle feathers and bruise egos. It had taken a while for David to get used to this approach. Was Evans really a tough cop, or a parody of one?

Lunch at David's club had softened Evans' attitude and relaxed his guard to the DG. There were times when he wondered if the tough cop approach was a reflection of social insecurity. Evans had come up through the ranks the hard way.

David was only too glad not to have to deal with the seeming endless avalanche of scandals that ate away at the integrity of the Met. On one occasion when he offered his sympathies about yet another scandal being splashed over the front-pages in full lurid detail, Evans smiled sourly.

'Yes. It is worse than I ever thought when I accepted the job. At least your people are hidden in the wings and untouchable.'

'On the face of it we should insert one of your people into the

Party. We want someone who has an academic bent and a Scottish background.'

'We don't have too many of those in the unit,' Evans responded.

'Not even north of the border?'

'No. Very few in fact. To be honest, David, I think it would be better if one of your people undertook this one. We are too thinly stretched on the ground and the demands on the unit at the moment are higher than they have ever been. It's not exactly a top priority is it?'

David smiled to himself. Evans had given him what he wanted without any argument. He was renowned for guarding his turf with a fearsome ferocity. His spats with the Home Secretary were legendary.

'The PM seems to think it's important.'

'A bit unusual for a politician to be thinking longer term, isn't it?' Evans asked with a wry smile.

'Yes, it is. That surprised me too.'

'Does he have an estate up there or something?' Evans asked mischievously with a glint in his eye.

In fact the PM's father-in-law had an estate in Ross and Cromarty but David chose not to respond.

Chapter Two

THE FOLLOWING DAY ANOTHER MEETING was held with Tom Bourne and Roger Gunn. After the initial chit-chat David got swiftly to the point. He was not renowned for his small talk.

'So who do we have who could fit the bill?'

'One person seems to stand out for this assignment: Murdo MacGregor.'

Roger agreed. 'Yes, he was the person who stood out on paper. I have made some gentle soundings and his department head rates him highly. His work on radicalisation of young Moslems in Yorkshire was outstanding. He is probably ready for another assignment.

'Father was in the FCO. Murdo was privately educated in Edinburgh when his father was on his various postings, predominantly in the Middle East. Went to Oxford and then joined us.'

'What you might call an Anglo-Scot. The Master of his College gave him an especially glowing reference. Unusual for a Master to write a reference.'

'Private life? Skeletons in the cupboard?'

'Engaged to the daughter of a City scion.'

'It all looks and sounds good – exactly the sort of person for the assignment, if he'll accept it. He may not welcome being sent to a far-flung part of the Empire,' David joked.

'His fiancee may not like that.'

'Yes, one for him to resolve, but he is ambitious. Wants to get to the top and all that.'

'Any indications of his political leanings?'

'Not that we know. I would say apolitical in the Party sense but probably right of centre. He wasn't involved in politics at university. More a games playing type.'

'He will need to start to re-cast himself as left of centre to fit in with Rodric's Party.'

A few days later Murdo was summoned to Sir David's office. He went with a sense of nervous trepidation realising only too well that someone at his level in the Service was rarely summoned by God. He began to wonder if he had made some massive error of judgment.

It was with a feeling of relief therefore when he was greeted by a relaxed and smiling Sir David who quickly put him at his ease with a sympathetic remark about the Scottish team's latest lamentable performance at Twickenham.

'How long is it since you lived in Scotland?' Sir David asked.

Murdo was unsure whether this was more casual chat or whether it was heading in a professional direction.

'Not since schooldays, Sir. My parents rent a holiday house in Crail, near St Andrews and we go up there once a year for a couple of weeks. My dad is a fanatical golfer.'

'Nice part of the world that, the East Neuk of Fife. And how well would you say you are acquainted with political developments in Scotland?'

Murdo began to see the direction of the conversation.

'I don't follow Scottish politics that closely. They seem parochial. Obviously I was well aware of the 2014 referendum campaign and the General Election result in Scotland the following year. I know that the Tory Party is not the first party of choice for about 78 per cent of the population.'

Sir David smiled. He liked Murdo's assurance and his wry humour.

'And where do you stand in all this if I may ask?'

'That is easy, Sir David, I am a unionist through and through. It would be a disaster if Scotland was to become independent. I am not even sure that devolution was a good idea. It created a climate of expectation that was surely a step towards independence.'

'Quite so, quite so. There are times when frankly voters don't know what is best for them but that is democracy,' said Sir David with a hint of weariness and vivid memories of the EU referendum which had stunned him and Whitehall.

'Let me get to the point. We need to insert someone into the highest level of the Party to keep us informed of their thought processes. You probably appreciate that there will be another referendum within the next eighteen months. We do obviously have other methods of knowing what is going on in the Party but we want someone to get as close to Rodric Fraser as possible.

'I am proposing that you go to St Andrews for a PhD, join the local Party and make yourself indispensable to Fraser in North East Fife. This will obviously take time – we are playing the long game here but the stakes, as you will appreciate are very high. This is about the survival of the Union nothing less, so you can see how important it is to us.

'You will need a few days to think this one over. I hope you will accept. You can see the importance of what is being asked of you. You are the right person for the job'

'I do appreciate that, Sir David. Give me twenty four hours to think through the implications. I am engaged and my fiancee works in public relations.'

'Yes, we know, Emma,' said Sir David with a smile.

Of course, he would have known that, thought Murdo.

'Good. That sounds promising. If you accept we'll have you starting at St Andrews next academic year. That will give you a couple of weeks to get your personal affairs sorted out. By the way, wasn't your father one of the so-called Camel Corps of retired ambassadors who wrote to the *Times* arguing that the intervention in Iraq would be a mistake?'

'Yes, yes, he was.'

'A man of sound judgment your father, given all that has happened in that part of the world,' said Sir David.

Murdo's initial instinct as he left Sir David was to accept the assignment. True, academia held little appeal for him now even if he would have no difficulty in choosing a topic for a PhD, several came to mind at once. His special interest had always been International Relations in the twentieth century. The undercover role appealed to him, not least because of its significance.

Justifying such a move to Emma, on the other hand, was fraught with difficulty. She was a Londoner through and through. Her family and friends were here. She delighted in the cultural life of the city with its museums, galleries, theatre and concerts. The thought of expecting her to move to a small grey town huddled against the North Sea was a non-starter. In fact, he thought there wasn't a cat in hell's chance of her moving there. He could already imagine the conversation. What if she refused? She would never leave her PR job which she was enjoying so much. She often referred, albeit jokingly to the Northern wastelands but behind this supposedly light-hearted remark there was a truth for Emma. Murdo avoided responding to the jibe.

Emma had of course visited the holiday cottage overlooking Crail harbour – so twee, she would tell her London friends. To visit for the odd week in summer when the weather was comparatively kind was not the same as staying in that part of Scotland with keen winds barrelling down the streets of St Andrews on a *dreich* winter's day.

There was little doubt that they loved each other deeply and were close friends if all the rest of what constitutes a relationship is set aside. Somehow he would need to win her over to the idea of leaving London and going into academia. Emma did, of course, know what he did and was proud of the fact but that was all she knew. Her family and friends guessed the truth by her oblique answers and slightly knowing smile. No further questions were asked: Murdo was in the Home Office and London based and that was that.

He decided to broach the subject when they were out for an after theatre meal. *War Horse* had moved them both deeply. Murdo's choice of venue was calculated. He knew there would be less chance of Emma making a scene in public. The one side of Emma that Murdo found difficult to cope with was her ability to let her feelings be known. Murdo hated a scene and was never quite sure how to handle the firestorms that affected their relationship. He wondered what had made her like this and often in quieter moments he tried to talk to her about it.

'I am a passionate person and I hold my beliefs firmly This is how I express myself.' Murdo knew that only too well. What interested him was *why* she was like that.

He waited until she had drunk just over half of her glass of Rioja Gran Reserva.

'I had an interesting session with Sir David the other day.'

'Oh, really? Does he really see people of your lowly rank?'

'This seems to have been ... well ... special.'

'And?' Emma's curiousity was roused.

'He asked if I would like to do a PhD in St Andrews.'

'My God, Murdo, you're joking aren't you? Whatever for? Are they easing you out or what? You haven't made some ghastly cock-up have you?' Emma asked with a growing sense of alarm in her voice.

'Not at all. Let's just say it is very important work they want me to do.'

'What? A bloody PhD in some obscure field that no one will ever read?'

'That is only part of it.'

Slowly, Emma's comprehension became evident from the look on her face.

'Oh, mmm, I see. It fits. If Sir David wanted to see you it must be very important.'

'Yes, you could say that. Shall we say that it is more important than you could imagine,' Murdo said in a low voice as he leaned across the table.

'And you obviously want to take it? What about us? If you think I am moving to that god-forsaken part of the world after London you are sadly mistaken.'

This was exactly what he expected. A period of gestation would follow and then in time a more balanced view would emerge. He decided not to say anything else about it.

'You don't have to accept it, you know. You could stay here. We are meant to be fixing a date for the wedding. We can't just drift on as an engaged couple. Mum keeps asking me if we have decided on a date. In fairness to them we need a decision.'

'True, but you don't often get the chance to have a hand in history.'

Another silence fell. He could see that Emma was working out the wider implications of what he was saying.

'God, it really is that important?'

'Yes. Really. Let's talk about something else. We both have some thinking to do.'

'Sorry, I think I'm beginning to understand. I'm not sure where that leaves us though. I am not going to follow you like some good little lady to the North. You must have realised that.'

'I don't expect you to. Many people have long-distance relationships nowadays.'

Emma was unconvinced. 'What you are really saying is that this... this assignment or whatever you call it is bigger than us, than our relationship.'

'I suppose so. That doesn't mean I want it to affect our relationship. Absolutely not. Of course, we would need to work out the practicalities.'

'Yes but how long are we talking about? It's obviously not months. It's bloody years.'

'At the moment the time-frame isn't clear but it could be for at least eighteen months.'

'I don't want that. We both need to reflect on this, on where our priorities lie. It seems that you've already decided to accept and I have to fit in with your plans or... we're finished.'

Murdo stayed silent – a ploy he used with Emma. Learning when to keep his mouth shut had not come easily to him.

Gradually, Emma's anger subsided. The conversation moved to other topics but it was awkward. It was clear by the following day that the tectonic plates in their relationship had slipped. Emma did mellow slightly. She accepted at face value how important Murdo's work was going to be even if she could not know the details. She began to think of ways to accommodate their relationship in the new circumstances. She did, after all, love him.

In the days that followed their love-making took on a new-found passion – the passion of a relationship on the brink, fuelled by insecurity. It was as though each of them wanted to leave an indelible mark on the other.

Chapter Three

THE SKIES WERE HEAVY WITH low clouds and as he approached St Andrews the grey of the granite buildings seemed to match his spirits.

Emma had seen him off at King's Cross as though he was going to Ulan Bator. They had parted in good spirits, both certain that their relationship would survive the dislocation. He had promised to spend as much time back in London as was practicable and Emma promised to come North as often as circumstances permitted. Talk of the wedding was quietly dropped until they saw how they would cope with this new set of circumstances.

Murdo's doubts about what he was doing increased the further the train got from London. By the time it was speeding through Yorkshire he had an urge to get off at Newcastle and take the next train South. Doing a PhD was not something he especially wanted to undertake. He had been glad to leave behind the rigours of student life and the endless hours sitting in libraries poring through piles of books. The idea of wading through reams of turgid official documents on Anglo-Egyptian relations between 1952 and 1956 lacked appeal.

The more he thought about the long-shot of starting at ground zero in the Party and insinuating himself into Rodric Fraser's inner cabinet, the more the chance of success seemed remote. It could all be a monumental waste of time for him. The idea of being away from Millbank did not appeal. He knew that once out the door the waves closed over. He wondered how failure would impact on his career. He may have been moderately ambitious but Emma's ambitions for him were supercharged. She came, after all, from a high achieving family. Failure was not a word in their lexicon.

The first few months were difficult. Student life had little appeal even although he mixed almost exclusively with post-graduates.

Dr Daish, his supervisor, was a dusty, diffident academic who seemed wary of him. Murdo wondered how much Daish really knew about why he was there. Perhaps he was one of the Service's placemen but if he was it was never evident. A perfunctory relationship was established without much obvious enthusiasm on either side. Daish did, however, have an expertise in the Middle East and Murdo learnt much from him at their weekly meetings even if there were times when Daish fell into a silence and slipped down in his chair until he almost disappeared under his desk.

On the political side, Murdo joined the local Party organisation. There was, of course, a student group but it was small in number in a university that had been a centre of Tory activism for many years. Many of Thatcher's policies had germinated here: privatisation, student fees and the poll tax had all been nurtured in the late sixties and early seventies. The high percentage of English and American students was also evident. The existence of a large Party grouping in the University was an improbability. For that reason Murdo joined the North East Fife Party group.

Rodric Fraser, the First Minister, announced in early October as predicted that there would be a second referendum on independence in the following September. Howls of anguish went up from the unionists while the separatists realised they had to start the grim slog up the hill again. The polls turned more positive for independence with time but victory was not assured – yet.

In the eleven months before the referendum Murdo worked painstakingly for the Party. He often wished he had a pedometer to tell him how many miles he tramped round the different parts of the constituency – was it the proverbial 500 miles – delivering leaflets and canvassing. It was hard and occasionally thankless work except when a door was opened by a supporter with a smiling face and words of encouragement.

Often he was faced with a sour face and a questioning look.

'Vote for that Rodric Fraser? You must be joking! The man is a Hitler. He should be locked up for treason.' The door would then be firmly slammed in his face.

'You must never take that personally, Murdo,' his mentor said. Murdo knew that this was true but it didn't make it any easier to face.

Slowly, gradually, he won the respect of the other activists who would tease him by referring to him as a PJ, or posh jock.

'Edinburgh private school, yeah, we know all about them. Now was it HMP Saughton you were at, Murdo?' they would laugh. But his hard unstinting work won them over. After eight months he had proved his dedication to the cause and became someone whose views were sought.

There were times when he worked alongside Rodric Fraser. At first it was in a relatively insignificant way – canvassing and leafleting – but the two struck up a friendship. Murdo found Rodric easy to talk to. He had a relaxed friendly manner that won people over. This was not the monster depicted by a Press hell-bent on demonising him but rather someone of the people, with no airs and graces but a man of quick wit and sound intellect whose commitment to the country was beyond reproach even if his political enemies and a significant section of voters regarded him as a 'chancer'.

Rodric began to entrust Murdo with small tasks and with time, he was given greater responsibilities. He felt that Rodric was testing him. This period lasted many months. Gradually, Murdo succeeded in making himself indispensable to the extent that when Rodric's deputy in the constituency fell ill no one was surprised that Rodric asked Murdo to take over the position.

The more Murdo got to know and like Rodric the more he felt deeply uncomfortable with what he was doing. The inner conflict grew more intense as the months passed. He liked Rodric and regarded him as a man of integrity, regardless of his political ambition for an independent Scotland.

Murdo's handler in London was delighted by his progress into the centre of the Party – a heartbeat away from Rodric. Over time Murdo carried out his appointed task of reporting Rodric's thoughts back to London. Often when he went to visit London and see Emma he would slip into Millbank and have a debriefing session. On one occasion Sir David asked to see him.

'Ah, do come in Murdo. I just want to tell you how delighted we all are by the work you are doing and how well it seems to be going. Dare I say it has been more successful that we had hoped? The PM has asked me to thank you. I am sure that one day you will get an Honour for this and you will be assured of promotion when you come out of the cold – literally and metaphorically, so to speak,' said Sir David smiling at his own joke.

'It seems that Fraser is more straight-forward in his motivation than we thought. Not for him the baubles of wealth and honours. The hunger for glory seems to be central to his motivation. These people are always more difficult to deal with. Most politicians can be bought by honours, preferment, titles or being appointed to boards.

Those who are motivated by a cause are the dangerous ones. Somehow in this country we don't tend to understand people motivated by causes. It's just not our style for some reason I have never quite understood.

'Now don't go native will you? That is always a danger. Remain detached – that is vital,' said Sir David as Murdo moved towards the door.

Murdo left Millbank feeling both honoured but also in emotional turmoil. In truth, he was feeling more susceptible by the day. He knew it was something he had to guard against at all costs – even if it meant asking to step down from what he was doing. He had always been a person who saw things in black and white but he was now aware that there were shades of grey too.

It was while working for Rodric that Murdo met Eilidh MacLeod, widely regarded as Fraser's likely successor. She was edgy, strong-willed and independent and had risen to the senior ranks of the Party despite her young age. Her presence lit up a room with her charm and smile. Murdo was especially taken by her eyes. Despite working together she rarely engaged him in conversation that was anything but Party business. Her body-language told him to keep away.

Initially he tried to win her over with charm and humour but she remained stony and suspicious. He began to wonder if she had a sixth sense and had already worked out who he really was. He decided to back off and watch her from a distance hoping that one day he would get to know her better. He began to realise that he was attracted to her and that, he knew too well, was danger territory. As far as he could tell there was no one else in her life but then he had never been able to talk to her about personal matters. She seemed private and utterly dedicated to the cause.

Once or twice their eyes met. She looked at him quizzically and with a slight scowl. He quickly looked away unable to meet her gaze. Her very distance somehow appealed to him. Her spirited, take-no-prisoners approach to life challenged him and all that he stood for. He grew to feel increasingly uneasy in her presence. For this reason it became imperative that he could neutralise her which meant getting to know her better – not something that seemed easy in the circumstances.

Rodric had a high regard for her and Murdo could see they got on well together. She laughed easily at his humour and seemed devoted to him.

Once when Murdo was canvassing with Rodric he steered the conversation round to Eilidh who was a few streets away.

'Eilidh's help this morning in getting all this literature together was really useful,' he said hoping to open up a conversation about her.

'Aye. There are few enough like her,' was Rodric's brief response.

Murdo felt he needed to be more direct.

'What's her background?'

'Ah, Murdo, you are not the first man to ask that. She comes from Skye where her family have a farm and a fishing boat. Her mother runs a bed and breakfast to make ends meet. It's not an easy life. Her grandfather is one of the oldest Party members. She went to Glasgow and studied Economics and Scottish History and then, a bit like you, came to St Andrews to do postgrad work. That enough for you?' asked Rodric teasingly.

'Just asking,' responded Murdo lamely.

'Aye, aye,' said Rodric smiling knowingly, 'And she doesn't seem over-fond of you either,' he added.

'You noticed that?'

'You have to be perceptive in politics, Murdo, as I am sure you know. A high emotional intelligence is required. She almost seems suspicious of you,' said Rodric teasingly.

Murdo quickly changed the subject and moved to safer territory. When he re-played the conversation with Rodric in his mind it was the word 'suspicious' that bothered him. He began to wonder if Rodric suspected him too. But then if he did why did he make him one of his closest aides in the constituency? He wondered whether or not to mention this to London next time he was down for a debrief.

Eilidh. The beautiful, talented, committed Eilidh whose playful eyes never set upon him without that look of disapproval, of questioning.

Control in the final briefing warned him not to form any intimate relations on this assignment but then laughingly said, 'Of course, you are engaged anyway. You have only got to look at the massive cock-up those undercover police made by forming relationships with women in protest groups to know how dangerous that is.'

The Met had had to pay out hundreds of thousands of pounds in compensation to the victims. Control missed the irony of the term cock up in the context – something that had made Murdo smile. He was swimming deep as they said.

However, the point was well-made. Professionalism and duty were paramount – the stakes in all this were so great that nothing else mattered. Or at least that is what Murdo kept reminding himself, almost on an hourly basis.

Over the months that followed he thought he detected a softening in Eilidh's stance towards him as they worked together for the Party. Then again, he cautioned himself. He recognised only too well his ability to mis-interpret signals through wishful thinking. Anyway, Eilidh was an irrelevancy in all this. He had his instructions and he had to carry them out as thoroughly as he could. There was no room for personal relationships that went beyond the professional. Not to forget Emma back in Notting Hill.

Chapter Four

MURDO CONTINUED TO SLIP DOWN to London every few weeks for a long-weekend. Emma's visits to St Andrews were less frequent. It had been three months before she had first trekked north to visit him during his first term. The town in the gloom of gun metal late November skies with a wind out of the Arctic tearing down the streets was to colour her attitude ever-after.

'God, how do you put up with this bitter cold and all this greyness, stuck up here on a limb into the North Sea. I've never been so cold in my life and then there is darkness in the morning and late afternoon...'

Murdo was not surprised by her reaction. In fact, he had expected nothing less. There was a dourness about the place in the winter months.

'No wonder you Scots are such a depressed lot and drink so much,' said Emma warming to her theme.

'Summer is different,' replied Murdo aware of his defensiveness, 'You know how you like it when you come up in summer.'

'Not so sure,' Emma responded, 'What makes you think I'll want to come back up then?'

Murdo was unsure how to take the remark. Was it a jest or did it have a more significant meaning and intention? There were times when he was unsure which way to read Emma. He let the remark pass.

They explored empty East Neuk villages in the gloom of winter. The charm of Crail, Anstruther and Pittenweem was less obvious on a bleak winter's day. Murdo realised that inviting Emma up in the winter had been a mistake. Yet she had been keen to find out all about his new life and see where he lived and worked.

'How on earth do people live up here?' Emma asked almost in exasperation on one occasion.

Murdo laughed. 'God Emma you are so metropolitan! They live well. There is a strong sense of community even if they say – wrongly – that you need a long spoon to sup with a Fifer. You metropolitan elites descend on this part of the world in summer in your 4x4s packed to the gills with golf-clubs. You can't get enough of the place then.'

'But that is summer. This is now,' Emma countered.

'Bloody Londoner,' he joked but the remark was truer than either of them would care to admit.

During that weekend Emma had plied him with questions on his academic work and his wider life. He told her about his supervisor which made her smile but he said nothing about his growing political involvement in the Party.

'I spend most of my time in the university library and move in post-grad circles. There are a lot of international post-grad students here and they are interesting to talk to. When I need some relaxation I ride my motorbike – there are some good roads around here.'

Emma remained unconvinced about it all especially when she picked up on a certain diffidence. Murdo never could hide his deepest feeling from her, no matter how he tried.

'You always were an Anglo-Scot. You belong in London as much as I do. Yes, for some reason, I have always found you lot appealing. Different but not too different. A touch exotic – that wild Celtic passion!' she joked.

'It was the kilt that did for you at Belinda's ball,' he riposted.

'It was what you weren't wearing under it,' she replied laughingly. The magic between them was still there.

'And coming back to Scotland after those years away?'

'I suppose as an itinerant Scot my roots were never especially deep here anyway. Yet I do feel a sense of belonging.'

'Ha! Bloody Scots. Always banging on about the country but living somewhere else and never letting you forget where they come from.'

Murdo knew what she meant. He had always tried to keep his Scottishness quiet. He never mentioned it unless someone asked him about it. Even then he said as little as possible. And yet, he was proud of his birthright.

At the end of the first term Murdo went to London for Christmas with his family as usual. He realised how much he had missed the buzz and energy of the capital, both absorbing and tiring. He had always loved the city with its culture and internationalism. Fewer and fewer people seemed to be speaking English around him. It was indeed now a world city as never before.

He and Emma threw themselves into Christmas preparations with an energy that surprised them both. They survived the crowds in Fortnums as he searched for a special bottle of wine for her father while she ordered a Christmas hamper for her parents, something that always went down well. They dipped into the Royal Academy and then he demanded time in Henry Sotheran's, the specialist bookshop, to soak up its rarefied atmosphere. He chose a book for his father. From there it was a blast up Regent Street to see the Christmas lights and then off to Kensington to the Conran Shop to choose new furniture for the flat Emma's father had bought for her off Haverstock Hill. They exulted in each other's company and the excitement of pre-Christmas in London.

When they got back to her flat they made love and slept until late evening. The sheer pleasure of it all made him marvel. This was life, this was the life he wanted yet he was only too aware that it was transient.

St Andrews seemed a world away. The research seemed utterly irrelevant. Even the assignment seemed to lose its appeal. This is where he wanted to be, not in some far-flung part of the empire. He began to wonder again if he had made a mistake in accepting the assignment. His desk job in London lacked the front-line immediacy but the other compensations of life here more than made up for it. The prospect of returning north in early January looked less and less appealing as the days passed. He knew his withdrawal symptoms would be acute once he returned north on that long, slow railway journey.

On Christmas morning they had brunch with his parents in Wimbledon. His father seemed to be ageing more quickly than he had imagined while his mother tore round the house with all the intent of a hostess at Christmas. His father was aware of his work and had guessed with a reasonable degree of accuracy why he had been sent to Scotland, although he did not discuss the matter with Murdo.

'Interesting times up North,' was all he said giving Murdo a knowing look.

'Yes, dad, as you say interesting.' The matter was closed although Murdo did wonder what his father's perspective was. On the face of it he was a dyed in the wool unionist. You can't be at the heart of the British establishment and be anything else, Murdo thought. The fact that he didn't volunteer an opinion made Murdo wonder exactly what his father's thinking was on Scottish independence. Perhaps age and retirement had softened his previously staunchly held views. Age and perspective together with an emotional return to roots in the latter stages of life often change outlook. Murdo decided not to pursue the topic. The fact that his father wanted to go and live in Scotland said something even if his mother was adamant he would go alone if that was his choice.

Murdo had always had a great respect for his father's knowledge of politics and international affairs. A career in the Foreign and Commonwealth Office ultimately as an ambassador in two capitals had assured him of that.

His mother was more concerned with his everyday life in St Andrews.

'A beautiful town with so much character and history,' she said to Emma who was helping her get brunch prepared. The two got on well. Emma chatted easily with Murdo's mother who had taken Emma to her heart.

'Did Murdo tell you I went to boarding school there?' she asked Emma. Of course, Emma knew already and had decided to say nothing about her visit there in November.

'We shall come up and see you next summer, dear. Dad will bring his clubs. He has been a member of that blessed Royal and Ancient for years now but hardly ever gets there. Of course, as a woman I can join now,' Kathleen said with a laugh and then added, 'Not that I would want to join that fusty club!'

They exchanged gifts, ate a hearty brunch, caught up on family news and then took their farewells to go to Emma's family in Hampstead which Murdo knew would be a rather less relaxed affair. Emma's siblings, partners and children would all be there. Chaos would ensue, noise levels would soar and then after the traditional Christmas dinner, the games that Murdo knew he would dread.

For him it was a matter of survival, forced jollity and some good wines.

Emma's mother, Connie, always made a fuss of Murdo. Will, her father, was more circumspect but seemed to like Murdo in a somewhat grudging way. Murdo rationalised it as a father and daughter thing. The 'no man is good enough for my daughter' syndrome. Emma worshipped Will even although she was only too ready to deflate his pretensions with an ironic humour that he could not help but appreciate.

Their two families could not have been more different. Murdo's parents were part of that great tradition of British public service, honours, and quaint club life while Emma's family had made their money in the City and represented all the new-found wealth generated by Thatcher's 'Big Bang' with its de-regulation. Not that they were flashy with their wealth, they weren't, yet the underlying prosperity meant that money was always available They were part of the moneyed establishment with all the privileges which that brought. Murdo admired the family's commitment to the Arts and to the endless charities they supported. Connie supported several local charities through her deep-seated convictions and faith.

Murdo admired them both even if he was never quite at ease with Will. The Presbyterian in him was suspicious of easy money-making that went on in the City, especially at the top and Emma's father was at the top. If there was a list of the twenty most influential City players then Will would have be on it. There was a certain smugness that Murdo thought he detected on occasions, a certain unspoken assumption of the rights wealth conferred and the doors it opened. Murdo watched all this from the outside with a sense of detachment. Any judgement he made erred on the charitable. It was, after all, only a matter of time before he and Emma were married and he became an integral part of her family.

Christmas came and went and after a raucous New Year Murdo

made his way North again. He was not looking forward to hours sitting in the library doing research in the cold, grey of winter. Yet there was his other work: the work for the British state. That, after all, was why he was there.

Murdo continued to go down to London as often as he could. His excuse was that he was going to the National Archives in Kew to further his research. He would spend a few days there each time. He enjoyed these visits. Emma was always delighted to see him and they spent happy hours wandering the city, enjoying its delights. Emma had taught him to broaden his cultural horizons considerably.

He was invited to Will and Connie's for Sunday lunch, a ritual of great family significance when everyone gathered round the large table and enjoyed each other's company.

On one occasion, after lunch as they were wandering in the garden Will asked Murdo about his academic research.

'So how are you enjoying undertaking a PhD after the Home Office? Sounds quite a challenge. Remind me what you are researching, something to do with the Suez Crisis and Egypt in 1956 isn't it?'

'Yes, exactly that. A fraught area of British Foreign Policy.'

'The start of our demise?'

'No, not the start but certainly a key milestone on that road.'

Will looked at him intently and said, 'But this Scotland thing isn't just about academic research is it? Don't worry, you don't have to respond. Emma hasn't said anything by the way. I have an instinct about these things. Keeping an eye on the Jocks probably. Volatile lot the Celts. Too many of them let their hearts rule their heads. I can see a time coming when there is a showdown. The Nats are doing rather better than London would like. Still, I think we can trust the majority up there. They have too much to lose if Rodric Fraser and his separatists become over-powerful and challenge the Union. The City will undermine the separatist case with ease. In the end it is the money that talks. Most Scots have their heads screwed on and understand that. They are not fools. It is not in any one's interests that the separatist case prevails – least of all ordinary Scots. If you pick up anything interesting don't hesitate to pass it on. You will be well-rewarded by my friends. I have said enough. Come on we should join the others for coffee.'

Murdo was surprised by Will's interest. He obviously had good contacts in the financial sector in Edinburgh.

'You and daddy seemed to be talking about more than his rose garden,' Emma observed.

'Yes. He was giving me his world-view on political and economic developments in Scotland.'

'Ah, ever the City slicker,' mocked Emma as she put her arm through his and they walked into the lounge. Emma could do no wrong in Will's eyes and that was not always good.

Later when back in the flat, Murdo ran through the conversation in his head. Will was no fool. He was a self-made man. Would money really determine the outcome of a referendum? He didn't doubt for a second that powerful vested interests would pour money into any unionist campaign. After all these people wanted to protect their considerable assets in Scotland. The prospect of an independent Scotland would cause uncertainty and a flight of capital – or that is what he had been led to believe. Yet the idea of the outcome being determined by big money, the full weight of the UK government and the three unionist parties did not appeal. Somewhere deep inside him something was changing. A curious fear and ambivalence was taking hold. Certainties were dissolving.

There was a side to him that would always support the weak against the powerful – an instinct shared by many of his compatriots. The idea that the outcome of a referendum could be manipulated by the financial and political elites and their media outriders left him cold. He may have been born into the establishment – however it is defined – but as time slipped by he began to realise he was not *of* the establishment. So it was that this seed grew and he began to question what he was doing.

Rodric and those who worked closely for him such as Eilidh and the wider Party and public were honourable people. They hoped for a better future for their country free from the stranglehold of Westminster. Of course, it would come at a price – that went without question – but it was a price many were prepared to pay for being in control of their country's destiny. No one expected a land of milk and honey on 16th September if the 'Yes' vote prevailed.

As the New Year gathered momentum the focus was on the referendum. Will's words and his none-too-subtle request for any inside information repeatedly buzzed through his mind. And then there was Emma. Their relationship had grown more fragile than he would have liked as their paths were diverging and it was clear that Emma had no intention of ever staying in Scotland for more than the bare minimum of time. The attractions of London with her social network and her somewhat patronising view of the country and its people was not encouraging.

'All tartan, shortbread and midges,' he over-heard Quentin, one of her school friends, say across the dinner table, 'And then there are the Scots.' There was general laughter. Emma then looked across the table and saw his pained expression. 'Oh come on darling, you are alright, you are an Anglo-Scot – one of us really.'

His pride was punctured and it took him all of his self-control not to respond. Later he was furious with himself for not speaking up. When he confronted Emma she laughed lightly and said, 'Oh come on, darling, it was a joke. I love the country and its people really. You mustn't be so touchy. God, you are not going native are you?'

Murdo may not have realised it before but he now had to accept that this is exactly what was happening. Emma's remark was more perceptive than she could have realised. He was forced to confront a new perspective within himself, a different narrative was unwinding in his mind.

At the end of the evening Emma's father, cognac in hand, came over to him.

'I want to apologise for Quentin's remark. It was entirely out of order and unforgivable. I have had a quiet word to him. You had the graciousness not to respond.'

'Thanks, Will. Yes, it was difficult to keep my mouth shut and not rise to the bait. I would find it difficult not to respond to a remark like that in future.'

In the following weeks he thought often about that evening. Was it Emma's casual, light-hearted remark that was the tipping point? Or was it the guilt he increasingly felt betraying the honourable people he was working alongside? Was it Eilidh with that fiery spirit and commitment to the cause? Yes, he admired her, no matter how prickly she was with him – justifiably, he knew – how could he let her down? Deep down he was still deeply attracted to her but could not show it. He was certain she would be contemptuous of any advance he made. She seemed awkward when he was in the vicinity and continued to be dismissive of him. He wondered if that was for self-protection. Maybe but then again maybe not. He dared not break cover and express his feelings for her. He didn't want to be humiliated and scorned. But sometimes risks have to be taken.

A new narrative developed in his mind: the British establishment had colonised Scotland over three hundred years as they had established an empire on which the sun never set and like any imperial power they had used divide and rule to subjugate the natives by promoting some of them within that power-structure, giving them titles and honours so that they became more like the colonisers than the colonisers. The success of this could be witnessed round the globe. But there were always those who did not benefit from imperial rule and who turned against their masters. This in essence was the story of decolonisation.

Curiously, some of the colonised emulated their former masters after independence. It was one of the ironies of history. But he cautioned himself against being too sweeping in his judgements.

Whether by accident or design relations with Emma were never quite the same. Yes, they still made love but somehow it lacked the passion of before. It was difficult to pinpoint precisely the nature of the problem. It seemed as though they were just going through the motions. Emotionally he felt increasingly distant from her. She sensed this and asked him outright.

'What's wrong, Murdo? You seem so remote as though you are on auto-pilot. What is going on in your mind?'

'Nothing, nothing,' he tried unconvincingly to assure her. But she knew that things between them were not the same. On another occasion after some desultory trysting she asked him if he had met anyone else. He assured her he hadn't. Technically that was true.

She came to King's Cross to see him onto the train. Each felt a certain coolness but tried not to show it.

'See you soon. I'll come up to St Andrews. Phone me when you get home.'

He assured her he would. As the train sliced through the country-side and as he gazed out of the window he began to accept that something had fundamentally changed within him. At first it was something he didn't want to acknowledge but as the days passed he had no alternative if he was going to be true to himself.

Chapter Five

IN LATE SPRING MURDO SIGNED up with Calum for an advanced biking course.

The two of them got on well. Calum's skills were imparted with ease and with his laconic, understated humour he managed to deal with Murdo's over-confidence. Calum would ride behind Murdo. Then every half-hour or so they would stop for Calum to suggest ways of improving Murdo's skills.

In time, the two became good friends and they frequently rode out together around Fife and Perthshire. There would always be a coffee stop and chat.

The appeal of biking was something deep down inside him. Being in control of a powerful machine with its challenges and the adrenalin kick-in of fast riding was a drug. The anonymity of the helmet meant that Murdo felt separated from the temporal world in a bubble outside time and space. For him, riding at its best it was an existential experience. All bikers understood this.

There was one set of bends that especially inspired him: sweeping with good visibility. Positioning the bike at the right point on the road to take the series of bends, controlling it and powering out of them at speed exhilarated him.

'Better than sex,' Murdo joked.

'Nae chance,' Calum responded, 'But a close second.'

The second referendum was now only weeks away and this time the opinion polls suggested that the momentum was with the 'Yes' campaign. That built up steadily as the weeks passed. The campaigning on both sides was every bit as hard-fought and bitterly contested as last time. Many had a distinct sense of déjà vu.

Murdo and Calum occasionally discussed the referendum. Calum was an agnostic but probably tilted more to the 'No' side. The discussions were always conducted in good humour and with a respect for each other's views.

What made this campaign different was the triumphalism of the Conservative Government elected in 2015, albeit with a small majority, and its implementation of English Laws for English Voters which helped to undermine the Better Together campaign. The fact that the recommendations of the Smith Commission had been watered down had angered just enough of the original 'No' voters who had believed the Vow made in the last campaign to push them towards 'Yes'.

Scottish Labour which had been almost pummelled out of existence in the 2015 Election reached the conclusion that its future was not as part of the UK but as a Party that would be better served by an independent Scotland. Support for Better Together Two ebbed away despite the furious media onslaught so reminiscent of 2014. Even the massive campaign funds of Better Together Two and the relentless advertising made few inroads into what was happening. Scotland was on the move again.

In London the Westminster political elite was divided between those for whom separation couldn't come quickly enough and those who were determined to prevent it at all costs. The Prime Minister worked hard to convince his Party that the disintegration of the UK would have profound implications in the eyes of the world. The rUK would be a rump state of questionable influence in the wider world. Or that at least that was what they thought. It seemed to be the final nail in the end of empire coffin, even if only a few spoke of it in this way.

Murdo was especially busy in these months, pounding the streets, canvassing, leafleting and working hard for Rodric. The 'Yes' campaign was buoyed up by the support they were receiving on the streets and on the doorsteps. Gone was the frequent hostility and occasional aggression of 2014.

Murdo managed one brief visit to London supposedly to the National Archives but in reality to report to Sir David personally who had now made Scotland his top priority.

Ushered into Sir David's office three weeks before the referendum he found all the key players in the drama present. The PM was not there – some distraction about EU negotiations within his Party, some of whom had not reconciled themselves to the final agreement with Brussels.

Murdo felt sickened by what he was doing – the stench of betrayal obsessed him. He realised more than ever that these were not his people. The only way he could justify his presence at the heart of the British establishment was that it might be useful to Rodric and his compatriots who were campaigning with growing confidence and success for an independent country. So he pulled his punches and dropped a measure of disinformation. Even although anyone who read the papers could see which way events were going. The gravity of the situation was all too apparent to Westminster.

'The PM has asked me to thank you again, Murdo. You are doing well. Your insights and information have been invaluable. I am not sure we could have done any more than we have done to reverse what seems to be yet another political tsunami from Scotland. It may well be that we have to take rather different approach as the PM has said.'

The meeting broke up. Sir David asked Murdo to remain behind.

'It can't be easy doing what you are doing. We understand that and we are deeply grateful. You will be pulled out in a matter of weeks now. If the present trend towards a convincing 'Yes' vote is not reversed – and here I emphasise that we shall spare no effort to prevent it in the coming days – then you should be aware that the final option is to declare a State of Emergency and impose Direct Rule before the referendum happens. We had to do that in Northern Ireland as I am sure you know.'

Sir David paused and watched Murdo's expression carefully.

'Does that surprise you?'

'No, Sir David, not really. I suppose it is inevitable given that the stakes are so high,' Murdo replied trying to sound nonplussed.

Of course, he should have guessed that this would be how it was going to be played out. What alternative was there? His stomach churned. The stakes had suddenly become higher.

He walked out of the building, along the Thames, his mind in turmoil. He realised he was privy to a secret so potent that it went to the heart of the deep state. Murdo walked and walked. He realised just how small a part he was in this drama being played out and yet his intelligence had helped shape the likely response of the Government. He had never felt such panic and shame. What had he become? Self-loathing gnawed at him. He was a mercenary, a collaborator. He was betraying his country and people he admired.

The final days of the campaign were every bit as febrile as in 2014, perhaps even more so as 'Yes' seemed to be pulling ahead – not in any dramatic way but incrementally. The odds reflected an increasing conviction that 'Yes' would win. The unionists understandably were appalled that defeat was staring them in the face. It was generally reckoned that the FUD – fear, uncertainty and deception – deployed in 2014 had lost its bite.

There was now only one course of action left for Westminster.

Chapter Six

ASUB-COMMITTEE HAD BEEN SET UP to prepare the detailed plans for the implementation of the State of Emergency and Direct Rule. It reported directly to the PM. Murdo may not have known the detail but it was not difficult to work out what would be likely to happen. He wondered if the state had the necessary resources to impose its will and achieve its goal. No doubt a proportion of those security resources had been sent North gradually to work with the assets already in place.

Murdo sat in his bed and breakfast looking out over the Edinburgh New Town with a glass of malt in his hand. He had been in the city for the last few days working at the centre of the referendum campaign as one of the First Minister's team. The 'Code Red' text warning of the imminent State of Emergency sent his mind spinning. Is this what he really wanted? The decapitation of the Party, its destruction and a declaration of its illegality as a threat to national security? He had always known that being a mole would cause inner tensions. These now came spilling to the surface.

He thought back over the twelve months. Yes, he had known he was going native. It was a drip by drip process. He couldn't betray Rodric and Eilidh. It had become personal.

Eildih, that fragile brittle woman to whom he was deeply attracted but who still refused to give him a smile or respond to his attempts to woo her with his humour and charm. The door was shut and he knew it. But his admiration for her commitment, dedication and spirit tormented him. She had given him nothing and yet he could not break her, betray all that she stood for.

And then there were all the activists who had opened their arms to welcome him, who had opened their hearts to him and with whom he had walked many miles on the campaign trail. They worked ceaselessly for what they believed would be a better country.

He thought back to the group photograph of campaigners taken in Ceres a few weeks ago in front of the monument to the local men who had gone to fight at Bannockburn. Looking back this was a pivotal moment. Standing there posing for the photograph he somehow felt infused with the spirit of these brave forefathers who were prepared to lay down their lives.

This was the moment he realised where his true loyalty lay. It was not to the British state and its political and economic elites in London. It was here. It was at this moment he knew he was above all else a Scot and he would not betray his country. Yes, he loved England and the English but this was about the fate of a nation.

As the night wore on and his mental turmoil increased a plan began to shape in his mind. He eventually decided to phone Eilidh.

'Hi, it's me.'

'Who? Oh you? What the hell are you phoning me about at this time? You woke me up.'

'Sorry. I didn't realise. Just something I wanted to tell you. I'll text you.'

'See you at Lachlan's tomorrow,' the text said.

A minute later the reply came through, 'Fuck off'.

Murdo hoped that Eilidh had the sense to realize what he was trying to tell her even although it was oblique. He had mentioned Lachlan to her several weeks ago. To suggest such a visit to Lachlan on the day of the referendum would surely alert her to something being badly wrong. Hopefully, she would have the insight to understand what he was trying to communicate to her.

Sleep was impossible. He didn't even try to go to bed. By dawn he knew what he had to do. It was the only way.

He texted Rodric: 'Sorry, need to deliver that document now.'

Two minutes later Rodric replied. 'Come immediately.' There was little to doubt that the referendum would be won as the most recent polls had shown a significant majority for independence. Last minute interventions by Westminster to offer concessions achieved had failed this time round.

Rodric couldn't sleep either. He knew a momentous day for Scotland lay ahead and he worked and re-worked a speech which assumed victory.

Murdo was sure that his text to Rodric would have been intercepted and hoped that it would not set in train the very series of events he hoped to avoid. He got the spare kit for the bike, put it in the top box and then kitted up.

Getting the First Minister out of Bute House to safety only had a slim chance of success. He was aware that security units would be on standby waiting for the 'Code Green' message.

Murdo needed about twenty minutes to get Rodric out of Edinburgh and across the new Queensferry Crossing into Fife. Then he would disappear into the maze of small roads and lanes which he had grown to know so well. He suspected a helicopter would be deployed with its heat seeking equipment and camera which would be ultimately impossible to outrun. Police motorcyclists would probably be quickly on his tail too. Once his direction was known road blocks would be set up.

His plan was to head out along the M8 and M9 towards Kincardine Bridge and then spin off to cross the new bridge into Fife. His only hope was that the security forces would be too pre-occupied with what was about to happen and caught by surprise. That would give him a vital few minutes head-start. Murdo left his phone in the room. He knew all about Covert Communications Data Capture which could pinpoint his location and intercept his calls and texts.

He approached Bute House slowly and decided to go round the block once to see where the security units were positioned. Their presence seemed well disguised: a couple of vans, two cars and a group of men walking around. He parked the bike.

Rodric opened the door. 'What the hell is going on?'

Murdo motioned silence and then pointed to the hold-all he was carrying and indicated that he should put on the gear while engaging him in small chat.

'Sorry, I should have brought this over much earlier. I was working on it and trying to get it just right.'

Rodric quickly grasped the situation and played along as he struggled with the kit. Fortunately the helmet fitted. Murdo realized that this scene would be playing in real time at GCHQ in Cheltenham and that the necessary orders to arrest the First Minister would probably already have been given. They had seconds to get out.

'So this is what it has come to,' was all Rodric could say as he struggled to get onto the pillion, 'I'm not surprised. They were never going to let it happen – were they? They had too much to lose.'

The motorcycle engine kicked into life. Out of the corner of his eye Murdo saw several men running toward Bute House waving at him to stop with what appeared to be weapons, but he accelerated hard and the machine powered out of the square. How many minutes or seconds did he have? He felt Rodric's body hunch low behind him.

The streets of Edinburgh were almost empty at that time in the morning and he took the machine up to 90mph in seconds, jumping traffic lights and heading out of the city to the west. Murdo surprised himself in getting out of the city so quickly. Once out of the city he took the bike up to 160mph, not something he had ever done apart from on a track day. It was settled and he knew he had more power on tap. The top speed was 185mph. Murdo knew that the security forces had nothing that could match it in speed but once spotted by drone or helicopter his position and direction would be radioed ahead. It all depended on where the security units were positioned. None, Murdo hoped, would be expecting a chase. They were expecting to arrest bewildered, sleep-worn people, pulling them out of their beds after using battering rams to force their way into houses and flats.

Murdo felt Rodric clinging on tightly behind him. The bike was not made for pillion passengers but at least it would not be for long. By the time they had left the M9 and were approaching the bridge, the first cracks of dawn were seeping through. As they surged over the bridge at 170mph Murdo knew that they had won the first round. He expected the helicopter to be in the air now searching urgently for them. He knew, too, that all the roadside camera records would be being scrutinized by computers with unparalleled urgency.

Murdo peeled off the M90 towards Kirkcaldy and then headed round Glenrothes towards Dundee. Lachlan's farm was up a track off the A92 near Rathillet.

By the time they got there it was 6.30am. They had taken less than 30 minutes. Murdo was at a loss to understand why the security forces had not been chasing them.

Lachlan heard the bike coming up the long farm drive. Murdo slowed down to a crawling pace to keep the noise of the bike's engine as quiet as possible. The last thing he wanted to do was to draw attention to a bike coming up the drive at this time of morning.

Rodric got off first and removed his helmet.

'Now would you tell me what the hell's going on? I have never been so terrified in my life.'

'You were about to be arrested, a State of Emergency and Direct Rule has been declared by London. We are not out of the woods yet. Lachlan is a close friend but he is a staunch unionist through and through.'

'So how did you know about what was about to happen?'

'You can guess First Minister.' Murdo usually called Rodric by his first name but he felt that what he had just done was not for a person but for the First Minister of Scotland and for his country. Rodric quickly realised that.

'Oh aye, I see it all now, I see it all now. And you've broken cover and joined us?'

'Yes, First Minister. In the end, I couldn't do it. My loyalty was to you and the country, not to London.'

'I don't know whether to punch you or shake your hand. At least you have come down on the right side, laddie. It takes a cold heart indeed to betray your country. I think you know why Eilidh regarded you the way she did.'

'Yes, I do.'

Lachlan came out of the farm and looked at Murdo and then glared at Rodric, a man he had never respected. He had been having difficulty sleeping since his farm tenancy agreement was coming to an end and the laird wanted to re-negotiate the terms of the lease.

'What the hell has brought ye here, Murdo? Dinna ye ken I'll haund ye ower tae the polis? Aye, I've just heard the Prime Minister's broadcast.'

He looked at Rodric slowly and deliberately, making up his mind what to do next. Rodric stepped forward and held out his hand. Lachlan shook it grudgingly.

'So whit dae ye want of me?'

'Somewhere to hide until this is over and I can move on safely,' said Rodric.

Lachlan looked uncertain and hesitated. The implications for him and his family could be a price he was not prepared to pay.

'For God's sake, Lachie, he is our First Minister. We owe it to him, to the country to protect him.'

'Aye, aye, we dae. I wis a unionist as ye ken but wi' the news leaking oot the nicht, I cannae support it. A State of Emergency? Huh. I kent we wis going tae lose but that is democracy. Ye'll be safe here First Minister. Get the bike oot the way – put it in the container by the barn. Come inside quickly. I'll wake Mhairi.'

A few minutes later Mhairi came downstairs and into the kitchen. She was a strong-minded woman who held different political views from her husband and was an ardent supporter of the campaign for independence.

Mhairi shook her head part in disbelief and part in confusion.

'Surely not? It cannae be. For heaven's sake – has it come tae this?
She clasped Rodric's hand in hers.

'Weel, the First Meenster, nae less. Welcome! Welcome! Thank God ye are safe.'

'Aye, Mhairi, but I don't want to bring trouble on your house.'

'There are times when we have to do what is right nae matter whit the personal cost,' Lachlan said.

'Aye, Lachie, ye are right. What will we tell the weans?'

'The truth, woman, the truth. They are old enough to understand whit is happening in their country. Why, they were independence supporters anyway.'

'Ye'll need something to warm ye up. Some porridge and tea?'

'Aye, that would be grand,' said Rodric.

Murdo walked across to Lachlan. There was a silence between them for seconds and then Lachlan grasped his hand tightly.

'Welcome, Murdo. It's guid tae see ye.'

'What's happening?' asked Jennie, Lachlan and Mhairi's elder daughter, who had heard the noise and came down the stairs into the kitchen. Isla followed her sister. Both were in dressing gowns and looked dishevelled from sleep.

Rodric got up to greet them.

'Oh my God, oh my God, I don't believe it!'

'We'll be looking after the First Minister for a while. A State of Emergency has been declared and Direct Rule has been imposed from London,' Mhairi said.

There was a silence momentarily and then Isla spoke.

'You are safe with us, First Minister, we'll look after ye.'

'Aye, we will that,' said Jennie.

'At least yer faither is nae a 'Yes' activist so they won't be interested in us.' They all laughed.

'I shall not stay any longer than I have to.'

'I have already worked out a plan to get you out of the country,' Murdo said.

'My place is here, Murdo, in this country. I don't want to be scuttling away somewhere else. I would rather take my chances here.'

Mhairi brought them porridge, boiled eggs and toast with home-made marmalade.

'Ye'll be needing this after what you've bin up tae,' she said as she laid it on the kitchen table.

Murdo and Rodric thanked her and they ate in silence for a while.

'I am still trying to understand you, Murdo, and what you have done. It will take me a while to reconcile all that in my own mind.'

'I am too well aware of that, First Minister.'

'Oh for God's sake, don't keep calling me that. Call me Rodric as you have always done. Whatever I am now it isn't the First Minister anyway.'

They finished their breakfasts.

'We have a lot of thinking to do. They'll be out searching for us now. No doubt of that,' said Rodric.

There was a silence for a few minutes as each of them was lost in thought. Gradually, the reality of what was beginning to happen was sinking in.

'We'll put ye in the holiday croft on the aither side o' the fermyard,' Mhairi said.

'Aye, that is the best place fer ye. Ye need to think whit tae dae next. There's a tele in there.'

A few minutes later they were in the croft trying to understand what they were facing.

'How do you feel?' asked Rodric who was curiously calm.

'Not sure. Apprehensive. Uncertain where this is going to end. Unsure of what will happen to us or to Eilidh and all the others. Lachie and Mhairi are good people. They will look after us.'

'How do you know them?' asked Rodric.

'Lachie is a cousin.'

There was a lull in the conversation as both men retreated into their thoughts.

'A storm of enormous ferocity is about to land. I hope our foundations as a people are strong enough. I suppose thinking about it, London's response was predictable. I've been naive. Far too naive.'

'Rodric, I have a document here you should read,' said Murdo tentatively. He handed over a large envelope.

Rodric opened the envelope and stared in amazement at the document in front of him.

'My God, Murdo, how on earth did this come your way?'

'It is better that I don't tell you. Just read it,' Murdo said quietly.

JOINT INTELLIGENCE COMMITTEE

THE PROBABLE REACTIONS TO THE INTRODUCTION OF

DIRECT RULE IN SCOTLAND

REPORT BY THE JOINT INTELLIGENCE COMMITTEE (S)

PART 1 – SUMMARY

It is not possible to predict reactions to Direct Rule at this stage. Reactions to Direct Rule would depend on how it was introduced and the timing. Scotland is deeply divided on the issue of independence as the 2014 referendum illustrated. Since then opinion has moved gradually towards independence. The polls show that a majority of Scots want independence. Our private polls confirm this.

Imposition of Direct Rule to avoid Scotland becoming independent would be highly contentious as a majority of Scots would feel that their democratic right to become a sovereign state had been denied by illegal means. It has to be borne in mind that the present UK government only has one elected MP in Scotland and that with a majority of a few hundred votes. A majority of Scots feel that Westminster does not reflect their political aspirations and the present Government's policies are deeply at odds with the prevailing mood of Scotland.

There is little doubt that the imposition of Direct Rule would lead to a backlash of some consequence and lead to serious political unrest and civil disobedience. It is impossible to tell how far reaching this would be and how long it would last for. The UK Government would have to be prepared to use considerable force to impose Direct Rule and this would shatter the political and social stability of Scotland. It is questionable that the security resources necessary to impose Direct Rule are available either within Scotland or the UK.

The response of the Police, Judiciary and Civil Service would be critical. While it is reasonably certain that the Judiciary and the higher echelons of the Civil Service would remain loyal to HMG there is not the same certainty about the rank and file of the Police Service who would be expected to implement law and order in the event of widespread protests that would certainly follow the imposition of Direct Rule. There is the very real danger that the security forces would be overwhelmed by lack of sufficient numbers.

Deploying the Army would be a high risk strategy and would be likely to inflame an already volatile situation. The reaction of the rest of the UK and the opinions of our allies would be questionable once there is a flow of images in the media of arrests and the imposition of Direct Rule.

The Scots are a proud people who could be expected to react with a degree of intense hostility to Direct Rule. Ways of reducing this hostility by the deployment of soft power would be essential although of marginal influence.

Signed JAMES STAMFORD Chairman, on behalf of the Joint Intelligence Committee.

Cabinet Office

THE PROBABLE REACTIONS TO THE INTRODUCTION
OF DIRECT RULE IN SCOTLAND

PART II: MAIN REPORT

CIRCUMSTANCES IN WHICH DIRECT RULE MIGHT BE
INTRODUCED AND POLICY ASSUMPTIONS

1. Direct Rule might be introduced because the territorial integrity of the UK is threatened in the likely event of a 'Yes' vote in the upcoming Scottish referendum. The major purpose would be to preserve the UK in its present form and to maintain the Trident base in Scotland.

2. The aim should be to take further power in Westminster's hands and to introduce new policies which would bind Scotland more closely into the UK and undermine both nationalism and the desire for self-determination completely.

The Assumptions:

3. We can assume that initially there will be a strong reaction amongst a significant proportion of Scots who want nothing less than full independence from the British state and a return of sovereignty to the Scottish people. It is difficult to know what forms that reaction will take, how severe it will be and how long it will last. It is wise to conclude that the worst case scenario is highly probable. This could involve civil disobedience and significant social and political unrest. It could include a significant section of the Scottish population being involved in a policy of non-cooperation with the agents of Direct Rule. There is always the possibility that some hardline separatists might start an armed struggle although there is no indication whatever of this from detailed intelligence reports. The whole thrust of separatist policy has been to achieve independence by peaceful means and with the consent of the majority of the Scottish people.

4. Those of a unionist persuasion will welcome Direct Rule and the positive aspects should be publicised to maximum advantage. The economic benefits of the Union and the economic disruption of independence should be constantly stressed. Prominence should be given to shared history and endeavour. This should include

references to the Second World War when the UK stood alone against Nazi tyranny.

5. It can be assumed that Direct Rule will polarise the Scots even more than they have become. These divisions will be deep, raw and visceral as they go to the heart of every Scot. Measures to try and lessen this polarisation are vital and urgent. A top priority must be given to this.

The Current Contingency Plans for Direct Rule:

6. These provide for a Minister (or Governor) to be vested with full authority for all existing responsibilities of the Scottish Government. He would exercise this authority through existing departmental machinery, including the civil service departments in Edinburgh, supported by a suitable staff of his own. It is highly likely that it will be necessary to introduce personnel from London on a large scale.

The Overall Separatist View:

7. Most Separatists would see Direct Rule as destroying the right of the Scottish nation to self-determination and regard the destruction of the Scottish Parliament and the recall of all devolved powers to London with extreme hostility. There would be a strong likelihood of support in the UN and EU for Scottish self-determination and HMG could expect to face considerable international opposition. It is probable that the international media will support the case for self-determination. The FCO would need to work hard to blunt criticism of the HMG.

8. It is a fundamental belief amongst Separatists that independence would not only preserve and strengthen Scottish identity but that political and economic power should rest in the hands of a Scottish Government and Parliament.

9. In the completely unlikely view that the Separatists react violently to Direct Rule there is reason to believe that any armed resistance to the security forces would be of manageable proportions. After the decapitation of the Separatist leadership and activist base we believe it unlikely that a charismatic leader would emerge in response to Direct Rule.

10. The discipline and morale amongst the Separatist camp is high. Resorting to violence is universally seen as counter-productive and regarded with considerable horror and would alienate those sections of Scottish society that would be needed to support independence. It is safe to say that the leadership and rank and file of the Separatist cause are well-aware of what happened in Ulster during the 'Troubles'. It is safe to assume that no one wants to go down that route.

11. The idea of a Unilateral Declaration of Independence has emotional attractions for some but the Separatists as a whole are unlikely to take the practical steps necessary to achieve this in the face of opposition from large sections of Scottish society and the British state.

12. An economically prosperous and politically stable

independent Scotland is virtually impossible to envisage even if the majority of Scots since the 2014 seem to have rejected that analysis. That point needs to be hammered home repeatedly. One plank of the HMG's approach must be to let the Scots know subtlely that HMG has saved them from themselves. Those parts of the UK media favourable to the Unionist cause can hammer this home.

The Civil Service and Judiciary:

13. The great majority of the Scottish Civil Service and Judiciary would be most likely to co-operate with Westminster.

Police Scotland:

14. Police Scotland would find themselves in a more difficult position than the Civil Service or Judiciary. Resignations are a distinct possibility although it is impossible to quantify the number. Whatever the circumstances Police Scotland would be likely to remain a cohesive force and continue to play its part in maintaining Law and Order. The imposition of Direct Rule and policing its aftermath would be critical to its success. The role and loyalty of Special Branch would be critical.

The Unionists:

15. It is probable that a small proportion of Unionists will welcome the ending of devolution and the Scottish Parliament. This group had always believed that

devolution far from ending the momentum of the Separatists to the splitting up of the UK that it would merely lead to demands initially for more devolution and independence in the long run. Events have proved them correct.

16. A larger group of Unionists would support Direct Rule but would be likely to regret the end of devolution and the Scottish Parliament. Opinion polls have for some years now shown that the majority of Scots want more devolved powers but within the framework of the UK. This group value their British citizenship highly and appreciate the social and economic benefits of the UK. They would be likely to accept Direct Rule for the greater good as separatism has too many risks for them both on a personal level and at a national level. The political sympathies of this group spans the three main Westminster parties although one would probably accept a federal solution.

Attitudes once Direct Rule has been introduced:

17. Direct Rule would give a breathing space to re-assess the damage done to the Union by the Separatists and a chance to return powers to Westminster. It would be absolutely vital that the initial security clamp-down on the Separatists would be linked to a charm offensive and largesse towards Scotland by Westminster. In this respect some high profile infrastructure schemes such as new motorways and an upgrading and modernisation of the rail network would be central. Defence procurement orders for the Navy would be helpful.

What might be expected to follow in the event of Direct Rule:

18. The spectrum of possibilities is a wide one but the following seem likely: initial political and social unrest amongst many followed by a gradual acceptance of Direct Rule; a return to normality within 4-6 months; a lingering and long-term sullen sense of resentment amongst a significant proportion of the population – this group has shown a resilience and a refusal to let the dream of independence die. How this would translate into political action remains to be seen. There is a possibility that all fifty-nine Parliamentary seats will be won by the Separatists at the next General Election.

19. There is a possiblity that if the Separatists win every Parliamentary seat in Scotland they will withdraw from Westminster and declare a Unilateral Declaration of Independence. In this eventuality the Separatists would not acquiesce in continued Westminster rule.

20. HMG should consider the possibility of an independent Scotland in the event of unsustainable pressure through civil disobedience and non-cooperation after the imposition of Direct Rule. This could lead to a healthier relationship between the consistuent parts of these islands. It would be a traumatic event for most UK citizens to see the break-up of the Union. The resultant ill-feeling and acrimony would take some years to dissipate.

DISTRIBUTION

UNITED KINGDOM

Cabinet Ministers (if approved by the Secretary of the Cabinet)
Secretary of the Cabinet
Secretary, Counter Subversion Committee
Chiefs of Staff: to take note
Metropolitan Police Office
Ministry of Defence: D of DOP
Secretary, Defence Policy Staff
Director, Communications
Electronic Security Group
JIC (A and B)
Secretary, Official Committee on Scotland
Sub-Committee on Contingency Planning

Military Commands:
Secretary CICC
Secretary, UK Cs-in-C Committee

United Kingdom Scotland Authorities:
Director of Operations, Scotland
Director of Intelligence, Scotland

Cabinet Office

After some minutes Rodric looked up. 'Well, well, well. What an insight into the thinking of our masters. I have to give them credit. They seem to know where they are going on this one.'

'Yes. They are nothing if not prepared.'

At 6am the Prime Minister went on national television and declared a State of Emergency and the imposition of Direct Rule on Scotland. Security forces moved into the counting stations and seized all the ballot boxes. The officials were ordered to return home and remain there. The arrests of leading activists had already started. Doors were battered open as security forces piled in to house after house and dragged bewildered men and women to waiting vans. Some, just a few at first, knew what was happening even before the Prime Minster went on national television speaking from Downing Street. Social media had sounded an alert in the early hours of the morning.

Rodric, Murdo, Lachie and Mhairi watched the broadcast with a sense of deep despair and anger.

Sutton's voice was sombre and his face grave.

"It is with deep regret that my government has had to declare a State of Emergency as our national security was about to be jeopardized by the Scottish referendum. It was clear to the intelligence agencies that forces had compromised the referendum process which my government on the advice of the Electoral Reform Commission has had to declare null and void. Dark forces were at work which would have disunited our kingdom and plunged it into chaos.

'The Scots themselves would have suffered most at the hands of these forces for whom the end justified the means. These are unscrupulous people bent on self-aggrandisement with no consideration for ordinary people. Our intelligence agencies with the help of our allies have brought to light dealings with foreign powers by this cabal. Intelligence will be made public in the coming days in Parliament.

'We have had to move swiftly to arrest the leadership of the 'Yes' campaign who, as I speak, are being interned. They have been guilty of treason and will be tried in due course. This country stands for the rule of law above all else. This is what has distinguished us from dictatorships around the globe. I am sorry to say that we have not yet arrested Rodric Fraser, First Minister, who has gone into hiding, but we are confident that he will be apprehended within hours.

I urge all Scots to go about their normal business and give thanks that this government has acted with decisive speed to end this folly and grave danger to us all. There will be a curfew throughout Scotland from 8pm until 6am until further notice. The forces of law and order have been instructed to act with the utmost severity against anyone who disregards the State of Emergency.

The State of Emergency will last until stability and calm is restored. Parliament has been recalled. Further announcements will be made in the coming hours to keep you informed.

God bless the United Kingdom and God Save the King. Thank you.'

They watched the television coverage of the imposition of the State of Emergency across Scotland. It was interspersed with interviews with unionist politicians, all expressing regret that the situation had left Westminster with no option but to pursue this course. It was deeply uncomfortable viewing: arrests, screeching sirens blasting from police cars marked and unmarked, Transit vans with the metal grills down to protect their windscreens, police in riot gear dispersing crowds who were shouting defiance and waving the Saltire.

'I must have been really naive ever thinking Westminster was going to allow independence. What a gross miscalculation on my part,' Rodric said. He was visibly upset at what he was seeing.

'These days will pass, Rodric. It will not end here.'

'Oh yes?'

'No. It won't end here. This is just another step along the road.'

'I wish I was so sure. I suppose we can be expected to be arrested within hours.'

'You are probably right on that, Rodric. I know full well the forces arraigned against us. Your chances of not being found and arrested are diminishing rapidly. The technology they can call upon is massive. Drones will be scouring the landscape even now. Helicopters will be airborne. They will know from roadside cameras that we crossed the Queensferry Crossing. They will already have narrowed down the search area. If we're lucky we have twenty four hours. More likely we have two to three hours.'

'Aye, but if ye move the First Minister ye can expect tae be stopped at road blocks,' intervened Lachie, 'It's best ye lie low here for some days until the search is reduced.'

'That will never happen. They'll spare no effort to find the FM. The longer it takes to arrest him the more foolish and inept they look.'

'Lachie is right. I shall stay here for a while and see how the situation develops.'

'Ye'll be fine here for a while. Mhairi will bring ye food. Just ask if there is anything ye want. Whatever ye do don't leave the croft. There is a television so yc'll be able tae see the news. I'll get ye both some clothes when I go into Dundee later today. Mon, these are grim times. Who wid hae thought it wid have come tae this?' said Lachie shaking his head.

Rodric thanked him. The television news was preceded by a short speech by the King from Buckingham Palace. He looked decidedly uncomfortable.

'Our nations have had a common history for over three hundred years. It has been a successful relationship in which each has added to the other. Together we are greater than our constituent parts.

I know Scotland well and Scottish blood is in my veins. Some of my happiest times have been spent in Scotland and I have a deep-seated admiration for its people. I am one of you. I can understand your pain and dismay but I have no doubt that there will be a settlement between the various parts of this kingdom which will be to the advantage of all our subjects.

Be patient and good will emerge from these difficult days.'

There was no mention of the State of Emergency or the thousands being arrested and interned at disused military bases around the UK. There was no mention of the First Minister or of the Scottish Parliament. The appeal fell on deaf ears for too many Scots. The situation was well beyond the point where the King could pour oil on these most turbulent waters.

To some the Monarch was the velvet glove of the 'deep state' which lay beyond the froth of Party politics and the Parliamentary shenanigans. It was the 'deep state' through its component parts in politics, the security network, society and business which ultimately controlled the UK and its destiny. It was a meshing together of various individuals and their shared interests: stability, continuity and control.

This group of disparate people through their networks controlled what – in their view – was in the best interests of the UK and worked quietly towards that end. They had the economic resources at their disposal and the contacts in all the right places to push the agenda forward.

An independent Scotland was not part of the agenda of the 'deep state'. The reverse was true. A disunited kingdom would have diminished the UK on the global stage and threatened powerful vested interests. The rest of the UK, or rUK, would have become an insignificant player and this was something the 'deep state' would not allow to happen, whatever ploys it had to adopt.

There were many who saw the King's speech for what it was and were unmoved. There were others who had a deep faith in the

Monarchy as a binding force for good. It was supposedly above politics, even if that image had been dented in 2014 when the last Monarch had 'purred' at the result of a 'No' victory. The corporate media's reporting of the Queen's 'I hope you will think carefully about it' as a veiled attempt to influence the outcome towards 'No' was reported as such by the gleeful unionist media. Many felt the whole occasion had been carefully set up and exploited for all it was worth by the unionist side.

The King's speech was followed by the news which gave a detailed account of what the Government was trying to do and the developing situation in Scotland. The newsreader interviewed some London pundit about the State of Emergency.

'The Prime Minister really had no alternative,' the pundit intoned with satisfaction, 'It was an issue of national security and if Scotland went it alone it would have endangered us all. We can't have that, can we? Then there were the economic implications – we only have to see what has happened on the markets in the last few days to realize what the implications would have been for UK plc. No, I have to say I commend the Government's swift and decisive action on this. Nothing like the smack of strong government.'

Rodric laughed. 'That is what we're up against.'

The Home Secretary was then interviewed. Again the questioning was mild and supportive of the government position.

'Can you tell us Home Secretary how many arrests there have been?'

'No, not yet. I would guess that by the end of the day we shall have several thousand separatist activists under arrest.'

'And what are they actually charged with?'

'The State of Emergency has given the government sweeping powers to secure the safety and stability of the United Kingdom. Of course, in time, all those detained will be charged. We are, after all, a country of law. None of this arbitrary imprisonment here, you know.'

Memories of the impact of internment in Northern Ireland lingered in the body politic even after all these years.

'Quite so Home Secretary. And can you say where those arrested are being detained?'

'There are holding centres throughout Scotland. In Glasgow, for example, those arrested are being processed in Hampden Stadium before being taken to military camps. Murrayfield is being used in a similar way. Of course, this is temporary and we shall make sure that detainees are well looked after,'

'And what other measures has the government put in place in this emergency, Home Secretary?'

'I am afraid we have had to censor the media, ban freedom of assembly and, of course, impose a curfew on Scotland.'

'You can imagine what will happen if they arrest you, Rodric. It may well be that they will decide that finding you and putting you on trial will inflame the situation here. It will depend on the reaction of the country in the next few days.

'If the decapitation of the 'Yes' movement is accepted and things quickly return to normal then their policy will have worked. If on the other hand there is large scale civil disobedience then things will get more difficult. The repression will grow uglier and harsher. If you become the focal point of resistance in whatever form it takes then the state will re-double its efforts to find you. A trial of sorts will follow and presumably a long prison sentence.'

'There is no way that I would want to plunge this country into a civil war. Look at the bitterness that Ireland went through in the last century. All those deaths of innocents. Civil disobedience – maybe.'

'Scotland is going to be a bitterly divided country now. That was always the risk – part of the price, whichever side won. There are many who will never forgive you for dividing the country, Rodric, as you must realise.'

'Aye, I have known that all along. It was going to be a high price one way or other. Violence is not the answer. We must seek to persuade.'

'That moment has gone now, Rodric. London and its allies up here are determined to bury the issue forever.'

'The country will never accept that.'

'It depends on the reaction in the next few days – whether they quietly go back to sleep or rise up in civil disobedience.'

'We have to accept that the movement is now leaderless and that all our key activists have been neutralised.'

'It will fall to the next tier down to fill the shoes of the ones who have been arrested. I believe that this will happen. London is not going to get away with this lightly. The Scots can be pretty bloody minded when their national honour is impugned.'

'Aye, perhaps, but we have always been a house divided amongst ourselves whether it was at Culloden or over the issue of devolution or independence.'

'It will all hinge on how the broad mass of the population react. We know that twenty-five per cent is staunchly unionist. It is how the rest will react that will determine what happens now.'

That evening Lachie came over to share a dram. He was by nature a taciturn man. Small talk was not for him. He was a man of the soil and the Kirk, upstanding and true and straight as a die. He was widely respected by neighbours and fellow farmers who valued his judgement and willingness to help others. Like most farmers he had been against independence. He felt there was too much uncertainty and too much to lose. Unlike Mhairi, he had never been impressed by the FM. Now to his surprise he found himself hiding and shielding the man he had thought would have brought the country to its knees. As the two men spoke, Lachie began to revise his opinion of Rodric, an opinion formed by reading the unionist press and speaking to fellow farmers. Inch by rugged inch Lachie was being slowly won over.

Rodric had always made a point of speaking to the farmers in his constituency and going to the county shows. He knew the issues that pre-occupied farmers and he could talk to them intelligently about their concerns. He was a good listener. This was not a man whose eyes glazed over when you spoke to him for more than two minutes. Rather here was a man who asked pertinent questions. Slowly, Lachie was realising that the media had denigrated Rodric for their own selfish ends. They had painted him as a shameless demagogue who would ruin the country. Lachie instead found a measured thoughtful man with a degree of humility and self-denigrating humour which surprised him.

Rodric and Murdo analysed every news utterance and endlessly dissected its meaning. Mhairi would recount the latest gossip from her friends and neighbours. In this small rural community the ties were strong. The divisions that existed in the wider nation were reflected here, yet people were respectful of each other and were careful not to be outspoken in voicing their opinions about what was happening to the country. Throughout the referendum campaign the majority had preferred to keep their views to themselves and so it was too with the State of Emergency. A few who had known each other for several decades could be more open and voiced cautious opinions.

'Aye, it's aw fer the best mind, we may nae like it but whit wis the alternative?' to 'This is adding flames tae the fire. The fire will spread the likes o' which we've never seen before. Mark my words.'

Both Mhairi and Lachie relayed what people were saying. When Rodric announced that he had cabin fever and had to get out of the croft and go for a walk Lachie spoke with a firmness that surprised him.

'Ye will nae dae that, Rodric, under any circumstances,' said Lachie firmly, 'It's far tae risky. There are people in the area I have nae seen before – walkers and the like – and they surely aren't

Scottish National Trust people. Ye can smell the security people a mile away.'

Murdo concurred.

'How long can we realistically stay here? Weeks? Months? Isn't it better to be on the move?'

'Aye, it may well be but travel exposes ye to risk. Everywhere is being watched closely. The security forces have mobile road blocks so ye never know where ye're going to come across one. Even the minor roads are being watched. Then, of course, ye've the fifth column keeping an eye out for you.'

Murdo could see that Rodric was not happy with this but realised he had little option until it was clear which way the wind was blowing. Rodric felt the longer he stayed in one place the higher the chances of being discovered but equally he was well aware of the risks in moving somewhere else. There was, too, the question of where he could go. The farm seemed as good a place as any.

Later that evening they watched the BBC News. The bulk of the broadcast centred round the Prime Minister's appeal for calm and assurances to the country that preserving law and order was the priority.

'I am prepared to meet the First Minister at any time and in any place to draw a line under these terrible events. Scotland will be given extra powers to govern itself. Of that there is no doubt. I appeal for the FM to contact me. I shall personally guarantee his safety. Meanwhile law and order is being restored and tomorrow will be a different day. The State of Emergency will remain in force until the government is satisfied that normality has been restored. This may take some while yet.'

'Aye, while they round us all up,' said Murdo, 'they can't be serious about negotiations. They want you arrested. The offer is just a ploy to quieten things down, not least the financial markets.'

'I am not going to come out of hiding to negotiate, given what they are doing on the streets. We go the whole way on this one. It is the usual ploy of divide and rule. They know that we are a divided nation and anything they can do to lessen our support they will do. You can fool a lot of people for a hell of a lot of time. That is what this is about. Nothing else.'

The following day was tense. Lachie ploughed the fields close to the farmhouse keeping an close eye on traffic movements on the roads and lanes within view. If he spotted anything untoward he was to phone Mhairi and say that he was coming home early. That was the alert that the FM was in danger.

Twice in the following day Lachie phoned to say he would be home early but the security forces never came to the farm. Lachie did wonder if the farm was being watched from a distance.

Chapter Seven

Eilidh was shaken awake by Kirsty, her distraught flatmate, at 6.45am.

'Get up, Eilidh, they are arresting all the activists. A State of Emergency has been declared and Direct Rule has been imposed. You'd better make a run for it while you can. They'll be after you. I'm surprised they haven't broken the door down yet.'

Eilidh jumped out of bed and grabbed her nearest clothes.

'Oh my God, this is what we were afraid of. The bastards. They were never going to let us get away with it. What has happened to Rodric? Has he been picked up yet?'

'No, he's escaped the net. Someone must have warned him.'

Suddenly it all came together in Eilidh's mind – Murdo's late night phone call and the text that followed. He had been trying to warn her. She needed to think fast. Why hadn't she been picked up already? Incompetence? Was she being left as bait? Were the security forces overwhelmed?

'Eilidh, you really need to get out of here. they could be round at any moment for you,' Kirsty warned.

'You're right. I'll grab a few things and head off.'

'Where to?'

'God alone knows.' Eilidh's first priority was to get out of the flat and lose herself in Edinburgh. If she went back to Skye she would surely be picked up at the ferry or at a road block on the bridge. She had to assume that all transport hubs would be watched closely.

She hugged Kirsty.

'Off you go. Quick. Good luck. Whatever you do don't try and contact me. Throw away your phone.'

'*Slán.*'

'*Slán.*'

Eilidh hurried out of the tenement entrance with her head down and her hood up. She was carrying a small bag with a few belongings and clothes. She made for the nearest ATM and drew the maximum she could withdraw in a day. She knew her ATM transactions would be located and so this had to be the last for the foreseeable future. She had to be conscious of CCTV cameras with their facial recognition capability at the station and in the centre of the city. The best she could hope for was that the police would be overwhelmed and that would give her a headstart.

It was 7.10am and the city was alive with the wailing of police sirens and the lumbering of army trucks and prison vans. People in the streets watched bemused, some were crying while others were yelling in celebration that Scotland had been saved from independence. Many shook their heads in disbelief and sorrow. How had it come to this? As she looked down the road she could see a police road-block. Cars were being stopped and searched.

She knew she had to do some clear thinking. First, she had to decide where to go and then how to get there. Eilidh decided to drop into an early morning cafe while she pondered her next move.

'Are ye aright, hen?' the barista asked, 'God whit a mess this is.' The television was showing footage of people being arrested and put in the back of police and prison vans. 'I cannae believe this is happening here. I mean would an independent Scotland have been the threat of a good example or what? I wis going to vote 'No' but this, this.' His voice tailed off.

'Aye, dark days ahead,' responded Eilidh, 'no telling where it will end.'

The few customers were glued to the television news. One or two applauded the arrests while others stared silently, traumatised by what was going on.

The re-assuring tones of the BBC reporter stated how it would have been disastrous for the Scots if the 'Yes' vote had prevailed and also for the United Kingdom. Unionist politicians expressed their sadness that a State of Emergency had been declared but all agreed this was for the best. The Prime Minister's speech was running on a loop and was being played three times an hour. The BBC newscaster set the scene.

'At 6am this morning the Prime Minister went on national television and declared a State of Emergency. Security forces moved into the counting stations and seized all the ballot boxes. The officials were ordered to return home and remain there. The arrests of leading activists have already started. We make no apology for re-broadcasting the Prime Minister's speech.'

Viewers watched doors being battered open as security forces piled in to house after house dragging bewildered men and women to waiting vans. A few knew what was about to happen even before the Prime Minster spoke from Downing Street and fled. In some parts of Glasgow and Dundee people stood outside their homes banging on pots and pans to warn their neighbourhoods about what was happening. Eilidh watched an interview with the PM. She mused how since the BBC Charter had been re-written by the government it had lost its bite and now sounded more and more like some broadcasting service in a one-party state.

'I did not take this decision lightly, I can assure you. Much was at stake,' the Prime Minister insisted in the most sincere tone. 'Our security and defence as a nation were at stake. Of course, I accept that many Scots today will feel deep sadness at what is happening. I hold my hand out in friendship to them and promise them that together we shall build a prosperous, secure United Kingdom. We are not against those who were going to vote 'Yes' but only their leaders who were without conscience and for reasons of self-gain, greed and ego were leading this great nation down a road that would only have led to disaster. No Prime Minister, no government could possibly have allowed this to happen.'

The BBC interviewer thanked the Prime Minister. There were no questions, no scrutiny of what was happening.

Eilidh drank her coffee and chewed at her morning roll. She held back tears of anger. Her stomach churned. She needed to think clearly. She had to disappear. As she thought she began to realise how near impossible this was. She knew only too well that with every step she took, every person she spoke to, every shop she went into she was leaving a trail that could be followed. She knew how advanced surveillance was and how drones were being deployed over the country even as she sat there. Her only hope was that the security services would be so over-stretched that it would take days, weeks even to arrest everyone on their black list. Eilidh even wondered half in jest if the security forces had named the key players of the 'Yes' campaign after cards in a pack as the Americans had done in Iraq. They had.

She thought about Murdo's last text. 'Going to Lachlan's'. Who was Lachlan? She knew two Lachlans. One was a childhood friend she had gone to school with on Skye while the other was an old boyfriend. In fact, she rarely ever said much that was of a personal nature to Murdo. Perhaps Lachlan was a code like a clue in a cross-word and she had to work it out. She racked her brain for any mention Murdo had made of a Lachlan over the last years or so. Nothing came to mind. She would let the name rest and perhaps, the connection would come.

The news broadcaster was now referring to the FM.

'The latest news is that the First Minister has gone into hiding and that the search area has narrowed down considerably. It is hoped that there will be a development later in the day.'

An interview then followed with a former colleague of the First Minister who had resigned a few weeks ago and joined the Better Together Two campaign.

'Rodric Fraser was a dangerous man, a self-willed, deluded, delusional politician who put his own career for self-aggrandisement above his country. That is the sort of person he was. People need to know that. I worked closely with him for several years and could see only too clearly what a flawed, dysfunctional person he was. If he had had his way he would have fooled the majority into voting 'Yes', and here I have to say that despite the recent opinion polls, I have every confidence that once in the polling booth good sense would have prevailed. The man was a bombastic chancer. Nothing more, nothing less.'

Eilidh shook her head. The denigration of Rodric in the media had become shriller by the day as the referendum approached and the 'Yes' campaign pulled ahead. The man they described was not the man she knew, nor the man so many people would have followed to independence.

A plan formed in her mind. She would go to Glen Clova on the edge of the Grampians. Susan, one of her cousins and now a widow, had retreated there when her husband died. She was an artist whose reputation had grown steadily over the years. Eilidh had not been in contact with her since Christmas and suspected she was a Better

Together voter but they had never discussed the issue. There was a chance Eilidh could be surprised. The problem was how to get there from Edinburgh. She guessed that her name would be near the top of the wanted list.

It would only be a matter of hours before photos of the wanted list were disseminated in the media. She decided she would need to take her chance and hope that she could slip through the security net. Time was of the essence. She hopped on a bus to Waverley Station. She planned to catch the first train to Dundee and from there make her way by bus to Alyth and walk the remaining miles to Glen Clova.

It was then it dawned on her who Lachlan was. She remembered Murdo speaking about a cousin who was a farmer in North East Fife, near the Tay estuary. His name was Lachlan. How the hell was she to work out the surname of the family or where the farm was? The electoral roll? At least she now had a sliver of information. This must be where Murdo and Rodric had gone.

She left the cafe.

'Guid luck, hen,' the barista called after her.

'Aye. I think we'll all need that now.'

She knew she had to throw her phone away but thought she had time for a quick phone call to Ian, her brother in Skye.

'Are ye awright, Eilidh?' Ian asked with concern in his voice.

'Aye, I am. I have to disappear now. Don't worry if you don't hear from me for a while.'

'Guid luck, Eilidh. Mind oot fer yersel.'

As she crossed the North Bridge she dropped her phone onto the railtrack below. She was now free, untethered and didn't quite know if she could survive cut off from phone and social media.

Eilidh managed to slip through the security net at Waverley. The police were overwhelmed by the rush hour crowds and although people were being stopped, Eilidh could see that it was being done half-heartedly. She boarded the train for Dundee.

She always enjoyed the rail journey to Dundee because of the views from the Forth and the Tay Bridges. She kept her eyes firmly fixed on her newspaper. There was no mention of the declaration of the State of Emergency or the imposition of Direct Rule as the paper had been printed before the news broke.

The headline on the front page predicted 'Yes' would win the referendum by a narrow margin and questioned whether this was enough of a mandate to lead the country down what it regarded as such a perilous path. It pointed out that many would choose to move South rather than live in an independent country.

The article also pointed to the turmoil on the financial markets with shares sliding in the last week as it became clear the momentum was with the 'Yes' campaign. Government borrowing costs increased markedly. It commented that the Prime Minister had visited Scotland several times in the last four weeks and spoken to carefully selected mainly business audiences. His appeal to Scots to stay in the Union had been both emotional and heart-felt. This was the genuine man, the article declared. No one could accuse the Prime Minister of not 'throwing the bathroom sink' at the issue. Ironically, the more he spoke the more support for the Union seemed to ebb away.

Several other articles focussed on the worst case scenarios for the economy: *Scottish GNP predicted to shrink by up to 15 per cent; house prices to collapse by 25 per cent as mortgage lending to dry up; large-scale job losses predicted in all sectors; Scotland left defenceless just as the Russian Bear flexes its muscles; State pensions in doubt* and *Food prices to soar in and independent Scotland supermarket bosses claim.* The state was clearly employing every weapon in the dark arts to put the fear of God into the Scots. It was Project Fear Mark III – nothing had been learnt since the Brexit referendum.

All the newspapers published in Scotland that morning published similar scare articles. It was as though the propaganda campaign had been carefully orchestrated from a single source and had reached fever pitch on the morning of what was to have been the vote. Now events had overtaken the print media.

This concentrated propaganda onslaught had been going on for weeks and intensified as the date of the referendum approached. The message was simple: don't risk what you have with a leap into the unknown – the consequences could be dire for every single person. Yet despite this, the 'Yes' campaign's momentum grew steadily, as the polls showed. It was a re-run of September, 2014.

To Eilidh this barrage had confirmed her worst fears about the Westminster political elites: they would stop at nothing to prevent the collapse of the Union but now, with the State of Emergency and the arrests, they had moved to another plane completely.

The passengers on the train were subdued. There wasn't much talk. People looked anxious and uncertain. Some of them must have known that friends and relatives were being rounded up and placed in custody – God knows where.

When the guard checked her ticket he looked at her more closely than she would have expected, almost as though he recognised her from some photo of her that had been published. He clipped the ticket and gave her a wink. The message was clear: I know who you are but I am keeping my mouth shut.

'Will ye need a taxi in Dundee?'

Eildih looked at his demeanour. Instinctively she trusted him. He was on their side.

'Aye I will,' she replied.

'I'll call ahead fer ye. My cousin, Dougie, is a taxi driver. He'll take ye where ye want to go.'

'Thanks, thanks.'

'It is nothing. Only tae glad to help.' They exchanged conspiratorial smiles. He gave her the thumbs up. 'Awra best.'

At 9.30 the train pulled into Dundee and Eilidh noticed several plain clothes security men on the platform near the exit. She wondered whether to stay on the train and hope for the best but decided she had to get off and take her chances. As she stepped onto the platform she saw the guard calling the security men to the other end of the train. It was then she realised what had happened: he had called ahead as he knew there would probably be security men on the platform and he was diverting their attention so she could get clear of the station.

Dundee was reputedly a city that would vote 'Yes' by some margin. In 2014 the vote had been 57 per cent in favour of independence. Now polls in the city suggested 66 per cent. Somehow as she made her way to the taxi rank she felt safer than in Edinburgh. The referendum had divided city against city just as it had divided individuals. Edinburgh was now enemy territory while Dundee was not.

Dougie recognised Eilidh from his cousin's description and waved at her to come to his taxi.

'Hi, Jimmy telt me that I wis tae collect a VIP from the station and take her tae wherever she wanted tae go with nae cost.'

'Aye. Great guy. Could you take me to the other side of the Tay? I am looking for a farmer called Lachlan or Lachie. I think his farm is off the A92 somewhere but I have no idea exactly where.'

'Nae problem, hen. I have a friend in Kilmany who may be able to help. Who wid have thought it wid have come tae this? It's a dark, dark day fer Scotland. Yer safe with me. I wis an early supporter of Rodric. A great man.'

'Not everyone thinks that.'

'Aye, more is the pity!'

The taxi swung onto the approach road to cross the Tay back into Fife. 'There is a chance of roadblocks. The radio has been fair full o' reports o' them. Keep calm they say and carry on. Who are they kidding? This is nae the end. It's the beginning. We'll never put up with this.'

Eilidh agreed but decided to say as little as possible. She must trust no one no matter how much they seemed to be on her side. If a reward was put on her head it could be tempting.

As they were driving across the bridge they heard a police siren shrieking from behind them.

'It's the polis behind us. We'll just have tae hope fer the best that it's nae us they're efter.'

Eilidh noticed her breathing became more rapid and felt her heartbeat quicken.

The police car sped passed and they both sighed in relief.

'Aye, ye can never tell if they're efter ye.'

They stopped at a small farm cottage in Kilmany. Dougie spoke to his friend who happened to know Lachie. Twenty minutes later they were driving up the farm track. Lachie spotted the taxi coming and phoned Mhairi to warn her that someone was coming.

The taxi pulled into the yard and Eilidh got out.

'Thanks, Dougie, ye saved me.'

'Och, it's nothing, nothing at all. Gled tae help. Nae charge. My pleasure. Guid luck. If ye need any help phone me.'

They hugged. Dougie got into the taxi and drove off.

Mhairi came out of the farmhouse with the two collies bounding up to Eilidh and barking a welcome.

'You must be Eilidh. Welcome, welcome. Come in. How did ye ken where to come?'

Mhairi hugged Eilidh spontaneously. It was the hug that one human gives another when they have common cause and face danger.

'Murdo sent me a text last night. I didn't realise what it meant until this morning. Where are Rodric and Murdo?'

'Come in lassie. They're in the croft but Lachie has told them under no circumstances to go out of doors. We have already seen drones flying over. They seem to know where to look.'

'I'll go and see them.'

It was with a sense of relief Eilidh hugged them both.

'Good to see you, Eilidh, very good,' said Rodric.

'And what took you so long?' Murdo joked. Eilidh was looking at him in a new light. He thought he detected a softness in her eyes. But he was cautious. He knew from experience that he often misconstrued the signals he received from women. Nonetheless he was pleased to see her and delighted with what appeared to be a new approach to him. Like most men, it was years before Murdo realised that it was the woman who called the initial shots in a relationship. He decided to bide his time.

'How did you know where to come? Are you sure you are not being followed?' asked Rodric. 'They might have been using you as bait.'

'I think I'm clean. I was careful. I checked that I wasn't being followed.'

'But they will have you on CCTV footage at Waverley and in the train.'

'Yes, but it will take them some time to get round to checking it all. The security forces are over-whelmed at the moment and likely to be for the next few days at least. We have time to work out our next move. We can't stay here indefinitely. We have to move. The longer we stay in one place the more vulnerable we all are.'

'I was thinking the opposite. As soon as we break cover we are more vulnerable and where the hell do we go anyway? Who would have thought it would have come to this?' Murdo asked.

'Aye, we were foolish. We under-estimated the forces of opposition – a fatal error of judgement on my part. Our cause has been set back for decades. It is clear that the British state will not allow Scotland to become independent.

'There is one thing I don't understand: if an independent Scotland would guarantee a permanent Tory government why is it so keen to preserve the Union?

'I think it comes down to prestige – national and international – I

don't go with this 'we are all one big family' myth that is being ped-
dled. If the unionist case is that we are Better Together – with which
a building tide of Scots disagree – the unionist press in England
repeatedly argue that the rest of the UK – or England in particular –
is not better with Scotland. It seems contradictory,' said Rodric.

'Aye it does that. I suppose too it is not in the interests of the
political and financial elites to let Scotland go. They have too much
of a stake in the Union. Think of the loss of face for the UK. It would
become the laughing stock of the international community, more so
since Brexit,' responded Eilidh.

The conversation returned to what course of action they should
follow. Eilidh was for moving and suggested Skye where she had
friends and relations she could trust. Murdo was less certain and
thought they should stay where they were for as long as possible to
see how the situation developed. Rodric listened to both points of
view.

'I don't want to be holed up here, pleasant though it is, for any
longer than I have to be. I don't want to endanger Lachie and his
family who will surely pay a high price if we are captured here. We
badly need to know who has escaped being arrested.'

Mhairi came over with sandwiches at lunch as they sat in silence
and watched the BBC which was reporting developments non-stop.
The headlines focussed on what appeared to be a return to normality
in Scotland with people going about their everyday business interspersed with yet more 'man-in-the-street' interviews expressing
satisfaction that the UK government had acted so decisively to
prevent catastrophe.

The Prime Minister was interviewed too and expressed his
gratitude to the security forces for the efficient way they were
conducting their difficult duties and the way in which Scotland had
returned to normality so quickly.

'Law and order was gravely imperilled but I am glad to say that the security forces prevented the disintegration of the UK by the separatists bent on their own selfish and grandiose schemes which could only have ended in chaos.'

When the Prime Minister was asked about the FM his reply was guarded.

'We have narrowed down the search area considerably and hope to have him and some of his associates in custody sooner rather than later.'

'Could you tell us which part of Scotland you have narrowed the search down to, Prime Minister?'

'No, for obvious reasons I am unable to do that.'

Rodric, Murdo and Eilidh had watched in silence.

'Do you think they know we are in Fife?' Eilidh asked.

'Probably,' replied Murdo, 'There has been a marked increase in helicopter and drone activity as the day has gone on. Mhairi noticed a lot of police activity when she went to the village shop and was stopped at a road block. It is just a matter of time before they start a house to house search and use dogs.'

'What do you think they will want to do with me if I am captured? A high profile trial would be reckless because of the passions and backlash it would create. Surely they would want things to calm down and play the long game?'

'Aye. The last thing they want is to inflame the situation. They want to dampen it down as quickly as possible. I suppose they want you to disappear completely.'

'An accident?'

'Possibly. It would certainly relieve them of considerable trouble and what is one man's death – even yours Rodric – in the broad sweep of history?'

'They could of course negotiate with you.'

'You really think that? No way. They want this whole issue dead and buried until the end of time.'

A silence fell.

'I wonder what is really going on out there,' Murdo speculated.

After the initial shock of what had happened crowds began to gather in the main Scottish cities to protest. The police seemed to lack the will or the resources to respond at first. By the middle of the day several thousand had gathered outside the Scottish Parliament waving the Saltire and singing. In Glasgow large crowds gathered in George Square full of energy and humour for which the city is renowned but it was coupled to deep anger.

Social media postings caught the spirit of the moment. It was awash with video clips and was drowning in comments condemning Westminster's imposition of a State of Emergency. Twitter surged – the 'Yes' campaigners were gathering. #stateofemergency was trending.

What Rodric was not to know was that flash demonstrations were occurring up and down the land – forming within minutes and dispersing before the security forces could arrive and kettle them. Shouts of 'Freedom' were commonplace and spread like a rash throughout Scotland.

The mood was fractured: some over-joyed and others cast down in despair that independence had been within grasp only for it to have been snatched away.

By Thursday evening as the crowds grew the security forces decided on a desperate ploy: to break the protests and demonstrations using maximum force. It was a high risk strategy sanctioned by Downing Street where it was realised that only firm and quick action could retrieve a volatile situation. If this failed the United Kingdom would disintegrate and some thought Scotland would slip into anarchy. It was decided that the crowds in Glasgow and Edinburgh would bear the brunt of the security crackdown.

A few cracked heads will be necessary for the greater good, the smack of firm government is what is required was the way the Prime Minister presented it at the emergency Cabinet meeting convened to monitor the situation, and then sotto voce 'Fucking Jocks,' which caused the Cabinet ministers on either side to smile, 'We'll sort them out.' From that point Scots became known as 'FJs' within Number Ten.

By 6pm the crowds outside the Scottish Parliament had swollen to 40,000 and the crowd in George Square was spilling over into the surrounding streets. The security forces had lost the initiative and had not acted early enough to prevent the crowds building up. The curfew due to start at 8pm was clearly going to be impossible to enforce.

The Cabinet Office activated COBRA, the acronym for the Cabinet Office Briefing Room. The televisual and electronic links were established with command centres in Scotland and in the Military Districts. The PM chaired the meeting.

John Langwith, Gold Commander at the Strategic Co-ordination Centre, was in constant contact with Downing Street as the day had unfolded giving an assessment of the situation on the ground as opposed to the slanted news media reporting. Langwith was in constant contact with Graham Melton, the Silver Commander, in Edinburgh.

'I am afraid, Prime Minister, we are losing control of the situation. We are too thinly stretched and police lines have been thinned by absenteeism. I am not sure we can count on the loyalty of the Scottish police anymore. There is only one way we can bring the situation under control.'

'And that is with armed force?'

'Precisely, although we should perhaps go in hard with tear gas first.'

'Try tear gas first. Use as much as possible. We have got to clear the crowds immediately. You have got enough of the stuff haven't you?'

'Large amounts were shipped North some weeks ago for precisely this eventuality, Prime Minister.'

'Armed force must only be used as the last resort. We are already getting very negative coverage in the global media. The last thing we want is people dying on the streets. This isn't some trumped up dictatorship. We have a global image to protect.'

By 9.30pm the crowds, bombarded by tear gas were beginning to disperse. The security forces moved in behind the curtain of tear gas and wielding truncheons, liberally split heads. Downing Street watched the result with grim satisfaction.

The members of COBRA continued to watch the live feed on the large television screen. It was not easy watching. Scenes from demonstrations in various parts of Scotland were playing out on the screens in front of the meeting. Sequences showing the police going in hard followed. It was barely watchable. There was the occasional sigh and a shaking of heads.

Attempts to corral the demonstrators in Glasgow failed as the police were outnumbered. The demonstrators seemed disciplined and despite frayed tempers, there was no sign of violence against the police. In a way this made it more difficult for the Government. Scenes of a robust police response to peaceful demonstrators would not play out well in the media or with international opinion.

'This won't be the end, Prime Minister,' predicted Neil Simpson, the Scottish Secretary. In truth he felt conflicting emotions at seeing such heavy handed methods deployed on the streets. Yes, he believed that Scotland should remain a part on the United Kingdom – for that was what was best for the country – but he empathised with his fellow countrymen who were now bearing the brunt of state repression. Such repression would surely be counter-productive and bring about the collapse of the Union it sought to protect. He had not gone into politics to see his fellow countrymen treated in this way, whatever the cause.

'Internment failed abysmally in Northern Ireland, Prime Minister, as I am sure you are aware. For every person interned a hundred turned to the republican side. There was, too, the issue of the wrong people being arrested which fanned the flames even more,' Simpson said.

'Yes, yes, Neil, we know that. The stakes are high but what else can we do to preserve the Union?'

Simpson got up from the table and walked across to the window. The room fell silent. Shortly, the PM joined him. He seemed to sense Neil's thoughts.

'I take no pleasure or pride in what is happening, Neil. I can imagine too well how difficult it is for you watching what is going on. We shall soon have regained the initiative and things will settle down.'

Neil turned to face the Prime Minister. Tears streaked his face. The Prime Minister put his hand on his shoulder. For all his puffed up self importance it hurt him deeply to see what was happening.

'I understand. I understand, Neil.'

'I have to resign, Prime Minister, I cannot see Scotland bear the brunt of this onslaught whatever my views on independence.'

'Take time to think this one through. In forty eight hours this will hopefully all be behind us.'

Two hours later Graham Melton, the Silver Commander in Scotland, reported that the crowds in Glasgow and Edinburgh had been dispersed but the security forces were now having to deal with flash demonstrations gathering quickly only to disperse before the security forces could make arrests. Tear gas was ineffective in dealing with flash mobs.

The PM was pleased that the police had regained the initiative without the use of armed intervention. The excuse for that was ready. 'Extremists opened fire on the security forces who had no alternative but to return fire to save lives.'

'This is not doing our image in the wider world any good, Prime Minister,' Ben Grant, Director of Communications, said.

'We really have no alternative on this one, Ben. Hopefully, it will be resolved speedily and the media circus will move on to feast on something else. That's why I think we have to apply maximum force. No matter how unpleasant and unBritish it may be, we must end this as expeditiously as possible. There isn't an alternative. If there was, I would choose it.'

'We must quell this within twenty four hours,' the Prime Minister added. Neil had already left the room. Others were beginning to wonder if they should do the same.

'With respect, Prime Minister, we may clear the streets and squares in the main cities but I very much doubt that will be the end of the matter. The blowback from this is going to outrage many people who were in the middle ground and, who knows, perhaps some of the unionists too.'

'What do you suggest we do then, Ben? Sit on our backsides and twiddle our thumbs and let the Union collapse around our ears?' Exhaustion was beginning to fray tempers.

'I think it has passed that point already, Prime Minister. There is no United Kingdom after this. Pandora's box has been opened and God alone knows where it is going to end up.'

'Steady nerves are required here, granted. History will judge us well, mark my words, Ben.'

'I am not so convinced, Prime Minister, in the worst case scenario it could end up in a civil war and you know how impossible they are to stop once they gain momentum.'

'I need to speak to Murray. I need a bloody tame Jock sitting in here to tell us how this is all playing north of the border.'

An hour later Murray, a Scottish political journalist working for the BBC, was ushered into the room.

'Ah, Murray, good of you to come at such short notice. We really need someone like yourself to interpret how these, er, ghastly events are playing out in the Scottish psyche.' They all resumed their seats and the sound on the television was turned to silent.

'What are your views on how this is going, Murray? Can we defeat this lawlessness? How do you think ordinary people will interpret this? The BBC is more than doing its bit to reassure the Scots that normality is returning even if we know this isn't really the case. Are we winning hearts and minds or is what we are seeing the beginning of the end of the Union?'

Murray, the Scottish face on the BBC network, took a deep breath. He didn't intend to pull his punches.

'You may be able to sweep the demonstrators off the streets but it won't end there. Once people get their blood up – as many already have – we are in for turbulent times. If we're not careful it is just a matter of time before lives are lost. Yes, the country is sharply divided between unionists and separatists. A policy of maximum force will fan the flames.

'This is going to have implications on the financial markets, in fact, as we speak the markets are reacting sharply. Investors are pulling money out of the UK plc. There are few people who are not going to react negatively to what is happening. In crude terms the state is crushing a butterfly and this doesn't play well. The Scottish sense of grievance is legendary as you know, Prime Minister. What we see happening on the streets will fan this exponentially. The worst suspicions of the separatists are now a brutal reality.'

There was a silence round the table as those present digested what they had been told.

'So what do you suggest, Murray?'

'The First Minister must be found. Negotiations must be opened with him immediately. An accommodation must be reached at all costs. Give them enough to think they have got their independence in name and throw them some scraps from the table but keep the real power here. It requires a subtle balancing act. It is entirely possible that we have gone beyond the point of no return. If you go on television tonight and announce that you are prepared to open negotiations with the First Minister then it is just possible the terrible events of today will recede.'

There were general murmurs of agreement from around the table. The Prime Minister thanked Murray and asked him to stay for as long as the BBC could spare him.

Graham Melton, the Silver Commander, came on the link to inform COBRA that 2,105 activists had been arrested and were being processed in Hampden Park and Murrayfield. Although the First Minister had escaped all bar two of the top tier of leadership had been arrested. The majority of the regional leadership had been rounded up although here, too, four key players had escaped. Most of the national opinion formers and shapers from the 'Yes' campaign had been apprehended. Detainees would be hurriedly processed and then dispersed to prisons and make-shift camps in Scotland and England within the next twelve hours.

The Prime Minister expressed his satisfaction and gratitude to both Langwith and Melton. A ripple of applause went round the room.

'The operation has succeeded beyond expectations, gentlemen. I am especially keen to get a sense of the mood on the street, John. Have the major demonstrations been quelled yet?'

'Yes, pretty much. The tear gas did the trick although we are still witnessing flash-mobs springing up spontaneously and then disintegrating before we can bring the security forces to bear. These are not large and can range from forty to a hundred or so people. Dare I say the mood is quietening down slightly? That said, it could still be a long night and we are thinly stretched. The fact that eighteen per cent of Police Scotland called in sick this morning has not helped although the reinforcements from south of the border could not have arrived at a more opportune moment.'

'Any progress on finding the FM? We have to get this bastard in custody as soon as possible. This is a top priority.'

'We have a dedicated team who have been working on this all day. CCTV and roadside cameras footage is all being scanned. It seems he was warned by Murdo MacGregor, one of our key assets who went native. Eilidh MacLeod hasn't been picked up either. The FM left Edinburgh on the back of MacGregor's motorbike in the early hours – footage confirms that – and they headed across the Forth Road Bridge and then onto the A92. After that there is no trace of them. They left all the main roads. We are working on the idea that they have gone to ground in Fife. We are going through the computer lists of all Yes supporters in Fife. They are probably in hiding with one of them. This may take time. They have clearly dumped their mobile phones and GPS systems. I have ordered the two drones into the area as well as the police helicopter. It is only matter of time before we have him in the bag.'

'Thanks, John. If there are any developments let me know immediately.'

'Yes, Prime Minister.'

'Fucking Jocks. We should have realised MacGregor had the propensity to go native.' The PM looked hard at David Manningtree.

'There was absolutely no indication in his record that that was a possibility, Prime Minister. Ironically, it was hard to imagine someone more of one of us. A Scot yes, but one of the establishment, an Anglo-Scot. Everything from his family background through his private schooling and Oxford career pointed only in one direction. His vetting was thorough and nothing was turned up that suggested that an aberration was possible. I had him re-vetted before sending him on this deployment and there was nothing untoward at all. It is impossible to under-estimate the appeal of a cause. Give a man a cause and he becomes transformed and little else in life matters.' Manningtree said in his matter-of-fact way.

'Too many FJs, no matter what their background, seem to have a propensity when push comes to shove to revert to type: disloyal separatists.

'Who is this woman Eilidh MacLeod?'

'One of Fraser's closest aides and a senior Party member. She comes from Skye, a farming and fishing background. Committed to the cause. Before MacGregor decided to go native he warned us about her: clever, perceptive and effective. She was the key member of Fraser's team and many within the party see her as the next leader should Fraser fall under a bus.'

'The time is ticking on this one. We have to take them out of circulation. I want the FM's head on my wall within hours.' The hunting metaphor was appropriate given the PM's love of fox-hunting.

COBRA dispersed for a few hours on the understanding that if the situation changed it could be re-convened at short notice.

An hour later Neil's letter of resignation was on the PM's desk.

'Fuck, fuck,' said the PM quietly to himself.

Emma got up at her usual time of 6.50am, put on the kettle and switched on the radio. Her thoughts were on the day ahead and the annual appraisal with her boss. There was, too, the meeting with the CEO of SARCO, to discuss the company's PR profile which had been taking a few knocks in the press for failure to deliver on public service contracts.

It was also the day of the referendum in Scotland and that filled her with a heavy heart as a 'Yes' victory seemed a foregone conclusion judging by the polls. Gradually she became aware of what was being discussed on the radio and it brought her up with a start.

The only news item seemed to be that a State of Emergency had been declared in Scotland and Direct Rule imposed by the Government. The powers of Scottish Parliament had been transferred to Westminster. This had all been done for the security and the territorial integrity of the UK according to the BBC political correspondent.

Emma was not a political animal but somehow this jolted her. Her first thought was of Murdo. Their relationship had gradually unravelled and together they made the decision to call it all off. There were no recriminations as both felt they had come to recognise and accept the obvious: the distance between them and the difficulty in spending time together had brought the relationship to a gradual, gentle end. It had run its course.

Emma suspected that Murdo had found someone else but he never said he had and she didn't want to ask for fear of what his answer might be. They phoned each other from time to time although the gaps between the phone calls became longer and longer.

After some months she accepted that the relationship was over and began to go out again. Her friends seemed determined to pair her up with a never ending list of male suitors most of whom seemed unsuitable. She began to realise that to find that one special person with whom she could feel a spark was more difficult than she had imagined. She was still grieving over the loss of the relationship with Murdo and it was hard not to measure every man against him.

She switched on BBC breakfast televison and watched the 7am news. The first item was about the State of Emergency in Scotland and that was followed by the Prime Minister's speech on why it had been necessary and his sorrow at having to go down this route. He spoke of his love of Scotland and reminded the nation that one of his grandmothers was Scottish. Emma thought his performance was credible and even touching. He seemed genuinely to care for the UK and the people of Scotland. He was clearly doing his best for the country.

Emma like many others had not really paid much attention to what had been going on in Scotland in the run-up to the referendum. It was only in the last few days when it began to appear obvious beyond all doubt that the separatists were going to win that she began to take notice.

Like many in England she could not understand the 'Yes' voters. Why on earth would they want to leave a successful Union which had served both the UK and Scotland so well? It was hard not to agree with the mainstream London press that the Scots were being led by politicians with only their own interests at heart. As someone who knew Scotland she felt sad that there was going to be a split. She even felt a degree of anger about it. Why had it come to this?

She decided to phone Murdo to find out exactly what was going on in Scotland. There was no reply. His phone was dead. Emma suspected the true nature of what Murdo was doing in Scotland. She was probably not too far short although Murdo had always made light of her questions and deflected them with humour.

She phoned her father. There was a dead line sound. It crossed her mind that either the mobile network had been shut down for security reasons or that it was on overload and couldn't cope with the sheer volume of calls. She phoned him on his landline at work because she knew that he would be at his office, given what was going on.

'Hi, dad, just thought I would phone you about the news.'

'Look, darling, really can't talk. Things are moving very quickly on the markets and volatility is horrendous. Talk later. I'll phone you when I can. Just to say the whole thing is a bloody disaster.'

The volume on the television had been switched down. There were clips of footage from Edinburgh and Glasgow of people going about their business, almost as though nothing had happened. Several were interviewed and, although Emma couldn't hear what they were saying, they seemed to all have smiles on their faces as though they were pleased with the turn of events. Emma was wise enough to know that it was what was not being filmed that was what was important.

At work Emma rushed over to talk to a colleague and friend who was from Edinburgh.

'Look, Emma, I don't really want to talk about all this. It has happened and it is probably for the best. I am too upset.'

'Have you been in touch with your family?'

'Yes, yes, I have. They're okay but things aren't quite going the way the media are telling us. It seems that there are more demonstrations than we know and also that arrests are being made. There is a strong security crackdown.'

'I suppose that is to be expected.'

Emma tried several times to phone Murdo but his phone still seemed dead. She texted him several times.

'R u alright? Love Emma.'

There was no reply. When Emma eventually phoned his university supervisor she was told that Murdo had not been seen for three days and had not kept an appointment.

As the day progressed it became clear that the Government's line of 'business as usual' in Scotland was not accurate. The turmoil and volatility on the financial markets was less easy to hide. Rumours swept the City of intervention by the Bank of England to try and restore calm. Other rumours spoke of significant sums being withdrawn by overseas investors. The City believed that the instability of the markets was a temporary adjustment and that they would soon settle down. The Chancellor made the necessary noises.

Will was astute enough to realise that when the Chancellor says one thing about markets you have a good chance of making money by doing the opposite. He decided to short the market. It turned out to be one of those days in the City that would be remembered for years afterwards – up there amongst the most difficult. Traders were to christen it 'Fraser Day'. Litres of Malt were consumed that evening to settle rattled nerves. Many wondered how the fate of a small and economically relatively insignificant country could spook the markets. Some surmised it was a symptom of deeper uncertainties over the economy. Of course, as always, there were some who had done well out of the day's gyrations and that included Will.

Chapter Eight

THE PM SLEPT BADLY AND was in a bad mood when he got up at 5.30am. This would be the pivotal day, he thought, and yet he had doubts about his government's course of action. He knew there was a real possibility that his smack-of-strong-government policies in Scotland would have the opposite effect and lead to independence. He thought long and hard about what Murray had said. The possibility of driving some unionists into the arms of the separatists was not to be under-estimated. He knew full well that the very future of his government depended on success in Scotland. Anything else and he would be spending more time with his family.

He phoned Langwith, who had been up most of the night and sounded exhausted.

'Melton reported a few hours ago that things quietened down in Glasgow and Edinburgh by about 2am. In Dundee protesters were on the streets all night and a morning shift seems to be arriving now.'

'We have got to nail this one today, John. Any progress on finding Fraser?'

'I am reasonably confident we shall find him within the next thirty six hours?'

'Too long. Find the bastard today. Top priority. Allocate whatever resources you need.'

At 8am Adam Montagu, the Chief Whip, arrived at Number Ten to discuss the appointment of a new Scottish Secretary. The PM got on well with Montagu.

'I thought the EU negotiations were bad, Adam, but this crisis is on another plane altogether. I always suspected Simpson was a wimp but as the only MP from our Party to win a seat in Scotland we had no choice. Well that's his peerage gone down the plughole. It looks as though we'll need to appoint an English MP as Secretary of State for Scotland. God, that is going to go down like a lead balloon. Can you think of any of our people who can take this one on, Adam? Ideally we want someone with links to Scotland, you know the sort of thing: at least one parent Scots or someone with a Scottish first name at the very least. Failing that someone who went to a Scottish university but for God's sake steer clear of Tatton, he will antagonise the Jocks no end.'

Tatton Wykehurst-Smythe was a backwoodsman of many years seniority in the Commons. He was the archetypal Tory MP from the Home Counties who happened to have vast family wealth and a castle in Angus. He had always been passed over for preferment, and it rankled with him. There is nothing that he would have liked better than to be made Secretary of State for Scotland. He now justified his existence by being a constant thorn in the PM's side.

'Tatton can keep pissing on the tent from the outside as far as I am concerned.'

Sure enough within five minutes of Neil's resignation being made public late last night, Tatton was on the phone asking if he could come down for a chat. Adam put the phone down and groaned loudly.

By mid-morning Stewart Wyndham was made Secretary of State for Scotland. At least his first name is Scottish, thought Montagu, although he didn't realise that Wyndham had never visited Scotland. Wyndham was delighted by his promotion. At last he was on that greasy pole, albeit at the bottom.

'We have been watching your career to date, Stewart,' the PM said smoothly to him. 'And I have to say that we are impressed. Your name was the first to be mentioned by Adam Montagu. Of course, I took other soundings as well.' Wyndham didn't realise that the PM was being economical with the truth. Montagu had scoured his MPs for a Scottish name or any links, no matter how tenuous, with the country. He had produced a shortlist of five and presented it to the PM who took a look down the list and snorted.

'God, is this all we have?' and then proceeded to write off three of the five on various grounds. That left Stewart Wyndham and Boyd Trend. At least both had Scottish first names. Trend was tentatively sounded out but, in his robust Yorkshire manner, responded that he needed to be Secretary of State for Scotland like 'a hole in the head'. So it was Stewart or Stewart.

'Of course, I realise that this is not an ideal time to be taking on this job, Stewart,' continued the PM at his smooth best, 'But look at it as a challenge. If you do well you will certainly be destined for higher things – no doubt about that.'

Wyndham was suitably flattered. The PM knew that gentle flattery was the oil that lubricated the workings of the Party. The vanity of Members knew few bounds. Massaging egos was what politics was about. Wyndham had always had a high opinion of his own abilities even if that was not universally shared. The first thing he did when he returned to his office was to phone his wife. She saw him as Party leader within a few years.

'You haven't accepted have you?' she asked incredulously. Why is it that wives have an amazing ability to deflate the male ego? Stewart wondered. Probably because they have good reason was his next thought.

When he assured her he had accepted she laughed.

'Oh God Stewart, are you mad or something? Can't you see what a poisoned chalice it is? I mean it is like Northern Ireland, a political graveyard, a job that no one else wants.'

Stewart assured Carol that he was the PM's first choice and that he had had an encouraging meeting with the PM over a coffee at Number Ten.

'Your weakness, my darling, is that you have always been susceptible to flattery. I mean what do you, or we, know about Scotland? We've never even been there. Do you have any idea of the geography of the place apart from knowing where Glasgow and Edinburgh are and that there are Highlands?'

'Look, I know this is a tough one, especially at the moment but I am sure I can do the job and do it well.'

'At the rate things are developing in Scotland, darling, there will be no Scotland within the UK of which to be Secretary of State.'

Carol had sensitive political antennae inherited from her father who had been an MP for thirty years. She met Stewart at the Young Conservatives and singled him out from all the other young bloods as the one most likely to reach the top. She married him as a result. And, yes, she did love him, for all his faults. She denied to her close friends that the marriage had been a political one.

'I mean, I love the man,' she told Susan, her closest friend, and then, 'Of course, he will get to the top. I can spot the killer instinct in him already.' She laughed. As always you never quite knew which part of what Carol said to take at face value and which was said ironically.

'You presumably realise that the line of 'business as usual and a return to normality' in Scotland is almost certainly propaganda?'

Stewart had to admit that had not crossed his mind.

'Oh well, I suppose you have accepted the bloody job so you have no option but to get on with it. You realise that this could be the end of your political ambitions, don't you? How many Northern Ireland Secretaries from the last fifteen years can you name?' Carol asked. The point was well made. 'When will you be going up to Edinburgh?'

'Probably on the first flight on Monday morning.'

The phone wasn't quite slammed down. Gradually the thought struck Carol that she would make a rather good 'First Lady' of Scotland and Edinburgh was full of interesting people. Mmm. On the other hand, she might be regarded as one of the colonists, a role that sent shivers down her political spine.

An hour later Carol phoned Stewart. Her tone this time was more positive and soothing.

'On reflection you were right to take up the challenge, darling. I mean, if you succeed your political star will be on the up. I know it is a high risk strategy but let's go for it. I'll fly up to Edinburgh as soon as I can after you.'

Stewart smiled. He liked to have Carol's approval as it didn't seem to come too often these days.

He reflected on what she had said earlier. He recognised her political astuteness and her ambitions for him. Somehow in accepting the job it was as though he had let her down. She was waiting for a greater prize. Her shameless schmoozing at Party Conferences with the top echelons inspired admiration and intense dislike in equal measure. Carol feared that Stewart's acceptance of the appointment would be mocked as a triumph of ambition over common-sense. There were many things that Carol could tolerate but being mocked behind her back was not one of them.

Stewart opened the atlas at a map of Scotland and called

Hatchard's for every book on Scotland they could recommend. He had homework to do and it was urgent. Then there were all those files. The thought of being at the centre of history in the making appealed to him.

'If you were to recommend one single book on Scotland which one would you recommend?' Stewart asked the sales assistant.

'Without a doubt it would be *Scottish Journey* by Edwin Muir and first published in 1935, sir.

I know Scotland well and I think you will find that not that much has changed since then.'

'Really?' asked Stewart incredulously.

'I think you'll understand when you have read the book and visited the country. Do read it before you go if you can.'

Stewart made a mental note to start reading the book as soon as it was in his hands. He would read it on the flight to Edinburgh.

That night when he got home he asked Carol to wrack her brains to see if they had any Scottish acquaintances they could ask round for a meal on Saturday. Somehow he had to find out what made the people tick. He would, of course, have a drink with Neil and then there would be the official hand-over, although he did get the message from the PM that Neil was 'no longer one of us'. Stewart wasn't sure if this meant that Neil had flipped and become a separatist or just that he had resigned. He regretted not asking the PM. Perhaps he would find out from Neil himself over that drink.

Murdo and Rodric watched the unfolding crisis develop. The BBC dropped any pretence of impartiality which had been highly suspect during the campaign anyway. Interviewee after interviewee praised London for its intervention. The whole issue of the referendum was now portrayed as an aberration and a distraction from other national issues.

Isla and Jennie came across to the cottage and chatted with Rodric and Murdo. They were proud in a quiet way that the family was protecting and hiding the First Minister. Isla joked they were hiding their Bonnie Prince Charlie.

After twenty four hours the country seemed stunned, unsure of itself, floundering even – all apart from the staunch unionists whose triumphalism was sprayed over the media with a glee that the majority found bitter to swallow.

It was Jennie who suggested that the true picture was more complex. Social media had replaced the corporate media – as it had done for much of the referendum campaign – and they could see the first stirrings of an opposition and spasmodic civil disobedience. The websites like Newsnet Scotland, Bella Caledonia and Wings over Scotland were blocked by GCHQ but others quickly replaced them and provided a focus for the reputed two million Scots who would have voted 'Yes' in the referendum.

'It's just a matter of time before the true feelings of the majority make themselves felt on the streets,' Murdo said.

'Aye, and what then?'

'If that happens there is no way that London will be able to control the outcome. They will lose. They have upped the ante. That was the risk they were prepared to take. The law of unintended consequences and all that. If that happens London will be determined to find you – they can't risk you coming out of hiding and leading the movement. It was made quite clear to me in London that they are out to destroy you one way or another, Rodric. You are a dangerous bombastic populist, a disrupter politically and economically. They are out to get you – preferably alive but it may suit their requirements if you were involved in an accident.'

Rodric knew that there was little doubt that what Murdo was saying was true.

Rumours spread on social media that the forces of law and order were split in Scotland over acting against demonstrations or civil disobedience. Many police refused to take orders from London and stayed at home 'sick'. Police from other parts of the UK poured into Scottish cities, especially Dundee and Glasgow. London was less concerned about Edinburgh which, although the capital, was two to one unionist.

Chapter Nine

THE PM HAD HAD LITTLE sleep for the third night. He was not someone who needed more than five hours but for the last three nights he had averaged two and a half. He was aware that the fatigue that was setting in was taking its toll on everyone dealing with the crisis. Surely, Fraser would be captured today? He was growing impatient with Langwith's confident assurances that Fraser would 'only be free for another few hours'. Last night he had asked the President if the National Security Agency could help locate Fraser. The President was sympathetic and said he would task the NSA establishment outside Harrogate with the responsibility. What he didn't tell Sutton was that they had already located Fraser at a farm near Kilmany in North East Fife. The President and the National Security Council were discussing the crisis the following morning and had yet to work out where US interests lay, given that the latest intelligence suggested London was going to lose Scotland. It was not in America's interests to swim against the tide.

The Cabinet Secretary and the PM's Chief of Staff were waiting for him as he came downstairs. Both could see that the crisis was taking its toll.

'Good morning, gentlemen. What's the latest? Have we got Fraser yet?'

On the third day of the crisis it was becoming clear to the security forces that, although the 'Yes' movement had been decapitated, power was passing into the hands of the ordinary people. There was a distinct possibility that the initiative would pass from the security forces to the 'Yes' campaigners – with or without leaders. This concern was discussed in the video link between Langwith and the Prime Minister in the late afternoon.

'How is it going, John?'

'Mixed, Prime Minister, if I am honest. The flash demonstrations are impossible to predict and are over in minutes. They have occurred in most cities and towns now. We are even getting reports in the most unlikely of places: small villages and at John O'Groats. Traffic on the new Queensferry Crossing ground to a halt heading North and delayed us getting our people into the search area in Fife. On the other hand, we have now picked up over two thousand key activists and their processing is going smoothly. We have airlifted about five hundred out of Glasgow and Edinburgh Airports to Brize Norton for dispersal. We are just holding the initiative. The next forty eight hours will be crucial. We have to bag the FM within that time. The last thing we want is the 'King over the water' syndrome.'

The Prime Minister expressed his satisfaction.

'Keep at it, John. We may be over the worst. Just let me know if you need any more resources. We have stripped most of the police forces down here to send you the manpower you need. How is the Scottish Police force reacting?'

'Mixed, depending on area. In some areas absenteeism has hit fifty per cent, notably in the Glasgow conurbation, Dundee and the central belt but even Edinburgh has not been immune.'

'So we're not really out of the wood yet are we?'

'Not yet, Prime Minister.'

'The longer this goes on the greater likelihood of a complete unravelling of the situation. The President has asked to be kept informed and offered any help we need. The Pope has expressed his concern. The King is most anxious that this is resolved within hours. No pressure, John. There is an aircraft sitting on the tarmac at Edinburgh to fly Fraser out as soon as he is bagged.'

Lachie came across to the croft in the early evening.

'The net is tightening. The area is crawling with polis and security people. It is only a matter o' time before they arrive. I can hear their dugs barking doon the glen. Mhairi and I have talked this one through. If ye want to stay we can dae our best to hide you but realistically ye're probably better to try and break through the security cordon if ye're to have any chance of avoiding being taken into custody. Ye have no chance at all if ye stay here.'

'Aye, Lachie, you are right. We have to take our chances and head for somewhere else.'

Over the next hour plans were discussed. In the end it was decided that Lachie would take them in the back of a farm trailer across the fields, through the wood and then along farm tracks avoiding all the roads for about ten miles. This, hopefully, would take them out of the main search area. He would deposit them at Rory Meikle's farm. Rory was a 'Yes' sympathiser.

They were to leave at 6am. The hope was that the security forces sweeping the area would not be in a high state of alert or much in evidence at that time in the morning. At best there would be a minimal presence. The drones, however, were a concern as they were constantly in the skies and could be seen at regular intervals as they criss-crossed the area. It would be all too easy for a drone to take pictures of their movement and direct security forces to stop them.

The question was where they would go. Eilidh was certain that they would be safe in Skye. Murdo and Rodric agreed with some reluctance that this was probably the best option.

Chapter Ten

A T 5AM MHAIRI ROUSED THEM for an early breakfast.
'Ye'd better eat as there is nae telling when ye'll eat again.'
Mhairi had built a fire in the kitchen and porridge was
already simmering on the stove.

'I owe you and Lachie such a lot,' said Rodric, 'Hopefully one day
you will be my guests at Bute House,'

'Ach, away with ye, it's nothing,' said Mhairi, 'It's only what anyone
wid dae. Lachie has become a true Scot at last,' she joked.

The three of them sat in silence wondering what the day would
bring. Custody? Freedom?

Isla and Jennie came downstairs.

'Get ye back tae bed,' said Mhairi.

'The noise woke us up. Are you all going?' asked Isla.

'Aye, we are. It's better that way,' said Rodric.

'We hope ye'll be safe,' Isla said.

'Dinnae worry aboot them and get back tae bed.'

The children crossed the kitchen and hugged all three of them.

'We hope we'll see ye again.'

'Thanks. Now back to bed as your mother said.'

Shortly later, they took their farewells with Mhairi.

'It has been a privilege to look efter ye, Rodric, Murdo and Eilidh. I'll hope for better days.'

'Aye, Mhairi, do that,' said Rodric.'Thanks, many thanks. You have a wonderful family and I'm grateful for what you have done for us. Our people will not tolerate repression on this scale – ever.'

They all hugged.

'Now be sure ye tak care o' yersells.'

The tractor and trailer pulled out of the yard and across a field that some days before had been golden with ripened wheat. The sun was struggling into the sky and light was darting across the landscape. The morning air smelt fresh and the slight chill hit their nostrils.

'I wonder what today holds.' said Eilidh.

After an hour moving slowly through the fields Lachie stopped the tractor in a wood and came round to speak to them.

'We'll wait here fer Rory. He should be here in the next twenty minutes and then he'll get ye oot of this area. There is a lot of air activity around. I saw some security people doon the glen – ye wuid have heard their dugs.'

'Aye, made my blood run cold. Stuff of nightmares.

'We have to assume that for some reason they know you are in this area, probably a combination of roadside cameras and aerial reconnaissance. The sooner you're away, the better.'

'I'm going for a pee,' Eilidh said and wandered into the forest. The smell of a new morning emanated from the forest. It seemed good to be alive to feel the presence of nature. Somehow the danger of their situation had heightened her senses to all that was around. She stopped to hear the birdsong and marvelled at it. It was as though she had never heard it before. She walked deeper into the wood to let its presence flood her senses. When she was a little distance from the tractor she squatted down.

Suddenly she heard movement in the forest as though someone was moving as quietly as possible through the bracken. There was the crunch of the odd branch. Eilidh stayed absolutely still and peered in the direction of the sound. It was then she saw about eight men in camouflage uniform, weapons at the ready, moving slowly in the direction of the tractor. There was no doubt that they had been directed here and were looking for Rodric.

Panic gripped her. If she exposed her position by running to warn the others she might be shot. Her gesture would serve nothing as Rodric and the others would be captured at the very least or perhaps even shot. It would certainly be easier for the State to claim that Rodric had resisted and had been shot while trying to escape – an excuse used so many times by governments round the globe. It was certainly a tidier option. Eilidh maintained her cover. The squad was moving through the forest to her left. They must have been about two hundred metres from where the tractor and trailer were parked.

Once the squad was within eighty metres they rushed the tractor and trailer screaming to Rodric and Lachie to freeze and put their hands up. She saw Rodric and Lachie raise their arms but could not see Murdo. Members of the squad were whooping exultantly. Within minutes more men in camouflage joined the squad. Then Eilidh could hear the approach of a helicopter. She could see Rodric and Lachie, their hands tied with plastic wire and hoods over their heads. The group started moving away from her towards a clearing in the forest where the helicopter was hovering and about to land.

Eilidh knew that she had to get out of the area before she was picked up too. She found a track leading in the opposite direction and moved swiftly alongside it, running hard and trying to put as much distance between herself and the clearing where the helicopter had now landed. She hoped that the security forces would be so pleased with Rodric's capture that they would drop their guard and leave it at that without searching for anyone else.

She could see a village in the distance and a road with heavy traffic. Eilidh decided to make her way to the road in the hope she could catch a bus back to Dundee. She needed to tell Mhairi what had happened to Rodric and Lachie. She walked across the fields and as she did so she saw the helicopter take off in the direction of Edinburgh.

She felt sick, physically ill. She wondered what had happened to Murdo. Why had she not seen him? Had he betrayed Rodric by directing the security forces to him? Eilidh dismissed this possibility. After all it was Murdo who had warned Rodric and helped him to escape arrest. Had he unknowingly been tracked by his phone even if it had not been switched on? Her mind was full of speculation. She knew, too, that she had to let Mhairi know what had happened to Lachie. Perhaps if she could get to Dundee she could use a public callbox even although she knew they were monitored.

The more she thought about it, the more she realised she would need to take her chances. She knew she would still be at the top of the search list although it seemed unlikely the security forces would be so diligent now that they had picked up Rodric. She made up her mind to return home to Skye as quickly as possible but how she was going to do this was another matter. She knew her family would be worried about her. Somehow she needed to let them know she was safe.

Eilidh walked down to the road towards the village about half a mile away. She looked at the timetable by the bus stop. The next one was not due for forty minutes. She felt exposed standing waiting so long and made her way to the garage which she could see had a cafe attached to it.

She ordered a coffee and a bacon roll. The television was on in the corner. A BBC reporter from Edinburgh was again assuring the world that things were returning to normal. The camera panned round and did indeed show people going about their everyday business. What Eilidh could not see was the crowd which had started to gather outside Holyrood or the other forming outside Bute House. Nor was there any reference to the Twitter storm.

The BBC reporter handed back to the London studio. A discussion followed between politicians from the three main parties all of whom supported the PM's declaration. All expressed sorrow at recent events and a desire to work together for the good of the United Kingdom. The last time the three main parties had agreed on anything was during the 2014 Referendum.

Eilidh's sense of outrage at the three parties in bed together was echoed in other parts of Scotland. Labour supporters watching the broadcast would be choking on their porridge. This was indeed a bitter pill for them to swallow: their Party in bed with the Tory Party. But then she smiled. She was remembering the *Masters of the Universe* Youtube clip when Scottish Labour MPs had been sent North in 2014 to preserve the Union and were mocked by a 'Yes' activist playing the *Masters of the Universe* tune from *Star Wars*. Wielding a loud-hailer, he shouted to the people of Glasgow to bend to their knees to welcome their Imperial Masters. She smiled too at the thought of the Better Together clip of what had become known as the *Patronising Woman* and its spoofs. The campaign for independence had humour that had brought smiles.

The two women behind the counter were arguing about what was happening. One was saying that tragic though the events were it was all for the best. The other argued that this was a dark day for democracy and that it would not end there. Eilidh imagined similar conversations up and down the country.

Just as she was about to leave the cafe a breaking news item flashed across the screens. It read 'Rodric Fraser, the First Minister of Scotland, has been apprehended in North East Fife. Further details will be released shortly.'

When Eilidh went to pay one of the women said, 'It's been a terrible few days for Scotland, my dear.'

'Aye, and for the UK too,' chimed in the other one.

Eilidh had expected Rodric's capture to be made public at some point in the day but not quite as quickly as this. Her stomach started churning again. She breathed deeply in an attempt to maintain her composure. There was no mention of Lachie or Murdo. No doubt a fuller picture would emerge later in the day.

Eilidh smiled non-committally at the two women and left to catch the bus which was due shortly. The journey to Dundee took nearly an hour. It passed through two road blocks the last of which was on the Tay Bridge. Traffic was backed up for several hundred metres. The passengers sat quiet, uneasy and edgy. Eilidh felt that the gloom could have been cut with a knife.

In Dundee she made her way to the station. From a callbox she rang Mhairi.

'We have had a bad morning with the tractor. Lachie won't be back for a while.'

'Aye, I thought something had happened. It's wall-to-wall on the tele. Take care of yersel. We'll meet up again some day.'

Eilidh then phoned home and left a voicemail.

'All's well. Holiday beach tomorrow three,' she tried to speak in a different accent to divert any suspicions. She knew too well that the security services had voice recognition capability.

Ian, her brother, who worked on the farm and also did some inshore fishing in his boat, listened to the voicemail with a sense of relief. He would take the boat to the beach at Allt tomorrow. Allt Dhiuirinis was a stream near Plockton on the mainland coast opposite Skye. The family had once owned land there.

She was safe. That was all her family needed to know. Fiona smiled at the good news and rushed into the farmyard to tell Alister, Eilidh's father.

'Thank God for that. We'll need to hide her until all this is over.'

'The holiday croft will be fine. We have nae mair reservations this year,' said Fiona.

'Aye, aye, that'll dae fine.'

Fiona then went to Rab's room. She knocked gently on the door. Rab had discharged himself from hospital a few days earlier and had come home to die. He wanted to die in his own bed. He wanted his family around him, the sounds of the farm he had worked for most of his life and Kyle, his sheepdog by him.

Rab was sleeping. Fiona stirred him gently.

'Guid news, faither. Eilidh will be wi' us tomorrow. She's safe.'

He smiled. Eilidh was his favourite grand-child. Yes, grand-parents are not meant to have favourites. Everyone knew that he treated his grandchildren the same and loved them all equally but his bond with Eilidh since she could talk had always been the strongest.

'Guid, I'm glad,' he said quietly.

Fiona had watched the visible decline of her father each day, never quite sure if this was to be his last. The family took turns sitting at his bedside even although Rab was now sleeping about twenty hours a day. He ate and drank little. Fiona, Alister and Ian knew that these were signs that the end was close. Nurses visited at intervals to make sure he was comfortable. Kyle hardly strayed from the bottom of the bed. He sensed that he had to stay close to his master.

Murdo had wandered a short distance from the tractor and trailer in the opposite direction from Eilidh. As he relieved himself he listened to the sounds of the forest – the breeze riffling the trees, and the birdsong. As his mind wandered he was suddenly conscious of branches and undergrowth being broken. He ducked down among the ferns and listened more closely. His heart leapt. He was sure that he could hear people moving stealthily through the forest to the right of him, perhaps forty to fifty yards away. He decided to lie low. The group – for that is what he imagined it to be – was moving in the direction of the tractor. Murdo knew immediately that they were security forces. There was no point in shouting a warning as Rodric and Lachie had no chance of escape. He decided that he had little option but to hide in the hope he was not captured. He wondered if Eilidh was back at the tractor.

He heard shouts as the security forces broke cover and ran towards the tractor where Lachie and Rodric were standing. In those few minutes of pandemonium Murdo scrambled away through the undergrowth in the opposite direction. He had no idea which way he was going. He only had one aim: to put as much distance between him and the security forces. He ran furiously, heart pounding, gasping for air – thank God all that exercise he had done over the last few years had kept him physically fit. After ten minutes of hard running Murdo emerged from the wood. He could hear a helicopter behind him arriving to collect Rodric and Lachie.

Rodric was taken entirely by surprise as the security forces broke cover and ran towards him hurling abuse. He and Lachie looked at each other in panic. Where were Eilidh and Murdo? Eilidh had gone off in one direction and Murdo in the other. Had they betrayed him?

'Get your fucking hands in the air, tossers!' The accents were not Scottish.

'That's the end of your little vanity project,' another sneered.

Rodric looked at their uniforms as they handcuffed him roughly with plastic cuffs. This was a unit of the special forces.

The two men were pushed around and mocked as hoods were pulled over their heads.

'You'll be out of circulation for a while now, Fraser.' Some of the squad laughed.

Rodric felt panic as the hood went over his head and tightened, as though they were trying to deprive him of air. He knew whatever happened he had to keep his dignity and show no fear. His position as FM demanded this.

The collective excitement of the squad eased as they congratulated one another and called for a helicopter. Rodric could smell cigarette smoke.

Rodric was pushed roughly into the helicopter which took off at once and headed towards Edinburgh Airport. Apart from minimal conversation between the aircrew and Edinburgh control tower, nothing was said. Rodric began to feel disorientated and the hood covering his head was making him nauseous. He gritted his teeth and told himself he had to get a grip. He breathed deeply to calm himself.

The squad leader contacted Gold Control.

'We've got Fraser, sir.'

Langwith jumped up and punched the air.

'Well done, well done! Congratulate your squad. The PM will be absolutely delighted.'

Langwith then phoned the PM with the news.

'Fantastic news, John. Absolutely bloody marvellous. Well done to your team! How did we find him?'

'Satellite reconnaissance and drones. We also narrowed the search area down markedly by looking through the footage from the road-side cameras.'

'Brilliant. The Cabinet will be delighted to say nothing of the King.'

The PM could not contain his pleasure at the arrest. He had a tendency to rise on his toes and wring his hands at moments of intense stress or joy. A press conference was called for him to make the announcement about the capture although the news was already trending on the social media. This was one press conference that he was looking forward to.

The flight to Edinburgh Airport was a short one. The helicopter landed some way from the terminal on the runway that ran South East to North East where private jets were often parked.

A short distance away a group of plane spotters watched the helicopter as it landed next to an executive jet. Their cameras with telephoto lenses clicked rapidly.

'My God, Andy, do you realise what this is? That guy with his head in the hood is the First Minister. I can tell by his walk. They've found him. Oh, my God!'

'Quick, we better get the hell out of here with these photos. The last thing the London government want is for them to be published.'

Within minutes the photos were uploaded to Twitter and Facebook and spilled into cyberspace. The photos of Fraser, hooded, being marched from the helicopter to the Gulfstream which had an American registration, were on social media and spread round Downing Street like a nasty rash. The PM was in a meeting with the National Security Council. It was interrupted by his PPS.

The PM's face darkened.

'I am afraid I have some bad news,' he announced, 'Pictures of Fraser in a hood being transferred from the helicopter to the other aircraft have been uploaded on social media and are now on the mainstream media. We need to get our spin on this out immediately. This can only inflame the situation. What a total disaster.'

The meeting broke up with Ministers at a loss as to how to try and deal with the approaching tsunami.

The sense of outrage was deeply felt as crowds gathered in the cities, towns and villages of Scotland. In Edinburgh groups assembled again outside Parliament while in Glasgow people were piling into George Square. Even many of the 'No' voters were angered by their First Minister being treated like a Guantanamo Bay prisoner. There was an acute sense of insult and humiliation. While many despised the man, to others he still represented the Scottish nation, regardless of his politics and policies. Many unionists now began to question where their loyalty lay: to the British State or to Scotland.

Once inside the executive jet and it was airborne, Rodric's hood was removed. The handcuffs, which were starting to chafe, were not. The aircraft was surprisingly small. Two men in civilian clothes sat in the cabin with him. Neither of them seemed keen to say anything to him or talk to each other. They sounded American. Rodric wondered if he had been handed over to private contractors.

Rodric looked out of the window as the plane climbed steeply out of Edinburgh airport and banked northwards over the Forth Road Bridge. Soon it was over the North Sea. He tried to see the position of the sun to work out the direction of the flight. It seemed to be North East. One of his guards decided to close the blinds.

If they were going South the flight would last no more than about ninety minutes to the southernmost part of England. It did cross Rodric's mind that he might not be going anywhere in the UK but perhaps to one of those 'black' prisons in Lithuania or somewhere else, which the CIA had used in its rendition programme after 9/11.

Over three hours later Rodric felt the aircraft start to descend. One of the men put the hood over his head again and the feeling of claustrophobia and mild panic returned. Breathing was not easy. When he complained he was told aggressively to shut up.

The descent was steeper and quicker than Rodric had expected. Once landed the taxi-ing took over ten minutes. Rodric deduced that it was a large airport and he was being taken to an isolated part of it. He did not hear other aircraft landing or taking off.

Once the plane came to a standstill the door was quickly opened and Rodric was hauled to his feet and manhandled roughly to the door. He noticed it was cool which suggested somewhere in the north. He began to think he was indeed at some 'black site' outside the UK's borders. He listened for the language being spoken but heard only English in the banter of the ground crew.

'We got Braveheart for you,' one said as Rodric was pushed into a vehicle.

'We'll soon find out just how much of a Braveheart he is. I've never heard of a sequel.'

Rodric's two guards laughed. They travelled for about six minutes and then stopped abruptly. Rodric was manhandled into a building. He was surprised that it all seemed so quiet.

His guards handed him over to a senior officer who ordered that Rodric's hood be removed.

'My name is Wroughton,' said the senior officer holding out his hand. Rodric noticed that his rank was Lieutenant Colonel. He was a tall, thick-set man with short, cropped hair and a quizzical look. 'And this is Mr Creyke,' he said, introducing another man in civilian clothes looking as though he was dressed for the warmth. Creyke looked every inch a policeman, probably Special Branch. He was stocky, well-built. He exuded hostility and ill-disguised menace. Crekye made no move to shake Rodric's hand.

'You will be held here for as long as is necessary, and you will be questioned.'

'About what exactly?' Rodric asked with his trade-mark look of disbelief.

'There's some reading material for you in your room,' said Creyke with a smile.

The men made no attempt to answer but Rodric heard Creyke murmur 'Smart arse.'

Rodric was taken to a cell – not a room – at the end of a long corridor. There was no natural light. The walls were painted ship-grey. There was a bed in one corner and a toilet in the other. There was also a small table and a chair. The table had a Bible on it and a pile of Treasury reports. Rodric wasn't sure whether to find this amusing or touching. There was a change of clothes lying on the bed, a pair of pyjamas and some toiletries.

As the door clanged shut Creyke said, 'We'll be having a chat sometime in the next few days. I recommend you read those reports after you've read the Bible.' He laughed at his own joke. Wroughton laughed too.

Lachie was taken from the helicopter to a prison van. He protested when he was roughly manhandled. His guard ignored the protest.

'Awra best, Rodric,' Lachie shouted to Rodric, 'This is nae the end. Only the beginning.'

'Aye, let's hope so. Good luck to you, too, Lachie.'

'One for you mate,' the military man said to the security guard as he pushed Lachie towards him. 'Where are you taking him?'

'To Murrayfield. There's a large holding unit there where all the activists are being processed.'

'Sort out these separatist bastards.'

'Aye, that and mair,' laughed the guard. It was now that he realised what it meant to be up against the might of the state. He felt utterly helpless for the first time in his life.

The guard pushed him into one of the cells in the van which set off at high speed. He looked out at the suburbs as the van sped along. The speed limit was ignored.

Lachie wasn't sure what to feel. Resentment? Yes. Fear? No. Foreboding? Perhaps.

At Murrayfield he was bundled out of the van, hood still on and frog-marched to a processing room.

'Another one fer ye,' said Lachie's guard handing him over.

'Fuck. How many more?'

Lachie was taken into a small room, de-hooded for the first time in over an hour, strip-searched, finger-printed, DNA swabbed and photographed – all within fifteen minutes. He felt like a common criminal and humiliated. The room smelt of sweat.

He was then marched to another room where he was ordered to sit on a chair, not speak and wait his turn to be interviewed. There must have been over thirty in the room – men and women of all ages. Several glanced in his direction and smiled encouragingly. Three gave him the thumbs up.

The irony of sitting amongst 'Yes' activists was not lost on him. He, who had been sceptical about the whole independence project, was now under arrest with all these separatists. He wondered how Mhairi and the girls were. He knew that by now they would be suspecting the worst. He wondered if he was allowed to contact them.

He waited three hours. There was a team of fifteen interrogators and each interview seemed to take about fifteen minutes. A series of questions was barked at the interviewees in a hostile, aggressive manner. Some of the voices were Scottish, others English. Lachie guessed they were security people trained in interrogation.

At last he was ushered across to one of the desks.

'Name, address and occupation?' asked a cultivated voice.

'Lachlan Murray. The Howe, Kilmany, Fife.'

'Occupation?' the hostility in the voice had increased.

'Bloody fermer.'

'And what is a bloody 'fermer' as you describe yourself Mr Murray doing supporting the 'Yes' campaign and hiding the First Minister? Bit odd wouldn't you say? I mean farmers weren't likely to gain from the whole independence farce, were they?'

Lachie bit his lip. He wanted to explain that he had been hostile to the whole idea of independence but he didn't. He now saw more clearly than ever why Mhairi held the views she did. Suddenly he was proud of her as he had never been before and, yes, he was now a separatist too.

His interrogator was typing Lachie's details into the computer.

'This says you were a Better Together supporter.'

'I wis but I'm nae one noo. I am one hundred per cent a separatist and bloody proud of it tae.'

His interrogator half smiled.

'Another fucking idiot!'

'Oor day will come. Nae doot about that.'

'I really doubt that Murray. I really doubt it. You have just moved yourself from a category three prisoner to category one. You should have kept your mouth shut. Mind you, I suppose anyone who hid the First Minister was always going to be a category one,' his interrogator said with tired resignation. He signalled to one of the SARCO security guards. 'Take him to the category one compound.'

'Sir.'

Lachie was marched into the stadium. As each prisoner was brought into the arena a cheer went up. Lachie waved in acknowledgement. He was herded into a large compound within the arena fenced with rolls of razor wire. He looked around the stadium. The place seemed to be surrounded by armed men patrolling up and down. The last time he had been here was for a Scotland versus France International earlier in the year.

As he was pushed into the compound one of the inmates came forward and shook his hand.

'Hi. Welcome to the Barlinnie road show. Name is Finlay, pal.'

'Lachie.' They shook hands. Lachie found himself facing a tall man with steely blue eyes and a bandana round his forehead. Defiance was written on his face.

'Where are ye from?'

'North East Fife.'

'Angus, fer me. Just outside Dundee. We fair put the wind up London.'

'Aye. We've done that and more.'

'Listen dinnae sweat o'er this one. They're on the back foot. Aye, perhaps we'll be out of circulation fer a while, but sure as hell we'll win. These bastards aren't going tae intimidate us. Just remember who we are.'

Lachie nodded. Instinctively he liked Finlay.

'Hey, come and meet the pals. We are the elite in this compound,' he laughed loudly. The SARCO guard at the entrance looked perturbed. He clearly didn't like Finlay and felt somewhat fearful. He was only doing this because he needed the money for his family. Two years of unemployment in austerity UK had weakened his resolve. This zero hours contract was not what he wanted but it was all there was and Christmas was not so far away now.

Four hours later security guards came across to the compound and escorted them out six at a time. The compound for category one prisoners must have had over fifty inmates. Over thirty were women.

As each group was escorted out Finlay stood by the exit and shook each person's hand in turn.

'Now ye keep strong. Ye understand? This is part of the price we're paying for independence. Dinnae let it bother you.'

A few hours later Lachie found himself in an RAF C17 along with Finlay and two hundred others taxi-ing to Edinburgh Airport's main runway. They had all been hooded again and plastic cuffs were attached to each one of them.

As John Langwith, the Gold Commander was briefing COBRA and the Prime Minister, an airport worker at Edinburgh was filming two long columns of 'Yes' activists hooded and in handcuffs boarding an RAF C17 transport aircraft. The cry *Saor Alba* went up followed by a roar.

Some of the aircraft maintenance people started clapping. Shortly later the footage was on Youtube. Once again public opinion was inflamed.

Once the doors were shut, Squadron Leader Ross Baillie started the engines and slowly the large aircraft lumbered along the taxiways to the runway. He was given the all-clear for take-off, opened the throttles and the C17 sped down the runway and lifted off.

Baillie found himself struggling with conflicting loyalties. Like all members of the armed forces he felt a deep loyalty to King and country and yet to see his fellow countrymen being treated in this way came as a shock. He had followed the events in the run-up to the referendum closely and had quizzed his friends and family in Edinburgh about it. His attitude was ambivalent. If anything he would have voted 'No' but like many Scots he was not without sympathy for the concept of independence.

When the aircraft reached cruising altitude the loadmaster came through to the flight deck.

'How are they?' Ross asked.

'They have been singing something about some flower of Scotland.'

Ross didn't know whether to laugh or cry. He did the former and switched on the address system.

'I want you to know it gives me no pleasure to be carrying out these orders. I applaud what you were trying to do.' There was a short silence and then a cheer went up in the hold. Singing broke out again and resounded loudly through the aircraft.

Ross' co-pilot, an Englishman to the core, lent across, shook his hand and said, 'I understand where you are coming from, Ross. It gives me no pleasure either. You Scottish bastards. We are breaking a butterfly. Don't worry. The spirit of a nation cannot be broken, you fucking separatist sympathiser.'

Ross smiled. He felt like turning the C17 towards the Netherlands and asking for asylum but instead he carried out his orders.

When the aircraft landed at Brize Norton, Ross could see the prison vans lined up on the apron. When the aircraft came to a standstill, Ross ordered the doors to be kept shut. He went into the hold.

'All the best and good luck,' he said.

The mood of the activists seemed anything but cowed. The opposite was the case. Morale was high. The doors of the huge plane were opened. Small groups were disembarked and taken to prison vans. The singing started again, even louder this time before.

The SARCO guards seemed phased by it.

'Fucking Jocks,' was the consensus. 'A spell in Belmarsh will shut them up quickly.'

Two days later Ross Baillie resigned his commission and made his way to Scotland. Whatever was going to happen to his native land he wanted to share it. Why hadn't he flown them to the Netherlands?

Murdo tried to take his bearings. The position of the sun helped. He looked at the landscape carefully to see if he could recognise any of it. In the distance he could see a road – probably the A92 from Edinburgh to Dundee at a guess. There was also a hamlet beside the road. He thought he recognised it from the bike ride with Rodric as they had escaped from Edinburgh. If he was correct he was about three miles from Lachie and Mhairi's farm. He decided to go back into the forest and hide until the security forces had gone. He was convinced they would stand down and return to base at Leuchars now that Rodric had been captured.

By ten o'clock Murdo felt it was safe enough to make his way back to the farm using the A92 as his reference point, but his intention was to keep to the fields. His mind was racing. What was happening? Where would they take Rodric? What would happen to Lachie? What would he say to Mhairi and the girls? Where was Eilidh? Had she been captured? What was the wider picture of what was happening in the country? Suddenly he felt tired. The strain of the last few days was taking its toll.

When an hour later he stumbled into the farmyard Mhairi ran out to greet him.

'Oh my God, Murdo, come in quickly. I've been watching the tele. Eilidh phoned a short while ago and told me what had happened.' She hugged him, 'Thank goodness you're alive. I've heard the sound of automatic fire in the last two hours. I feared the worst.'

Murdo told Mhairi exactly what had happened in the wood. He wondered how the security people had known so precisely where to find them. It certainly didn't seem like chance.

'You must stay here in the croft again until things quieten down before you decide what to do,' Mhairi assured him.

In fact he had no idea what to do next. He was a hunted man. There was no telling how long the State of Emergency would last or how effective it would be. He asked Mhairi if she knew what was really happening in the country.

'I've only heard snippets frae neighbours and the odd phonecall, Murdo. All I can say is that it is far from the way Westminster and the media are presenting it. There is evidence of a campaign of civil disobedience emerging nationally. Things aren't quietening at all. The reverse is true. There is nae telling what will happen next.'

Murdo stayed indoors. He didn't initially fear for Rodric's life – he was too valuable to Westminster alive, especially if they had to use him as a pawn to quieten things down. Little did they realise the true nature of the man. No amount of intelligence data could reveal his strength of character. Murdo did wonder however how hard they would try to break him. Perhaps it would have been better if he had been 'shot while trying to escape'. Yes, there would have been an almighty outcry but in time it would have died down and Westminster would not have had to deal with him. They would have found a more compliant politician who would have protected the interests of the United Kingdom first.

He asked Mhairi where she thought Eilidh would go if she had not been captured.

'I think she'll probably try tae get home tae Skye. That is what I wid hae done. Her family will look efter her and hide her until this is all resolved,' said Mhairi.

'Do you know where in Skye her family live?'

'Isleoronsay between Broadford and Armadale on the Eastern side. You can find out by looking up her family name in the online phone directory.'

'Is that a good idea? The inquiry will be traced back to your computer and address.'

'Aye, I suppose it will. It's terrible to think how we're all monitored so closely in these days.'

Murdo was unsure how long to stay. He didn't want to endanger Mhairi and the girls and it was surely only a matter of hours before the security forces arrived at the farm to search it from top to bottom. After a few hours he had made his decision.

'Mhairi, I can't stay here any longer for your sakes. It won't be long before the security forces arrive and you have problems enough with Lachie in custody.'

'Ye're right but I think we have time before they come here. Their other priorities are much more pressing than us but ye're right. Ye need to move for your ain sake. Where will ye go?'

'To Skye to see if Eilidh is there. If she has been captured at least I'll be able to see her family and tell them what has happened to her.'

'And then?'

'Who knows?'

The Sunday papers were full of the crisis with lurid tales of what the separatists had been hoping to do. There was universal praise for Sutton, the PM who had saved the Union. There was also approval that Fraser was in 'protective custody' somewhere (no one quite knew where) to save him from the 'ungovernable wrath' of his own people. Some spoke of a possible treason trial. The slant on what was happening in Scotland was predictable: a return to normality – thank

God. *The Observer* gave particular prominence to the internment of several thousand activists – the number ranged from two thousand to five thousand but no one really knew the total.

Unusually for a Sunday, the National Security Committee met. There was a sense of relief that the situation might be being brought under control.

'We must not become complacent about this,' the PM told the Committee. 'We need to remember that it was a close-run thing and that the separatists could well be regrouping. The security people are keeping a close eye on developments.'

The PM turned to Stewart Wyndham, the new Scottish Secretary. 'How do you read the situation, Stewart? A calm before the next wave of the storm, or has the storm completely abated?'

'The national mood is surly and depressed, PM. We were right to go in with maximum force and decapitate the movement. There are now 6,000 activists in camps and under guard around the UK, mainly in disused military camps. SARCO has excelled at providing the guards necessary for these establishments. We owe Sir Michael, the CEO of SARCO, particular gratitude. Perhaps recognition in the New Year's Honours List, PM?'

The PM smiled thinly. 'As you know, Stewart, I could not possibly comment on that one.'

Polite laughter followed.

The PM then asked Walter Goldsmith, DG of GCHQ, if social media could be shut down as the Egyptian Government had done during the Arab Spring in 2013.

'Technically, the answer to that PM is yes, but we would be entering the realms of a dictatorship. The State of Emergency would give us the cover we need, but I doubt it would play well with the country, even in these difficult times. It would be much better to use social media to our advantage and bend it as much as possible to our narrative.'

'Mmm, I suppose you're right on that one although it may get to the point where we have no option. I want to leave that option open.

'There is a certain irony in all this. For so long we have set the national agenda and controlled the media either directly or indirectly, and now fucking social media has taken power from the top and given it to the grassroots in a way we can't control,' the PM said grimly.

There was a pause, then Wyndham continued.

'The State of Emergency must be ended as soon as possible to underline a return to normality. We can do what we want under the provisions of Direct Rule anyway. The Scottish Parliament will not meet for the foreseeable future, if ever again.'

There were murmurs of approval around the table. The commonly held belief in the party was that Labour's policy of granting devolution to Scotland to quell nationalism had the exact opposite effect and even encouraged and sustained it. Now that the Scottish Parliament was closed and its powers recalled to Westminster the status quo prior to devolution had been re-established.

'I agree totally with you, Stewart. We survived this challenge to the Union by the skin of our teeth. Our priority now must be to strengthen the unionist position in Scotland, to win over the fence-sitters and undermine and destroy the separatist cause entirely; to do, in other words, what we have done to Labour. A few sweeteners are necessary: orders to shipyards, that sort of thing; new infrastructure projects; a modernisation of the Scottish rail network; perhaps extending HS2 to Glasgow and Edinburgh. We must make the Scots feel more of a part of the UK. I shall discuss a few more visits by the Royals when I go to Buckingham Palace next.'

There were yet more murmurs of approval.

'How long are we going to keep the activists in preventive custody, PM?' asked the Home Secretary.

'For as long as is necessary, but not a moment longer. They should be individually screened and assessed for their commitment to separatism. Only when they have given us a written guarantee of no further political involvement of any kind will we release them. I don't envisage this starting for at least three months; time enough to cool their political ardour, and only then will they be released in small numbers. The whole process could take at least eighteen months or more. That's how we should proceed, in my view.'

There was suppressed amazement that the PM had already seemed to have thought this one through. Either he was thinking quickly on his feet – something he was renowned for even if it did get him into political scrapes later – or he had been well briefed by someone.

'I think we need to start a charm offensive North of the border. Perhaps you should go up first, Gavin. As Chancellor you could spread a little largesse, I'm sure: a few photo opportunities with all sections of Scottish society. You could even make amends for your last visit there.'

There was a ripple of laughter. His last visit had been a public relations disaster. The Chancellor's phrase that the Scots were benefit junkies had not gone down well.

'I would be delighted to go and spread some largesse, Prime Minister, as long as our English voters don't feel that the Scots are being treated over-generously,' the Chancellor responded.

In private, he had a low opinion of most Scots and Scotland and believed that the country should have been cut loose, if only to live with the consequences of independence which he was certain would have been disastrous. Neither did he have much time for Stewart Wyndham and his ghastly wife, who had a grossly inflated opinion of her husband's political abilities and future career. The light at the end of the tunnel for Buckland was that Wyndham's political career would surely come to an abrupt end in Scotland and he would not be a rival for leadership of the party. Buckland smiled: there was some justice after all.

Dame Juliet had never seen the PM use so much strong language in such a short time; a reflection of the stress of the situation and the high stakes for the United Kingdom, being rent asunder. Yes, there was an irony in all this. The Security Services knew everything there was to know through monitoring of electronic communications and their carefully placed 'assets' in Scotland. In their complacency Whitehall and the mainstream media had completely underestimated the appeal of independence to the Scots. How had it come to this? How had they got it so wrong? There was an irony, too, in the fact that while the Security Services had used social media to keep a watch on the mood of the country – a sort of updated Mass Observation Project that Whitehall had used in the Second World War to see beyond the war propaganda – social media with its immediacy and freedom from control was now being used against the State. It was an irony not lost on those at the meeting.

'Draft a statement for the media, Ben, will you? We need this to go out now,' ordered the PM.

'What line are we going to take on it, Giles?' The fact that Ben Grant called the PM by his first name was noted with disapproval. Grant was not popular. Directors of Communications rarely were.

'That Fraser has been arrested and is being held under the State of Emergency for his own safety because of the righteous anger of the Scottish people.'

'I don't really think that will wash, Prime Minister,' said Dame Juliet. 'Whatever else the Scots are, they are not fools. They will see through that one. Just keep it that he is being held under the State of Emergency until further notice. The photos of him being transferred from the helicopter to the aircraft with a hood on his head are the most damaging thing we have to deal with. That's what's causing such an outpouring of anger on the streets.'

'You will have to deal with questions on that, Prime Minister, at the press conference,' said Sir Crispin. 'You just need to say that it was an over-enthusiatic member of the security forces acting beyond orders, and that the case will be looked into by his superiors. Then give every assurance that Fraser is being well treated and looked after without revealing where he's being held.'

'Good point, Crispin, we'll play it that way,' the PM responded.

An hour later the PM appeared at the press conference. The questioning was uncharacteristically sharp and unsympathetic. Even the natural allies of the Government seemed sceptical of the line they were being fed. Events on the ground suggested that there was no relief in the State of Emergency, in fact the opposite was the case. Unrest was still sweeping through towns and cities. What had been a series of spontaneous flash mobs had become large-scale demonstrations with the security forces unable to cope with their scale or frequency.

'Can you give us the Government's perception of events in Scotland in the last twenty four hours, Prime Minister?' The question came from the political correspondent of the *Telegraph*, which had campaigned hard for a 'No' vote, and whose Scottish edition had done its part in churning out lurid headlines for the Better Together's 'Project Fear'.

Goebbels once said that the press represented the long-range artillery of the regime, and so it had proved during the referendum campaign when the *Scottish Mail* and every other arm of the media owned outside Scotland had campaigned vigorously for a rejection of independence. It was almost as though each tried to out-do the other with its endless dict of scare stories. But as Goebbels also said, 'Propaganda, to be successful, has to fall on fertile ground'. That ground had proved increasingly stony as the campaign neared its climax. Ironically, this time the propaganda of the mainstream media had produced a backlash amongst a sufficient number of Scottish voters who saw it for what it was: an orchestrated propaganda campaign of lies and half-truths from London and Whitehall.

'Well, thank you for asking that, Justin. As you probably know the situation is more fluid than we would like but I have every confidence that things are settling down, albeit more slowly than we would hope. I think by the end of the week we shall see a return to almost total normality. I can understand that the State of Emergency is difficult for some Scots to accept when they thought they were about to win what they call *independence*. Of course, we all realise that true independence is illusory in this world of capital markets and the constraints of the European Court of Human Rights. None of us is an island, Justin, are we?'

The PM was pleased that he had been able to end his answer with a little quip. The assembled journalists did not respond.

'Where is the First Minister now, Prime Minister?' asked the Political Correspondent of the *Sun*, a man whose finger on the political pulse was more sensitive than many of his colleagues, and all the more respected for that.

'Ah, Bill, I'm so glad you asked that. He's in good hands and is being well looked after by units of our security forces. We disagree strongly with what he was trying to do – dismantling our United Kingdom, our family of nations that has been so successful for hundreds of years – but we must respect his views no matter how misguided he is. The damage that would have been done to Scotland and, indeed, to all of us in the UK, would have been considerable. We would all have been diminished if Scotland had gone its own way.'

The journalists realized that the question had not been answered.

'With respect, Prime Minister, you have not told us where the First Minister is being kept,' another journalist commented.

'No, it would be wrong of me to do that for security reasons. I'm sorry about that, but I am sure you will understand,' the PM's answered.

There was a noticeable groan from some of the journalists present. National security was wheeled out regularly when the Government wanted to shut down discussion. The questions then moved to the implications of the State of Emergency for the UK as a whole.

'We are a democracy with a free press and rule by law. I, for one, do not want the present situation to last a minute longer than necessary.'

'Under what circumstances will it be brought to an end, Prime Minister?'

'Once things have settled down in Scotland and normal life has resumed for a period of time. We cannot have political instability in part of the United Kingdom that threatens our economic progress and social cohesion. Let me give this assurance: the State of Emergency will end sooner rather than later.'

A number of other questions followed, broadly along the same theme. The tone of the questioning remained sceptical. These were after all, hard-nosed journos who had been following the vagaries of the political process for many years. They all had their inside sources who usually told them a rather different story from the one spun at the PM's press conferences.

'How do you think that went?' the PM asked Bennett.

'Let's just say, PM, that it was a damage-limitation exercise that, on the face of it, went satisfactorily. How the journos report and spin it is another matter. I think the media are onside, of that there is no question. I am getting reports though that some powerful people are getting a bit anxious that we haven't shut the situation down yet; worried about their estates in Scotland and the financial markets,' joked Bennett.

Chapter Eleven

Eilidh made her way to Inverness and then to Duirinish. She was surprised that it had been so easy and that she hadn't been apprehended. Yes, there were plain clothes police at the stations watching the crowds who swarmed through the barriers. It seemed to Eilidh who watched them from the distance that they were just going through the motions as they had done at Waverley.

The passengers on the train were quiet. Few wanted to talk even with friends or relations. Minds were elsewhere. Even the ticket inspector was subdued and elaborately polite. Eilidh tried to take her mind off what was happening by looking at the magnificence of the scenery. The mountains stood as silent witnesses to Scotland's history – yes, they looked down on Culloden and no doubt shed a tear for the carnage of that day – just as now they they were witnessing the present troubles.

Yet for all the beauty of the landscape, Eilidh's mind was in overdrive. She wondered about what was happening to Rodric. Where had Murdo gone? Had he been captured? She asked herself this repeatedly. The time they had spent at Lachie and Mhairi's farm had somehow formed a bond between them in a way she hadn't expected. She had developed feelings for him. Yes, her early suspicions of him seemed justified. She had to acknowledge, too, that in those initial minutes of their first meeting she had formed a view of him that was negative and defensive. They had little in common apart from their nationality. He was the product of privilege in education and wealth and his connections with the establishment went deep. Why would he turn away from that? Why did he join the Party? Why did he work so hard on its behalf? It seemed as though he was turning his back on his roots and Eilidh wondered why on earth anyone would do that. But then she knew only too well that people sometimes reach a tipping point when their lives take a completely different direction. That was the only way she could explain Murdo to herself.

He had been only too keen to make her smile and talk during those hours in the farm cottage. She was also aware that her ingrained hostility to him had slipped, even if she didn't drop her guard and reserve completely. She was not a person who ever wanted to appear weak, especially to men. It crossed her mind that this was a case of opposites attracting each other. But then the reality was that she was unlikely to see Murdo again.

After Pitlochry two plain clothes policemen moved through the train asking people for some form of identity whether it was a driving licence or a bank card. Eilidh felt panic as the men made their way up the carriage towards where she was sitting. Surely, this was it. Arrest appeared imminent. The officiousness of both men was apparent. Often one or other of them would speak into their communications link and ask for further detail on an individual.

'Where are you going?' one demanded when they reached Eilidh.

'Inverness,' she answered trying not to betray the nervousness in her voice.

'Proof of identity?'

Eilidh handed over her licence. The policeman looked at it carefully and then handed it back with smile. He must have realised that she was on the wanted list as the names of Rodric's top thirty closest aides which were fixed on the minds of all the security officials. Much later she learnt that she had been designated the 'Queen of Hearts'.

'Thanks,' said Eilidh unable to hide the relief in her voice.

'You take care, lass,' the policeman said as he made his way further up the carriage.

It took many minutes before Eilidh regained her composure. She was quietly amused that there were those in the police force who were in sympathy.

The slow train journey from Inverness to Duirinish went through some of the bleakest, most remote and yet awesome scenery in the country. It was not difficult to feel humbled by the grandeur of the mountains which placed human experience in perspective: small, fleeting in time and lacking permanence. Life was momentary and illusory, so elusive to hold onto as one inconsequential event followed swiftly on the heels of the next. Meanwhile the hills stood in silence watching as clouds and weather patterns formed and re-formed.

She was the only person to get off at Duirinish. She walked from the station down towards the bay where she hoped Ian would be waiting. As she approached she could see a boat at anchor close to the beach. Her heart leapt: Ian was waiting there.

'So good to see ye!' he greeted her with a huge hug, 'We've been worried sick about ye. Dad has turned in on himself and hasn't been saying much. I have never seen Mum so anxious.'

'And grandad – how is he?' Eilidh asked anxiously.

'Rab is waiting for you. He knows he is dying and discharged himself from hospital. He wants to die at home. You'll be shocked when you see him. He's wasting away before our eyes.' Ian turned away from her as he edged the boat out of the bay.

A silence fell. Eilidh had always been close to her grandfather. Ever since she was a child it was as though there was a mutual conspiracy between them. He adored his grand-daughter and was so proud of her. When she visited Skye from Glasgow they always went off for days together to walk in the hills and talk and talk.

As a child it was from Rab that she had learnt about Scottish history: the Declaration of Arbroath, Bannockburn, Flodden, Culloden, the Massacre of Glencoe, the Highland Clearances, William Wallace, Robert the Bruce, Rob Roy. She imbibed these stories with an eagerness that delighted her grandfather. Rab seemed to bring each episode alive as though he was talking about something that had happened the previous day and he had seen it all with his own eyes. He had a gift for telling stories.

'Tell me that one again, grandad,' became a frequent request and so he would tell it all again embellishing one part more than the other.

It was from her grandfather that Eilidh learnt of the Clearances in Skye in 1853. Again, he spoke about them as though they had happened only a few days ago. Eilidh was twelve when Rab told her that story and the clearances and the injustice of it all touched Eilidh deeply. It was to influence the course she charted for her life.

'You see, Eilidh, Lord MacDonald was deep in debt and thought that if he cleared his land of people for sheep his financial problems would be solved. Thirty two families were evicted from Suisnuish. They were evicted and the roofs of their crofts were torn down, the doors barred and their meagre furniture thrown out. Most emigrated never to return. Some fled to the hills and then came back to rebuild their crofts only to be evicted a second time. Long columns of people were in tears as they left their homes.'

He reached for an account written by Sir Archibald Geikie, a geologist, who had witnessed the aftermath of the evictions:

'A strange wailing sound reached my ears ... I could see a long and motley procession winding along the road that lead north from Suisnish ... there were old men and women, too feeble to walk who were placed in carts; the younger members of the community on foot were carrying their bundles of clothes...while the children, with looks of alarm, walked alongside ... A cry of grief went up to heaven, the plaintive wail, like a funeral coronach, was resumed ... the sound re-echoed through the valley of Strath in one prolonged note of desolation. It was a wailing that went all the way to heaven.'

Eilidh sat beside Rab, her attention wrapt and in her imagination she pictured them all walking away from their homes in such despair.

'But why, why grandad?'

'It's what happens when money is put before people. It is a story as old as history itself.'

Eilidh reflected on the story.

'Could anything like that happen again, grandad?'

'Aye, my lass. It could. But never in the same way. It is happening now somewhere as we speak. Something like it happened in the 1980s in Scotland and other parts of the UK too.'

Eilidh remembered these stories vividly. She was instinctively on the side of the weak. Other stories followed and Eilidh carried a version of Scotland's history in her heart.

Later she persuaded her grandad to take her to Suisnish and Boreraig where the clearances had taken place. The ruins of the crofts were a stark reminder of those terrible events that seared the history and collective memory of Skye. For tumbled stones represented lives: each one was a testimony to the collective suffering. Eilidh would not forget this nor other similar deeds which were inflicted on her land.

There is little doubt that these stories were central to her choosing to read Scottish History as part of her degree. For her Glasgow was vibrant, edgy and with people whose wit and kindness were legendary. Of course, she also knew the city had its darker side.

Gradually she realised that Rab's stories were more complicated than he had suggested and his interpretation was from a particular standpoint: that of a proud Scottish separatist who had been one of the earliest members of the Party. Nonetheless as her understanding and learning grew Rab's interpretation of the sweep of Scottish History held truth for her.

Hanging in her university room was a facsimile of the Declaration of Arbroath of 1320.

'Yet if he (King Robert Bruce, Robert I) should ... agree to make us or our kingdom subject to the King of England or the English, we should exert ourselves at once to drive him out as our enemy ... for as long as but a hundred of us remain alive, never will we on any conditions be brought under English rule. It is in truth not for glory, nor riches, nor honours that we are fighting, but for freedom – for that alone, which no honest man gives up but with life itself.'

Her university friends who came to her room and saw the Declaration hanging on the wall were bemused.

'Do you really believe that nonsense?' was a frequently asked question.

'Yes,' Eilidh would say with a smile. She joined the Party and campaigned in Glasgow: knocking on doors, delivering leaflets, going to meetings. But she never talked politics with her friends unless they initiated the conversation.

She wanted to be on the side of the under-dog, which led her into a Law degree at Edinburgh. Her focus was Family Law and soon she was dispensing advice at a walk-in Law Centre in Leith.

It was a pivotal experience for her. The day to day hardship, poverty and hopelessness she encountered struck deep. She dealt with cases of eviction, domestic violence, discrimination at work and housing. Then she began to see that the answers to many of these issues lay in politics and so she made the first hesitant steps in that direction.

Those initial months and years in the Party were grinding and exhausting but slowly she began to make headway. It took her twelve years to win her first seat in the Scottish Parliament in what had been a Labour stronghold.

Her talents were quickly recognised by the Party hierarchy and soon Eilidh was a close advisor to Rodric Fraser. She was widely liked for her approachability and her ability to understand the lives of ordinary people.

And she listened. She listened more than she spoke – a rare gift in a politician. She was tireless in her work for the dispossessed. Her sharp mind took her to the heart of issues which left many of her colleagues floundering. Some spoke of her as the leader in waiting but there were others who thought she was too smart, too quick. For some she was just another politician out for personal aggrandisement.

In the run-up to the second Referendum the unionist press labelled her 'the most dangerous woman in the UK', because of her closeness to Rodric Fraser. It was an accolade which quietly amused her. The more the unionist media focussed on her with attacks which became ever more ridiculous the more her standing rose with the Party and her supporters.

As Eilidh absorbed the news about Rab, Ian pointed the bow of the boat out of the bay towards Raasay.

'God, it is good to see you, Ian. I have so much to tell you. But first you must tell me what is happening nationally. Where is Rodric? What are the media reporting?'

'It's not good. You know I've always been ambivalent about inde-pendence although both Dad and Mum are for it. Dad put up the biggest 'Yes' flag he could find on the road near the house. I think in a way he was supporting you. He never said much about what you were doing but I know he is deeply proud of you. Mum is too and she speaks more about it to her close friends. Of course, it has been divisive. Many have kept their opinions to themselves – it's safer that way. I think we've lost friends on this one but, on the other hand, we have made some new ones.

'Nationally, the State of Emergency is not working. It is being defied widely – despite what the BBC and the media would have you believe. As for Rodric all we know is that he has been taken into custody but we don't know where. The security forces are too thin on the ground to control the situation. They are concentrated in Glasgow especially and to a lesser extent Edinburgh.

'I'm proud of you, Eilidh. My little sister in the thick of it all! Who would have thought it? On the list of the thirty most wanted people in Scotland!'

'What is it like in Skye?' Eilidh asked.

'Split, like everywhere, I suppose, but there is a head of anger building. There are lots of people who are not prepared to accept the State of Emergency. There have been peaceful protests in Portree. Dougie, the policeman, stood by and watched them. Some are talking of going to Glasgow to George Square to join the flash mobs. Corralling by the police apparently failed as the crowds grew so large that the police had to withdraw. Their tactics aggravated people and word spread round the city to go there and protest.'

'How do you know this?'

'Morven phoned from Glasgow yesterday.'

The boat pulled out into Loch Carron. It was a clear day and Eilidh could see across to Raasay and Skye with the Cuillins towering in their stark mystic beauty. As they edged out into the Minch and passed the small island of Eilean Mor Eilidh felt an overwhelming sense of relief: she was going home, to where she belonged, where she would be safe.

Eilidh barraged Ian with questions about family, the farm and friends. Ian replied with the patience of an elder brother who at times had despaired of his head-strong sister. The cause of independence ran so deep in her. He knew where that impulse had come from. Even as a child Eilidh had always had a deep sense of justice. That was what propelled her to devote her life to the cause of independence even if others didn't interpret the world in quite the way that Eilidh did. He fretted over her idealistic, take-no-prisoners approach to life which made him fear for her.

'You mustn't be so naive, Eilidh, the world doesn't work like that,' he told her so many times over the years, knowing full well that there is nothing more powerful in a person's life than a cause. Independence was the cause for Eilidh.

'The people who have shaped the world and events, Ian, are not the fence-sitters and equivocators but those who have strong beliefs in the rightness of their cause and are prepared to give everything for that cause. That is how the world moves forward. My God, if it hadn't been for the suffragettes women might not have the vote yet!'

Eilidh absorbed the intense beauty of the seascape around her. Was there anywhere more beautiful in the world?

Ian watched her sitting silently as the boat edged past Scalpay and into Loch Sligachan to the slipway at Sconser.

'What are you thinking?' he asked, even if he could guess the answer.

Eilidh turned to face him. Tears were running down her cheeks. It was then that he began to understand what she and many others were going through: they were witnessing the rape of their country. All the tensions and fears of the last few days had spilt out. He motioned her over to his part of the boat and put his arms round her as he had done many times over the years. He didn't need to say anything, his presence and his hug were enough. Ian also knew that the State of Emergency would fail and that somehow the country would rise up against the powerful, not with violence as in Ireland but in protest and civil disobedience, the likes of which the United Kingdom and the Westminster establishment would never have experienced before.

'You can't defeat the spirit of a people, Eilidh.'

When the boat was moored they got into the old Landrover and drove to the farm which had been in the family for three generations. It was a hard living which Ian augmented with lobster fishing. Alister, their father, had been worn down by the heavy physical work and was now inclined to do less and leave Ian to do more.

Eilidh had not been home since Easter. At that time of the year Skye looked even wilder and seemed more remote. She had intended to return at some point in the summer but events had overtaken her. She hadn't expected to be returning in these circumstances.

'For your safety, Eilidh, it will be a mistake if you stay in the farmhouse. Mum and dad have prepared the holiday croft at Tokavaig. Fortunately it has been empty for the last week and there are no more bookings at the moment. Remember how we used to play over that side of the peninsula when we were kids? You should be safe there until all this dies down. You'll be on your own there but you will see one or other of us at least once a day and if we feel it is safe you can come across to the farmhouse. It will take a while for all this to blow over and it's better you keep out of sight until that has happened.'

Eilidh remembered the croft well. The only access to it was a rough farm track. It had sweeping views across to the Cuillins.

Ian drove the Landrover up the driveway to the farmhouse. Megan, the sheepdog, came out to welcome them followed by Alister and Fiona.

'Thank God you are safe,' her father said as he hugged her tightly. 'Ian will have told you about Rab.'

'Yes, he has. There's no hope?'

'No. None at all,' Fiona replied as she hugged her daughter. They went into the large farmhouse kitchen.

'Oh, my lass, thank God you're here. Come in, come in.'

They sat round the kitchen table in silence. Hesitantly Fiona told her about her grandfather.

'Looking forward to seeing you has brightened him up more than I can say. You had better go and see him but be prepared for a shock.'

Eilidh climbed the stairs unsure of what she would find.

Rab called her to come into the room. His voice was not as strong as she remembered it. She pushed open the door. Her grandfather was in bed, propped up on the pillows. His face had shrunk and there was a greyness to his pallor that frightened Eilidh.

'Come in lass,' he said quietly, each word an effort, 'and take a seat. I'm sorry you find me in this state. It has all happened so quickly. I've known I was ill for a few months. I didn't want to tell anyone.'

Eilidh hugged him and tears rolled down her cheeks.

'I am glad you're here now. Your father tells me you are number three on the thirty most wanted list. That makes me very proud of you. I would expect nothing less from you, lass. I have always known you are destined for great things in this country. We'll get through in the end. I've no doubt about that but I won't see that day with you.'

She sat with Rab, holding his hand. He drifted into sleep. After a while Fiona came into the room.

'I'm afraid that he spends most of his time sleeping now. Even when he's awake it's difficult to hear what he's saying. We can only understand a little of what he's saying.'

After a meal they all got into the Landrover and drove to the cottage. Eilidh took a pile of books and paper for writing. Her intention was to record everything that had happened.

'Can Megan come with me?' Eilidh asked her father, 'I could do with company.'

Alister pointed to the back of the Landrover.

'I think she has already decided that.' On hearing her name Megan wagged her tail. She had been in the family for ten years and Eilidh had always regarded Megan as her dog. The feeling was mutual. She was Eilidh's dog. It was as simple as that.

'They will be looking for you and will be sure to come here. If Rab's condition changes we'll come and get you,' Fiona said as she hugged her goodbye.

The croft was ideal for Eilidh. She was exhilarated to be home with her family even if Rab was fading. She wanted to be with him as much as possible. She knew in time the security forces would be scouring the area for her. Hopefully, given their other priorities she had a few days at the least.

Eilidh's mind was still in over-drive. What sleep she had was disturbed: dreams vivid and full of violent images.

Chapter Twelve

THE HOURS AND DAYS THAT followed were psychologically demanding. Rodric lost sense of time as his watch had been taken away. Mentally he struggled to reduce his level of anxiety and sense of claustrophobia. He wanted out of this small space. He decided he would need to impose a disciplined exercise routine and do deep breathing exercises to still his panic. He tried to divide his time into hourly units as best he could. He would read the reports on the table for one hour, exercise for half an hour, do deep breathing and meditation for an hour and then return to his reading. There was a supply of paper and a pen on the desk. He was tempted to record his thoughts but he knew they would be read and held against him; a sign of whether or not he was cracking. He wondered how long it took for people to weaken psychologically. He thought a few days for most. Torture was not necessary. Psychological pressures were surely all that were required.

In front of him were fifteen Treasury reports of 1,400 pages in length, about the economic consequences of independence for Scotland and the UK. Issues like trade, the Scottish financial sector, fiscal matters and the currency were all dealt with and analysed in some detail. He knew what the thrust of the reports was without reading them: economically, independence for Scotland (and indirectly the UK) would be a disaster. It followed from this analysis that the UK Government would spare no effort to defeat the concept of an independent country.

The hours passed painfully slowly. He was forgotten, even by those who had detained him. He understood now how repressive governments dealt with dissidents: took them out of circulation and threw away the key.

Every day Rodric was escorted out of his cell to a large yard with a high fence and razor wire. The building seemed to be surrounded by conifer trees and sand dunes. In this yard he took his exercise. Apart from giving him an indication of the day's weather he had no other clues about where he was. He began to think that given the length of the flight he was somewhere in Eastern Europe, but that was total supposition.

After two days they delivered newspapers to his cell. They were all a day old when he received them. The news told the story of a triumphant Westminster, the collapse of the independence campaign and a return to normality in Scotland. Dozens of Scots from all sections of society had been interviewed and announced their delight and relief that the campaign had collapsed, and their unremitting gratitude to London. There were also short articles – barely more than a hundred words – reporting arrests of small groups of demonstrators around various parts of the country. Rodric noticed the financial sections and articles had been either cut out or redacted.

The delight of the King was made evident in front-page articles, although he did express a concern for all his subjects, unionists and separatists alike. His television broadcast to the UK was widely highlighted and praised for its measured tone. Yes, he understood the appeal of an independent Scotland. Did he not have some Scottish blood in him? But, in a dangerous and uncertain world, it was better that the Union stayed united. The shared history of the constituent parts of the UK made it something worth preserving and, yes, more power would be devolved anyway. Stronger together, that is what we are.

Rodric read the newspapers with a profound degree of scepticism. Weren't these the very same newspapers that had been the long-range artillery of London? He saw the newspapers in the same way as he saw the Treasury papers: an ill-disguised attempt to undermine his self-belief in the cause to which he had committed his life.

On the third day Rodric was taken from his cell into what seemed to be an office at one end of a long corridor. Two men stood up as he came in. Creyke didn't need to introduce himself. The other man, a tall, thin man with a donnish look about him, did.

'Ah, Rodric. I hope you don't mind me using your first name? Do come in and have a seat. My name is Crispin Bennett. The PM has asked me to convey his good wishes to you,' he said in a relaxed manner. Bennett exuded that charm and self-assurance of the Mandarin class of civil servants who had run the Empire at one time and now ran Whitehall. Rodric had a profound mistrust of this class of people. It seemed to represent everything he disliked.

He held out his hand in greeting. Rodric shook it firmly with a degree of reluctance but he knew he had to maintain the moral high ground as much as possible.

'Now I do hope you are being well looked after. Any complaints? Creyke tells me that you are eating well and that you are getting exercise and the daily papers.' It was obvious that he did not expect the question to be answered.

Rodric decided not to respond so Bennett continued unruffled, in his urbane manner.

'Have you read the Treasury papers we left in your cell ... I mean room?'

'Yes, I have.'

'They do make interesting reading I think even you would agree, don't they? I mean, I fully understand that your side had to present the upside of independence but, in truth, the economic risks were dangerously high, and not just for the Scots. You see, the UK Government had to act. It was in the interests of us all that it did, wouldn't you agree?'

Rodric smiled. This was beginning to sound like one of his university tutorials at St Andrews with his Pol Econ tutor, a clever mild-mannered man. Rodric began to wonder what this interview was about. What was London trying to achieve? A capitulation from him? A rejection of what he had devoted his life's work to? Was this softly-softly approach a reflection of the growing difficulties London now had with Scotland? Perhaps this return to normality was a lie. Perhaps London needed him to bring back calm. If anything made the Government jump it would be the financial markets and the large-scale withdrawal of capital from the UK. The newspapers had their financial sections removed, while other articles, which he took to be on the economy, had been redacted. There was only one conclusion Rodric made from this: the markets were volatile. Just how volatile was something he could not know.

'You can't expect me to accept that, Mr Bennett. Of course, we had to present the best case possible. That's what all politicians do and have always done. Our supporters knew there were risks but they were risks we were prepared to take. To control your own national destiny is worth sacrifice and economic turbulence. It would all have settled down eventually.'

'I'm not sure I can agree, Rodric. There were too many, even of your own people, who didn't agree with you. A nation divided against itself is not a good start now, is it?' The question was rhetorical.

'The very people who supported your cause most vehemently were the same people who would have suffered most with independence, as you would have had to cut expenditure or raise taxes, or do both. That, after all, was confirmed by the Institute for Fiscal Studies report whose objectivity is well known.'

'With respect, Mr Bennett, I'm not sure what the purpose of this interview is. I'm not sure of the intention behind it. I see no purpose in continuing it.'

Bennett's calm, relaxed and reasoned approach seemed to falter. A look of annoyance momentarily crossed his face. He had been warned what to expect from Fraser and these warnings had proved entirely justified. He stood up from his desk and held out his hand.

'I'm sure we shall be having more conversations again soon, Rodric,' he said, now that he had regained his composure. 'Do show the former First Minister back to his room, will you, Mr Creyke?'

The fact that Bennett called Rodric by his first name was not lost on Fraser, neither was the prefix of 'former' in front of First Minister. Rodric was well versed in the subtleties of Whitehall to know what was going on.

Creyke marched Rodric back to his cell without uttering a word. He slammed the door hard after him.

Rodric went to his desk. The white noise seemed to get louder, or was it his imagination? He was acutely conscious of how paranoid he was becoming. He thought over the short interview and its purpose. Then it dawned suddenly: they wanted him inside the tent not outside it. They were trying to find a way forward, to see how they could facilitate that. This gave Rodric hope that whatever was going on in Scotland, it was not a return to normality.

Part of Rodric's degree course had covered the history of the Empire and the gradual dis-engagement, not through choice but circumstance. He was well versed in how the servants of Empire functioned through divide and rule, trying to undermine the case for independence by bringing the local power elites into the tent. Honours and titles were usually showered upon them. Garden parties, military bands of strutting Marines and the Monarch's birthday party celebration were used unabashedly to soften the Opposition, to win them over, so that they ended up like their occupiers with the same worldview and set of values.

The irony was that while these elites stubbornly refused to be led into the tent, as soon as independence was declared they often became more like their former masters than could have been dreamt. Rodric had always felt this was the case in some sections of Scottish society.

Rodric had a good understanding of the background of the independence movement in India. He was also familiar with the results of the Winds of Change that had swept through the British Empire. His thesis had focussed on the unravelling of British rule in Kenya with the Mau Mau. His perception of these events had influenced the way he had come to view his own country and its relations with the London Government. Of course, the parallels could not be taken too far but they were there nonetheless.

Somehow he felt that the initiative was not entirely lost, even if he was without any real knowledge of what was happening on the ground. If the situation was not exactly as it was being presented in the mainstream media, Rodric believed that there would be negotiations either with the unionist opposition inside Scotland on forming a coalition government or, if his hand was stronger than he realized, with him. This was perhaps why the softening-up process was underway.

Bennett was looking for weaknesses in his position. He had obviously been tasked to find out what Rodric's negotiating terms would be short of outright independence. The Treasury reports were part of that softening-up process to make him see the folly of his ways and influence his negotiating position. That is if Whitehall decided that it couldn't get another option more to their liking.

The following day the SARCO guards hauled Rodric into another office. Creyke and a man who didn't introduce himself was sitting behind a desk. There were no pleasantries.

'Sit down, Fraser. Playtime is over. The gloves are off. Bennett has returned to London.' Creyke said in a brusque, no-nonsense way.

Rodric sat down wondering what was coming next.

A picture was put on the desk. It was of Rodric and someone who could have been a party activist. He struggled to remember where the photo might have been taken or who the person was.

'Do you know this man?' the man beside Creyke asked aggressively. Rodric took him to be another Special Branch officer.

'No. Is he an undercover policeman?' asked Rodric with a smile on his face.

'Don't be a smart arse,' Creyke barked …

'I have no idea who he is or where this photo was taken.'

'We want to find this man urgently. Should we believe this Scottish bastard who is renowned for his lies?' asked Creyke turning to his accomplice.

'No, I don't think we should for a second.'

'Now, I have to warn you that if we find proof that you have links with this man you will be prosecuted.'

'For what exactly?'

'We have never had any difficulty in finding reasons to prosecute people in the past.'

Rodric felt the aggression coming from the two men. In different circumstances they might have struck out at him.

'Well, once you have had time to think a bit more you may want to tell us more about this man.'

Creyke called the guard. Of course, he realized that they knew the answer to the question they had asked. That was usually the way these people played it. If the man in the photo had been of any interest to them they would know everything they needed to know about him, just as Rodric knew that they had a thick fat dossier on him and every phone call and email he had ever made or received.

In his cell, Rodric thought hard. He was being truthful when he said he didn't know the man. After all, he had met thousands of party members and activists over the years. Was this part of the softening-up process, to make him feel edgy and under suspicion for dark deeds? He knew if they wanted to frame him with some imaginary crime they would. He knew, too, that there would be many out there who would believe them unquestioningly as the press would act as their proxies and spill all sorts of rumours calculated to undermine him in the eyes of the UK, and of his supporters more particularly. He decided that this was a sign of weakness and to regard it as such. His conscience was clear. He had never done anything outside the law.

The possibility that London would manufacture a trumped-up charge – guilt by association or some such thing to denigrate and destroy him personally – was a distinct likelihood. He knew there were many people out there, both in Scotland and the rest of the UK, who would be only too ready to believe the worst of him and accept whatever line the Government wished to take.

The next day they marched him back down the long corridor to the office. This time it was different. He was greeted with a warm smile and handshake by Bennett.

'Ah, do come in, Rodric. I hope all went well with your chat with Mr Creyke and his colleague yesterday?'

'I shall be completely open with you, Rodric. Now, of course, we know only too well that you have staked out your position on independence clearly, and we realise that in the heat of the referendum campaign things were said that were ... well, shall we say *economical with the truth*? You must know that the course you were advocating with such passion and dare I say, skill, was fraught with serious flaws and real dangers. Many people would have suffered the serious consequences that would have followed independence. You know, as well as I do, how devastating these consequences would have been to many of your supporters, do you not?'

Rodric knew that the interview was being taped and was not to going to admit to any of the weaknesses in the advocacy of independence. He was aware of what they were, but his view was that independence came at a price and that price whatever it was, it was one worth paying. Five years later things would have settled down and the dire warnings of economists on economic Armageddon would be proved false. The world would move on, accommodations made, the new realities accepted. Scotland would have taken its place in the world's family of nations.

'With respect, Mr Bennett...'

'Do please call me Crispin, Rodric. We are civilised men, after all,' Bennett said. 'We both want the best for our country regardless of how differently we perceive that. I'm sure we can find some common ground and work together for the good of our nations. The PM believes that all this can be settled to the mutual advantage of all in the UK, without any loss of face. I am not saying a formula will be easy to find, but it is not impossible with goodwill on both sides, I'm sure.'

'Can I just get this right? You are, in effect, trying to negotiate with me on the PM's behalf?'

'Well, let's just say I have been asked to sound you out, to find out how the ground lies, so to speak.'

'I am sorry to disappoint you both, Mr Bennett, but there is nothing to negotiate. Scotland will be independent. There can be no equivocation on that. The polls put us ahead in the referendum campaign. Any negotiations between Scotland and the UK will start with Scotland as an independent country with its own currency, central bank and head of state. I'm sure that once that is accepted our two countries will enjoy close cooperation in all spheres of life; a sort of social union.'

'Ah, yes, its own currency and central bank. That is where it all fell apart in 2014. I think you had a close shave there, to be honest.' Bennett couldn't hide a smirk. 'But at least you were keeping the Monarch as head of state last time. The thought of an elected President, like France, the USA or Ireland, is too horrible to contemplate. Look at the list of utterly ghastly people they have ended up with over the years.' This was the first time that Bennett had made his feelings clear.

'We have a respect for the Monarch but not the principle of monarchy, in which one family through dint of birth holds such a significant position. It's an anachronism even if individual monarchs have done their duty over the years. It's a throwback to a distant era.'

'We shall agree to disagree on this one, Fraser.' The fact that Bennett had reverted to Rodric's surname was an indication of his feeling on the matter.

'Nothing personal against the King; we have spoken many times and I admire much of what he is trying to achieve, but that is what he stands for: a deferential, class-bound society of privilege, honours and patronage.'

Bennett's patience was wearing thin. 'The Monarchy has served us well, Fraser. You shouldn't forget that,' he said curtly.

Who the 'us' was was not specified but it opened up an interesting line of thought in Rodric's mind.

Rodric was about to ask what honour he had received, but decided to keep his mouth shut.

Bennett switched tack and tried to sound reasonable and relaxed again.

'I want you to think about what I've said. We shall discuss this again on another occasion.'

'Am I under arrest here?' Rodric asked.

'Good lord no. Whatever made you think that? Shall we just call it self-protection from the wrath of certain elements of society? Of course, there is still a State of Emergency in force and that allows internment.' There was a tone of irony in Bennett's voice.

The ambivalence of his answer needed no further clarification.

'I think we'd better leave it there for the moment. You need to accept that the longer this goes on the more Scotland, and indeed the UK, will be damaged. I'm sure you don't want that.'

'We shall speak again perhaps later today or tomorrow. Are you comfortable? Got everything you need?'

Rodric was escorted back to his cell. He was in no doubt what they were trying to do: to soften him up, break his spirit and then force him to make concessions which would retain the status quo and the Union. These were, after all, high stakes.

But the conviction was growing in Rodric that they needed him more than he needed them. Bennett had even begun to sound conciliatory. Gone was the harsh tone of Rodric's first few days in custody. Creyke had obviously been taken out of the loop; another sign that Rodric's negotiating position was changing. But then there was nothing to negotiate as far as Rodric was concerned. He hadn't taken Scotland to this point in time merely to march back down the hill and call it all off. Westminster must surely know that.

Rodric found yesterday's London and Scottish newspapers in his cell when he got back. There was now also a television in one corner. This was London's attempt to undermine him for he was in no doubt about the line they would take: normality all round; Scotland saved by a generous and forgiving Westminster. With nothing better to do, Rodric decided to look at the papers. Every one of them was predictable in the line it took: the UK has been saved by the three Unionist parties to the relief of all its subjects and the wider international community. The President, the Pope and the

Australian PM all spoke of their relief that the Union had been saved. Even the *Guardian*, which had shown some understanding of events in Scotland, was singing the praises of the Government. The *Financial Times*, a paper which had shown a mild degree of balance – and it was mild – had come out strongly in favour of the Union on economic grounds, even although it had argued at one point that Scotland could be an independent country with a viable economy. Its editorial pulled no punches about the 'Yes' campaign's route to disaster.

Rodric turned on the BBC *News at One*. Jim MacCallum, the BBC's Scotland Correspondent, interviewed several people mainly in Glasgow and Edinburgh, who in a ratio of four to one expressed pleasure that the UK Government had stepped in. Even the few who had been interviewed with another point of view were mild in their criticism of London and the State of Emergency. They had been interviewed for *balance*, but there was little doubt about the skewed reporting. The BBC was, after all, the *British* Broadcasting Corporation.

Rodric, however, knew a few of their Glasgow staff who would have had deep reservations about the role the BBC was playing. He could imagine only too well the tensions within BBC Scotland's offices. It was, like the Labour Party, merely a branch office of London.

Rodric knew too that it was not what the cameras showed but what they didn't show that mattered. A parade of politicians from around the globe seemed to have been lined up to express their satisfaction that separatism had been undermined. Too many of them faced similar problems at home. The Spanish Prime Minister received more air time than the others as Catalonia had been champing at the bit for years, and support for secession had grown steadily. The difference between Scotland and Catalonia was that the social, political and economic elites in the latter had, for the most part, supported secession. That had not been the case in Scotland.

Rodric was acutely aware that he had failed to win over sufficient support from those sections of society in 2014. They were, after all, comfortable with what they had. Why should they vote for a change that could leave them materially worse off? To Rodric they had put self-interest first before the Holy Grail of an independent Scotland free to make its own decisions and face up to its economic choices. He was contemptuous of their self-interest. He had never accepted that their unionist sympathies were underpinned by their view of what constituted the best way forward for the country. To Rodric it was self-interest: nothing more, nothing less.

The hours passed slowly in his cell. The white noise started again, just as he was about to go to sleep. He tried hard to blank it out but the more he tried the more difficult he found it. He decided to turn on the television in the corner, as he knew the best way to counter one noise was to do so with another one. Eventually he fell into a fitful sleep full of vivid dreams: he was a child walking along a beach holding his father's hand. Then a powerful wave came crashing up the beach unexpectedly and swept them out to sea.

He woke up with a start and heaved a sigh of relief. How did the narratives of a dream form and weave themselves together? He laughed. Freud and Jung would have had their say on that one. These sharply defined nightmares were now part of every sleep. He was conscious that the small camera in one corner of the ceiling was recording everything in the room. Someone would be watching and listening.

Rodric was increasingly aware that his isolation and confinement were taking a toll on his mental health. He wondered how long his incarceration was going to last. He still wondered where he was. He was increasingly certain he was outside the UK in some 'black site' outside the remit of law. Whatever else was wrong about the Union, Rodric did have respect for the independence of the Judiciary, however misguided and bizarre some of its rulings could be. In this situation, however, he knew that they had no option but to uphold the State of Emergency and all that flowed from it.

Somehow he had to steel himself to sit this incarceration out. His isolation and the fact that he had no time scale as to how long he was going to be held made it psychologically difficult. Time passed slowly. He did not see Bennett for several days. He tried hard to keep his mind active and his thoughts positive. In truth, the isolation stripped his morale bit by bit.

He gave himself mental exercises: thinking of various periods of his life: of the times of happiness and fulfilment; of Shona and the family as well as friends. He thought about his childhood in Dundee where he was brought up. Jim his father was a carpenter, and Nessie, his mother worked in the Co-op.

One of his uncles was a casualty of the closure of Ravenscraig Steel Works in Lanarkshire while the other was arrested during the Miners' stike. These events had traumatized the family and confirmed their political credentials.

Rodric remembered one heated conversation between his father and a friend about economic policies. One line remained etched in his mind even although he must have been in his late teens at the time.

'There is nae getting awa' frae it, capitalism moves from one crisis tae anither. And tell me, who are the victims of this? Aye, we aw know the answer tae that.'

Rodric had rarely heard his father speak with such vehemence. 'Ye know why the working class is stuffed? Because industry will always move to where the wages are lowest. We'll hae a rentier economy in nae time at aw and tens of thousands of us will be on the scrap heap, on the dole. The working class cannae resist the strong forces of capitalism. That's why we need socialism. Only then will the wealth be shared properly – nae mair of this ten percent owning ninety percent of the wealth stuff. Only the Labour Party can look efter us yins.'

Rodric was brought up by his mother with an impressive attendance record at St Andrews Kirk, close to the tenement. The Ministers seemed learned, compassionate individuals whose sermons had an intellectual rigour that appealed to the young Rodric as he reached his late teens. At one time he even thought of going into the Kirk but that idea gradually died in Edinburgh when he became politically involved. At first he followed his father's footsteps and joined the Labour Party. The Tories had declined in Scotland after Thatcher. It was Labour that controlled the heartlands.

Rodric's schooling gave him a life-long love of study and especially history. Donald MacPherson, his young, charismatic teacher taught him to question conventional wisdom and standard interpretations.

'You should never accept the views of others without scrutinising them under a microscope. History tends to be written by the victors. I am interested in the history of the grassroots, not top down history but from the grassroots up. Never trust elites. They have their own agenda.'

Rodric and his peers imbibed their first taste of intellectual freedom with all the enthusiasm of youngsters being introduced to the world of ideas, analysis and intense debate. These were glorious days when they stood on the threshold of new worlds. Everything seemed possible. It was with that deeply held self-belief that they went to university.

It was here that Rodric's socialism received its first jolt which ultimately led him in a different direction entirely. It was a tipping point. Rodric was open-minded, always prepared to listen to argument and debate issues. It was while attending a student debate that the change came. The motion was 'This House believes Scotland should be independent.' The motion was heavily defeated by sixty eight votes to nineteen but what unsettled Rodric was the argument and the vigour of the motion's proposer. She was a firebrand of a woman who spoke with a commitment that inspired him. Her arguments made sense. The kernel of the argument was that Scotland needed to be able to make its own political and economic decisions to create a just and fair society.

When the result was announced Rodric went up to sympathize with her. Cheers echoed through the hall followed by cat calls and jeers as the proposer waved to the audience. Rodric introduced himself.

'You mustn't let that bother you. You were brilliant.'

That brought a smile to her face.

'Ach, well, that's all right then. I'm Shona MacKay, pleased to meet you,' she said.

Rodric was struck by the look in her eyes: quizzical, lively and yet betraying a slight uncertainty.

Rodric joined the party as a foot soldier at a time when the furrow being ploughed was singularly unproductive. It was salutary to have door after door shut firmly in his face as he canvassed the wealthier parts of Edinburgh during election campaigns. It gave Rodric an inner toughness and strength that would serve him well in the years ahead. Rejection and defeat were fundamental parts of the political process.

On graduation Rodric and Shona married. It was a partnership based on a common cause and a deep mutual compatability laced with an irreverent sense of humour. Rodric initially worked in the financial sector, to the hostility of his father.

'Ye have sold out tae mammon, sold yer soul,' Jim would say with disgust on repeated occasions before retreating behind his paper.

Yet from behind his paper there was an unspoken admiration for Rodric's political direction. At first, Jim accused him of selling out to nationalism, 'A vicious political philosophy which puts nation before the brotherhood and unity of mankind,' was his description of it.

Rodric knew his father well enough to know that there was little point in contesting his deeply held life-long views. Far better to adopt the drip by drip approach.

It was four years later that Jim was openly converted to Rodric's viewpoint. It was Blair's neo-liberalism and the Iraq War followed by Brown's disastrous term that finally buried Jim's loyalty to the Labour Party. Jim was not alone as the 2011 and 2016 elections to the Scottish Parliament proved.

Rodric slowly rose through the party ranks. He stood for Parliament twice but was defeated. In 2010 he was elected to Parliament and from that point onwards his political career began to soar. No one doubted he would be the leader of the Party one day.

The media lambasted him. Here was the Michael Foot of the separatists, a dangerous and misguided man who would bring the country down. Fraser was Mugabe personified, they screeched. Yet there were too many ordinary people who admired Rodric for his moderation, his good sense and his ability to connect with people. No one could doubt his commitment to the country. The viciousness of the personal attacks made him philosophical.

'The greater the intensity of the attacks the more they obviously fear me and what I stand for. It could be worse. They could ignore me altogether,' was his verdict. He was going to need the thickest of political hides tempered by a strong dose of humour to survive in the political jungle.

Rodric constantly replayed these thoughts. There was an irony about it all: had he not attended that debate all those years ago he probably wouldn't be sitting in a cell waiting to be summoned for another round of interrogation. Life, after all, turns on a sixpence. He thought about fate and destiny.

Who knew how the bigger picture was going to play out. He was a mere cog in this huge wheel. His life was of little consequence in this scheme of things. He was a bit-player, nothing more. That, however, was not how he was regarded by his interrogators or by Westminster.

He worked hard to think through how the situation would develop. Perhaps a tame interim government in Edinburgh appointed in a cross-party agreement for 'the benefit of all'. Yes, he imagined all the worthies being called to save their country from catastrophe.

As the days passed his sense of reality became fragile and his dreams even more vivid and alarming. They seemed so real that they almost took physical possession of him. In these dreams the deep-seated anxieties and insecurities of his life plagued him. His self-doubts rattled round his mind. Perhaps the successful politician and man of the people that he was to the wider public were mere projections, with no substance. Yes, it was true in his moments of reflection, even before his incarceration, he had wondered if his public life was a fantasy, a bending of reality. Now, in these circumstances, his anxieties and doubts doubled.

Being in a room with no windows was clearly meant to disorientate him, to help in the dismantling of his personality. Although he realized this, he felt that the process was well in train and he was powerless to stop it.

Any human contact, no matter how minimal, was seized on with alacrity. Most days the guards whose unidentifiable uniforms seemed indeterminate would open the door, put his meal on the table and say nothing. They didn't answer his questions. The door was then slammed shut and the lock turned not once but three times.

There was an exception: one guard with a Geordie accent always said 'Hi' in hushed tones and gave Rodric a smile. On one occasion when the white noise was intense the guard said, 'Tough it out, First Minister. Scotland is behind you.'

These words of hope raised Rodric's morale. Suddenly he no longer felt alone. It was as though a couple of million Scots were in there with him. He felt he had a duty to survive for them.

He tried to engage the guard in conversation always making sure that he was facing away from the camera. The guard signed to him that he could not reply.

On one occasion though, the guard managed to let him know that the State of Emergency and Direct Rule had caused serious ongoing unrest.

Rodric wanted to ask him more. He needed to know what was going on. If there was opposition to the State of Emergency he wanted to know as much about it as possible.

But then the guard stopped bringing Rodric's food. He had obviously been transferred. Perhaps his sympathies had been detected by the surveillance equipment in the room.

Rodric's state of mind soon relapsed. His short exercise bouts within the confines of the perimeter fence were but a brief interval in a routine of unremitting psychological harshness. The confinement regime made sure that his exercise periods were not held at regular intervals, thus chipping away at this sense of time and disorientating him. He was woken up in the small hours of the morning and kept awake with loud music. Physically he felt drained and exhaustion set in.

He guessed that it had been several days since his last interview and he began to suspect that London no longer regarded him as part of the solution. Probably – given his intransigence – they were wondering what to do with him next.

Each day he was taken from his cell and into the exercise yard outside his block. Sometimes it was during the day often it was at night. There was never a sign of other prisoners or indeed any human life apart from sullen guards who gave abrupt commands.

He was allowed to walk within what seemed to be a large fenced-off area. It was impossible to tell from the nondescript landscape where he was, yet in Rodric's mind it could have been Tentsmuir Forest a few miles from St Andrews near the estuary of the Eden.

These interludes outside his block lasted about twenty minutes. A guard always followed him and allowed him to walk by himself. Often he was at least a hundred metres away. They were obviously confident that Fraser could not escape.

Chapter Thirteen

'ON'T GO NATIVE,' WERE CAROL'S last words as he left the house and got into the taxi.

Stewart Wyndham was on the 6.30am flight out of Heathrow to Edinburgh. An official car collected him at 5am. This was either his start up the greasy pole or the end of his political career. Carol hoped it was the former.

Some twelve senior civil servants seconded from various Ministries were on the aircraft with him. They would be implementing direct rule from St Andrews House. They had been chosen for their abilities and were all high-flyers, keen to cut their teeth on this new and difficult assignment. There was a general feeling of trepidation. All had visited Scotland at one time or other. Ironically, only Wyndham, the new Secretary of State, had never visited the country. Some amused comments flew between the Civil Servants to that effect.

Once in the air Stewart pored over paper work. George Crosby, the senior civil servant in the team, sat next to him.

'What do you make of all this, George?'

'Not sure. It's not an easy task. A lot of feathers have been ruffled at St Andrews House. We'll need to proceed with sensitivity and caution. I've been in daily contact with Eric Mountbank, the PPS. He is a reasonable man and has a sense of humour which I suspect he'll need in the coming days.'

'I have accepted this poisoned chalice for a reason as I am sure you will have guessed.'

'Yes, Minister,' Crosby replied with a smile.

'Do call me, Stewart, please.'

'Yes, Minister.'

'Have you read Muir's *Journey through Scotland*?'

'No Minister.'

'Oh do call me Stewart, George. You should read it. Quite outstanding even although it was first published in 1935. I've been told not much has changed since then.'

Crosby was uncertain whether the Minister was attempting humour and was unsure how to react. He smiled thinly.

'Yes, the section on the Anglo-Scots makes for interesting reading.'

Crosby knew that Wyndham was ambitious to get to the top. He suspected that the Scots would soon be experiencing the smack of firm government. Wyndham was going to be noticed if nothing else. Crosby had made extensive soundings amongst his friends in the Commons trying to get the measure of the new man. He often thought that the most dangerous politicians were the ones who wanted to make a name for themselves and leave some legacy behind them.

Crosby's irreverent sense of humour had helped him cope with the vagaries of politicians and their bickering, back-stabbing ways. He had nicknamed Wyndham 'the Gauleiter of Caledonia' to Marjorie, his wife.

'Really, George! You'd better not call him that outside these four walls,' she cautioned with a laugh.

The more Crosby thought about the nickname in the weeks that followed the more he seemed to have chosen the right one: Wyndham, the Gauleiter of Caledonia – it had a certain ring to it.

The BA flight banked over the Forth as it made its descent into Edinburgh. Stewart was sitting on the left-hand side of the aircraft and so caught his first sight of Edinburgh Castle, Arthur's Seat and the Scott Memorial. It looked impressive. He wondered what sort of reception he and his Civil Servants would receive.

Wyndham and his party were escorted off first. Stewart could see three official black Mercedes lined up at the bottom of the steps. I am going to like this posting, he thought.

Eric Mountbank met the party at the bottom of the steps and welcomed them to Scotland. It was a brisk, cool day but the sun shone, albeit weakly. George thought Eric looked strained and tired. His welcome was not what could be described as warm. The word perfunctory came to mind. Perhaps this was not surprising.

Wyndham, Crosby and Mountbank, travelled in the first car.

As their driver closed the car door after Wyndham got in, he winked at the driver of the car behind and mouthed a disrespectful, 'Fucking idiots.'

The driver of the second car smiled.

'Take me to Bute House first, driver,' Wyndham commanded trying to adopt informal tone but ending up sounding imperious.

'I'll drop my stuff there, have a quick look round and then come over to St Andrews House.'

It was hard to ignore the unease in the car as it sped into Edinburgh, its police motorcycle escort lights flashing. The cars and the police escort gave the new Secretary of State a feeling of self-importance. He had never experienced that before and he liked it.

Wyndham did not have much in the way of small talk and wanted to get straight to business. Mountbank was subjected to a barrage of questions.

'Bloody, Gauleiter,' Crosby thought. He was beginning to wonder if the delights of working in Edinburgh would be undermined by having to jump every time Wyndham said jump.

Mrs MacConnell, the housekeeper at Bute House, met Wyndham on the steps. She was not a political person and had not voted in the 2014 referendum. She had considered voting this time but it had been cancelled. She felt that what was happening was wrong. It upset her to think that Bute House was no longer going to be occupied by the First Minister of Scotland. She had always got on well with Rodric and Shona who treated her as one of the family. The events of recent days had saddened her more than she could say, to the extent that she was thinking of resigning.

Her initial impressions of Stewart Wyndham were not encouraging. He was abrupt and too full of himself. It was made clear to her that she was just a housekeeper and the relations between them would be conducted with the utmost formality. It was like *The Jewel in the Crown*, a dramatisation of life during the Raj with Wyndham as the new Viceroy.

An hour later Wyndham's car sped across to St Andrews House with the police outriders, lights flashing. The other three cars with the civil servants had joined the cavalcade. Stewart had decided that they should have a chance to check in at the George Hotel nearby before joining him. There was something about the new rulers being seen together in this way, a sign of power perhaps.

As he looked out of the window he counted three people give the car the V sign and it wasn't the victory sign either. Stewart had been warned that the Glaswegians had a robust sense of humour but somehow hadn't expected this in Edinburgh.

'Ach, dinnae take it personally, Sir. There are a lot of upset people just now.'

'Yes, I can imagine that. Somehow it doesn't fit with my image of Edinburgh.'

The driver said nothing more on the short journey to St Andrews House. When the car pulled up there was a short line of Civil Servants waiting to welcome the London contingent. Although they were all Civil Servants it didn't feel as though they were on the same team.

'Here is the army of occupation, our new masters,' Mountbank whispered out of the side of his mouth to James Rushmore beside him.

In truth, the same thought was going through the minds of others. Mountbank hadn't been a separatist until that moment. His conversion hit him in a flash. Suddenly, so many things fell into place. It was a revelatory experience. He had surprised himself.

Wyndham worked the line, shaking hands saying a few words to each person. He had clearly done his homework and knew everyone by first name. Few doubted that he was a man of purpose who would take no prisoners – that was communicated in his body-language and steely gaze.

'Interesting days ahead, methinks,' Mountbank said to Rushmore.

'Yes. Think I'll keep a low profile.'

Half an hour later Wyndham addressed all the departmental heads. His short speech was a masterly combination of the velvet glove and the brutal.

'Of course, we all have the best interests of Scotland at heart and that is a Scotland in the UK. The alternative would be too horrendous for all concerned, not least the Scots who above all want stability and economic prosperity. I am well aware that Westminster needs to build bridges and much of my focus shall be directed in that direction. Any questions?'

There were none.

Once back in his office Stewart phoned Number Ten. Sutton

sounded his smoothest when Wyndham told him about settling into the new job.

'We are so grateful that a man of your standing in the Party has taken this on, Stewart, we really are. I am conscious of the debt I owe you. It will be repaid one day. Believe me.'

'What news from John Langwith? I haven't had time to speak directly to Graham Melton yet – he is due here in half an hour. The streets of Edinburgh seem quiet and there is no obvious sign of trouble that I could see.'

'The situation is far from settled yet, Stewart. Just because you don't see anything in Edinburgh doesn't mean things are not happening. Langwith warned us about that. There may seem to be a degree of normality but there are obvious undercurrents. Glasgow and Dundee are on a knife edge. Do be careful. I know you have security people with you round the clock but these days one cannot be too careful. Speak later, Stewart.'

He then instructed Jane MacKinnon, his secretary, to make a list of twenty prominent Scots and invite them to a dinner party at Bute House in ten days time. He had little doubt that Carol would want to be the gracious First Lady and start a vigorous assault networking the elites of Scotland. He knew she could make a significant difference to the outcome – just as Edwina Mountbatten had in the dying days of the Raj.

The tone of their phone conversation that evening was altogether different. Carol was emollient and could see that she had a role to play in networking for the Union, as she liked to think of it. She was determined to play her part.

Two days later she was in Edinburgh working the city and its people. She had the political nous to engage with all sections of society and made sure that wherever she went the Press were tipped off to take the obligatory photos which then appeared plastered over the pages of the papers the following day. She made a point of homing in on charities, especially for the homeless for whom she felt genuinely concerned.

Anne, their elder daughter, teased her mother on the phone.

'When is the Durbar mum? I am so looking forward to it.'

Carol laughed but the point was made. This was not India. This was not the Delhi Durbar in planning. Still, a Royal Visit to settle the nerves would not go amiss – once the security situation was settled. Yes, Carol was beginning to relish the role. She began to see it as a practice run for Number Ten.

'I think I like the Scots,' Carol said as they got into bed, 'God this bed is lumpy. I'll order a new one tomorrow.'

'Perhaps it's time we christened the bed.'

'Yes, as they say power is an aphrodisiac and you are the man with the power,' Carol said nuzzling up to him.

The following day Stewart discussed which Orders in Council he could issue. He wanted maximum impact – high profile stuff that would be reported nationally. This was about self-publicity, nothing else. He had to remind his colleagues in Westminster that not only did he still exist but he was a potential leadership candidate in the future.

'What do you think, George? Obviously, we need some high profile security Orders in Council – the smack of firm government always goes down well with the media and Downing Street. Beyond that? Milk for all primary school children? That sort of thing. We need to reverse the image Lady Handbag gave us up here. We need to be seen as caring and compassionate.'

George smiled and nearly said, 'But you are not.' He kept his mouth shut.

'Yes, that is a good idea, Minister.'

'What news from Gold and Silver Commanders? And how are you getting on with the Edinburgh box wallahs?'

The true answer was not encouraging but Crosby decided to play down the obvious ill-feelings that were beginning to surface. Resentment floated through St Andrews House like an iceberg.

Chapter Fourteen

THE POLITICAL CRISIS TOOK A sharp turn for the worse on Thursday. A twenty vehicle nuclear convoy en route from Coulport on the Clyde to Burghfield in Oxfordshire was brought to a standstill on the M8 going through Paisley. One of the trucks carrying the nuclear warheads broke down and came to a standstill. The police escort immediately closed the motorway.

A reluctant Bennett was the bearer of the news to the PM.

'What? Do you mean to say that no one at the MoD thought to cancel the convoy with all this unrest going on? This is bloody unbelievable! There needs to be an immediate news black-out on this.'

'I am afraid, Prime Minister, it is too late. It is already trending on the social media.'

'I really can't believe this. The Scots have always been extremely touchy on this whole issue. We have got to get this sorted immediately before the security of the convoy is put at risk.

'Langwith has ordered all available police units in the West of Scotland to go to the convoy and secure it until it can move again.'

'Any idea how long it will take to repair it?'

'No idea at present.'

'This is absolutely the last thing we need. If this can't be resolved in an hour we must send in special forces to protect the convoy. This is an absolute priority above everything else. Get me Langwith on the phone will you?' the stress in the PM's voice was pronounced.

Less than a minute later Langwith was on.

'Just how serious is this, John?'

'It couldn't be more serious, Prime Minister. It isn't an exaggeration to say that we are now dealing with two crises that could conflate into the biggest crisis the UK has faced in peacetime.'

'Thanks for that, John. Exactly what I needed to know.'

'I am getting reports that hundreds perhaps thousands of people are on the motorway and gathering around the convoy in a growing sit-down protest. CCTV cameras in Paisley show more people heading in that direction.'

'You have my full authority to break up the protest with as much force as you need but you must do it now. Use as much tear gas as you need. We have to secure the convoy at all costs. You have my authority to shoot over the heads of the protesters if we can clear the motorway.'

'With respect, Prime Minister, that will inflame an already extremely volatile situation not just in Paisley but in Scotland generally.'

'We have no choice, John. Do it. There is a meeting of the National Security Committee in an hour. I'll brief them and get them on board. For God's sake if you have to use live ammunition don't kill anyone.'

Within an hour of the convoy grinding to a halt there were a few thousand sitting on the motorway both in front and behind the trucks. They were no closer than a hundred metres away. Armed police and Marines kept the protesters at that distance. Many of them were wondering if they would have to fire their weapons in anger. If the convoy was endangered they had no alternative but to open fire. Opening fire on unarmed protesters was not a scenario they had anticipated.

The PM was cursing the fact that he had not ordered the mobile and social networks to be closed down.

The senior officer guarding the convoy walked towards the protesters and spoke through a loud-hailer.

'I have orders to shoot anyone who endangers this convoy. If you approach closer than you are now you will be given one warning then shots will be fired above your heads. If you continue to advance towards the convoy you will be shot.'

This was followed by hoots of derision and disbelief by the protesters but the point was made. The officer repeated his announcement at both ends.

A helicopter landed with a maintenance crew who immediately started trying to repair the forty four ton truck with nuclear warheads on the hard shoulder.

The National Security Committee meeting was even more tense than the previous one. Wyndham was concerned that the whole crisis was spinning out of control.

'This stand off could be disastrous. If we can't regain control of the convoy we are in...'

'Yes, yes, Stewart. We all know that,' Sutton said cutting him off impatiently.

The meeting was attended by Michael Hutton, the top Ministry of Defence official responsible for the nuclear convoys. The PM fired questions at him.

'What are the risks here? What exactly is the possibility of nuclear contamination with these convoys if there is an accident?'

'The risks are infinitesimal, Prime Minister. We haven't had a major problem in the last fifty odd years. We have, of course, carried out contingency exercises with the various worst-case scenarios and I am confident that we can do no more in this respect,' Hutton answered with measured confidence.

'So what exactly would the consequences of a worst case scenario be?'

'With respect, that is not going to happen, Prime Minister.'

'That is not what I asked. Answer the question, please. Who thought a 9/11 scenario was a possibility until it happened?'

Members of the committee held their collective breath.

'Well, if the warheads are breached – and I stress this is not a realistic possibility – depending on which way the wind is blowing they would release up to thirty millisieverts into the immediate area and less with distance. There would be a cigar plume. People would be advised to stay indoors and we would have to put restrictions on farms.'

There was a silence as members of the committee absorbed what they had been told.

'How much of a security risk is this breakdown near Paisley?'

'None, Prime Minister. The security is total. Those guarding the convoy are well versed in what to do in extreme situations.'

'You mean shoot to kill if the integrity of the convoy is endangered.'

'Yes, Prime Minister,' replied Levisham who was surprised that he was even asked the question.

'We need to get the repair of the truck done as quickly as possible and get the convoy moving again. I think we all agree that this is a top priority. I am sure John Langwith already has this in hand.'

The crowds at both ends of the convoy stayed where they were to great relief of the PM and the National Security Committee. There was still the matter of getting the convoy underway once the repair had been made. After three hours a large recovery vehicle started moving into place to tow the broken down truck away.

The protesters were in party atmosphere. Loud music was playing and drinks were handed around. The consensus was emerging amongst them that they had made their point. Never had the UK's nuclear weaponry seemed so vulnerable. It was a message that went deep. Even some who supported the UK's possession of a nuclear arsenal were beginning to have second thoughts.

At 9pm the demonstrators dispersed good humouredly as a police line in full riot gear moved towards them.

'Hey you, Jimmie, see that nuclear warhead over there? That's tae protect our foodbanks and our homeless,' one demonstrator shouted. General laughter and derision followed. Another unfurled a sheet with 'Nukes of Hazard' written across it.

By 9.30 the convoy was again on the move at a few miles an hour but at least it was moving. The PM, the NSC and COBRA heaved another collective sigh of relief that would have lifted Nelson's Column.

In Scotland the episode made a deep impression on many whether they were involved in the campaign of civil disobedience against the State of Emergency or not. In Paisley the day was celebrated as Nukes of Hazard Day in bars that night. The town's reputation had been cemented.

Eilidh watched the confrontation on Ian's smart phone. She remembered one of these convoys on the A68 two years ago near Jedburgh. At first she didn't realise what it was and then when she did, she felt sick. It was a spine-chilling moment that she hadn't forgotten. She vowed to herself that she would campaign to have these weapons of mass destruction removed from Scotland's soil.

Chapter Fifteen

Two days after Eilidh arrived Ian came to the croft at 6am. The sharp knock on her bedroom door woke her up with a start.

'Come, Eilidh, quick. Rab is slipping away.'

Eilidh sat bolt upright in the bed. She dressed hurriedly.

'Oh God! Will I be in time? Please, God, don't take him before I get there.'

'Just hurry will you?'

It was still dark but the first hints of dawn were spreading like a gentle wave over the landscape. They jumped into the Landrover and Ian drove along the pot-holed lane like a demon possessed. A drive that normally took twenty minutes was done in fifteen.

Eilidh rushed into the farmhouse and up to Rab's bedroom. Alister and Fiona were sitting quietly at the bedside. They rose and hugged each other.

'We have called the doctor,' her mother said. Her face was

tear-stained. There was a deep sadness in her eyes. Her father was stony faced, grief etched on his face. He said nothing.

Eilidh looked at Rab. His breathing was laboured and his eyes closed. She took his hand and held it tightly.

'I'm here, grandad, I'm here with you.'

He nodded. He said something she couldn't hear. She put her face closer to him to try and hear. He was struggling hard to get the words out and Eilidh was struggling to hear.

'My ... my time ... is over now ...' A silence fell for what seemed to last minutes. The dawn light was creeping into the room.

Then his final words: *'Chath mi deagh chath, chriochnaich mi mo chuairt, gleidh mi an creideamh. Saor Alba!' (I have fought the good fight, I have run the course to its end, I have kept the faith. Free Scotland)*

Then he departed. The room suddenly felt very empty. Rab's life force had left the room.

Ian had just come in. The four of them hugged. Eilidh's tears rolled down her cheeks. Her mother sat down on the chair beside the bed. She wanted to be alone. The house drowned in silence. A chill descended and no one knew what to say.

'Take your mother a cup of tea, will you Eilidh? Ian, we have got to tend the cattle. Come now will you?' Alister said.

Ian looked at Eilidh. They both understood that this was their father's way of coping with the weight of grief and loss.

'We'll be back in an hour or so. Don't leave your mother until we are back.'

Eilidh took up the cup of tea and tiptoed into the room.

'Thanks, thanks. Leave me here. I'll stay until the doctor comes. Get yourself away.'

Eilidh closed the door quietly behind her. Rab was physically gone, she knew, but she had a strong sense of his presence, as though he was still with her. His spirit rarely left her in the days after. It was as though they had not been parted. Eilidh found herself conversing quietly with him and, somehow, he answered in her heart. That consoled her as the waves of grief came over her from nowhere like a storm brewing far out in the Minch.

Childhood memories overwhelmed her. There was hardly a part of the farm or surrounding landscape that did not conjure up a memory of him and his laughter and things he had said to her. She wished above all else that he had lived to see through these dark days. She had so wanted him to see the dawn of independence which would surely have come had the referendum been allowed to take place. Eilidh needed his encouragement, his perspective on the difficulties and uncertainties they faced. She needed his strength.

She imagined him saying, 'Stand firm like a rock, lassie. The waves will batter you, the storms and gales will sap your strength and will, but stand firm. Remember who you are, what you stand for. Worse days have befallen our people before and these days will make us stronger, more determined. The day will come, of that there is no doubt.'

The wider community came to pay their respects. Visitors were sensitive not to ask about Eilidh although there were widely held suspicions she was in the vicinity.

There was some discussion about whether she should attend the funeral.

'They'll be waiting for you when you come out of the Kirk,' Alister warned, 'They won't let this opportunity slip.'

'So be it, Dad. There's no way I'll miss grandad's funeral. It is as simple as that. I won't be intimidated.'

The family knew better than to try and dissuade her.

The funeral was held a few days later. The Kirk was full. Rab was well-loved although not all agreed with his politics. They respected him nonetheless.

When the coffin was carried from the hearse into the Kirk, Eilidh noticed several security people trying and failing to look inconspicuous. Someone was obtrusively taking photos of her. Malcolm MacMillan, the Minister, noticed them too and had anticipated this. Malcolm was a tall man in his middle years with a kindly, smiling demeanour. His parishioners liked and respected him and he was a pivotal figure in the small community.

Before they entered the body of the Kirk he whispered to Eilidh.

'You'll be leaving by the back door, Eilidh. That will give you a few minutes headstart. You must go to the Manse and hide in the loft. It has all been arranged.'

She thanked him although she knew she would not witness the interment.

No one in the congregation seemed surprised to see her. Many smiled at her in a show of support. Others averted their eyes.

Immediately after the funeral Eilidh exited by the back door, ran to the Manse and hid as she was told. She stayed there for several hours and only when Malcolm told her that the coast was clear did she emerge from hiding.

'Thank you, Malcolm. Thank you so much.'

'Don't even think about it. Rab would have haunted me for the rest of my life if I hadn't hidden you,' he joked, 'And anyway, your work is not finished. It has only just begun.'

Ian collected her in the early hours of the morning once the security forces had given up hope of finding her. John Langwith, the Gold Commander in London was incandescent that Eilidh had slipped the net and told Melton, the Silver Commander, in uncompromising language.

While she was still on Skye Eilidh would go frequently and sit in the Kirk. It was the one that the family had attended for generations. She was brought up as a church-goer and had attended every Sunday with her parents and Ian. It was a small congregation close knit and supportive.

Eilidh's early years of Church-going had left a deep impression on her although when she left Skye for Edinburgh she had drifted away from organised religion. Sometimes you have to move away from something to be able to gain a perspective on it. The tradition of Psalm singing and its haunting beauty was something that never left her. Psalm 121: *I will lift up mine eyes unto the hills...* Many, many times she recited the words of the psalm to herself.

The Psalm singing in Gaelic had left a particular mark on her for its haunting beauty, a beauty that spoke to her soul. There were times over the last few years when she had faced personal difficulties and sadness but, somehow, listening to Psalms in Gaelic put her life in perspective. They seemed to touch the void.

She found the stillness and quiet of the building brought her inner calm. She prayed. She felt the weight of the prayers that had been offered in that building over its three hundred years. It was in this building, in stillness and quiet that she discovered her spiritual self. It was in this building that she found the faith and strength to carry on.

She also did something that was to lead to questions later. She took a candle into the Kirk and put it beside the communion table where she lit it. She knew that in other Christian churches this was done and she liked the idea: the idea of the light of Rab's life illuminating the darkness. The darkness would never overcome the light of her Rab's spirit.

On one occasion as she was sitting in a pew, Eilidh heard the creaking of the door open. She heard footsteps and then someone sat down in a pew behind her. The silence resumed. When Eilidh got up to leave she saw the Minister, Malcolm MacMillan, sitting there praying. She decided to wait outside for him even though she knew that she was not meant to be seen.

'Ah, Eilidh, I cannot say that I am surprised to find you here.' He spoke with that lilt of the Hebrides.

Eilidh smiled broadly. 'Thank you again for what you did for me the other day. There are times when it feels right to say a prayer.'

'Yes, Eilidh, there are. And I have to say that I guessed it was you who lit the candle two days ago. You can't imagine the questions and theories there have been about it. I have to say that I had my suspicions,' he chuckled.

'Tell me are you safe? Are you well?'

'Yes, I am thank you.'

'And long may that be so. You know what has happened to this country is a terrible thing. Even many who opposed independence are upset. I shouldn't be talking like this but I know you will understand. Goodness knows where it will all end.

'Our country has a long history. Our people are strong. We'll come through these days. I'm an optimist. Now you must go because they are still searching for you. You know where to find me if you need me, Eilidh.'

Eilidh made her way back to her cottage over the fields with Megan following closely at her heels. She felt uplifted: her spirit was strengthened.

That evening she walked across to the farm. She felt in need of company and Megan was happy at the prospect of another walk.

The BBC national news had just finished.

'They're still searching high and low for you, my girl. They even showed pictures of the top thirty activists they had either arrested or were still looking for. It's not safe for you here, Eilidh, especially not at the farm house or the croft for that matter either,' Fiona said with concern.

'Aye, your mother is right. You need to make plans.'

'Was Murdo MacGregor one of the people they are still looking for? Do you remember?' Eilidh asked.

'Aye, he is. Yes, that name was one of them wasn't it Ian?' Eilidh's mother asked.

'I'm sure it will all be repeated on tonight's BBC news,' said Alister, 'This has all been an eye-opener to me and to us all.'

'And why do you ask about Murdo?' Fiona asked with a wry smile, 'He's no your man is he?'

'No, he isn't,' she replied unsure of whether he was or wasn't.

Ian laughed. 'Aye, I ken ye too well my lass!'

'We had a visit from Dougie, your policeman friend in Portree, this morning asking if we knew where you were. We told him we had no idea. He said 'Good, I don't expect we'll be seeing her around these parts.' with a knowing smile,' Alister reported.

'Dougie? I always liked him as a person but, well, not in any other way if you see what I mean, dad.'

'Aye, I ken whit ye mean, lass.'

Dougie and Eilidh had been in the same year at school. Eilidh always thought that Dougie fancied her but she never reciprocated his advances. Instead they became good friends. Dougie and Ian went fishing together so he followed what Eilidh had been doing in the campaign and admired her for it.

'How are things on the farm, Dad?' Eilidh asked.

Ian tried belatedly to sign to her not to ask. He rolled his eyes heavenwards.

Alister told her about the difficulties they had had over the last two years when their income had been so low.

'But for the bed and breakfast, this cottage and Ian's fishing we would have struggled even more than we have. And what of you? What are you going to do now?'

'I don't know at the moment. It depends how things develop. I realise I can't stay here indefinitely whatever happens nationally,' Eilidh responded.

'You know Eilidh your Mum and I are more than happy for you to stay as long as you want but the net must be closing in on you. We'll look after you as will Megan.'

Megan's tail wagged at the mention of her name. They say that sheepdogs are the most intelligent and Megan was certainly both intelligent and intuitive. She kept watch over Eilidh and instinctively seemed to understand her every move. Megan made a good companion for her and slept outside her door each night as though guarding her. Together they would stride along the beaches with Megan never leaving Eilidh's side by more than a few yards. When Megan went ahead of Eilidh she would turn round frequently to see that Eilidh had not changed direction. She understood what Eilidh wanted by the tone of her voice.

The days passed slowly. Eilidh established a routine and kept to it unswervingly. She would get out of bed at 7am, shower, breakfast while listening to BBC Scotland news and then walk Megan for an hour or so. There was nothing about Rodric save that he was in custody. Each day the news programmes stressed how quickly Scotland had returned to normal and how glad people were after the recent events. The PM repeatedly assured the country that the State of Emergency would not last a day more than necessary. When pressed at Prime Minister's Questions how long that would be his answer was evasive citing 'known unknowns'.

Eilidh knew that all was far from being settled. She listened to what Ian and her parents told her from telephone conversations with friends elsewhere in Scotland. In the West, Glasgow was in ferment. In the East it was Dundee and in the North it was Inverness. Edinburgh was for the most part calm although Leith was on the boil. What seemed to be happening was a grassroots 'Arab Spring' or 'Velvet Revolution' which the authorities, despite all their pleas, were powerless to prevent.

The announcement that the Scottish Parliament whose existence was dependent on Westminster's permission was to be prorogued until further notice angered many people of all political persuasions. To many the sovereignty of the Scottish people lay with Holyrood and not Westminster no matter what the latter claimed.

Eilidh looked at what was happening on the financial markets which were showing extreme volatilty. The FTSE had dropped twelve percent in the last four days. On the sixth day it seemed stable but on the seventh it dropped another three percent. Sterling was also dropping more dramatically than ever before.

Eilidh had asked Ian to buy the *Financial Times* in Portree if he could. It was clear that investors were withdrawing capital from the UK on an unprecedented scale. In the two months before the referendum there had been an outflow of £33B but, in the space of a few days since the State of Emergency was declared, the outflow had been £34B – a figure that no government could ignore. The UK was haemorrhaging capital at an unsustainable rate. There were hints that the Bank of England was going to have to raise interest rates appreciably within days. It was clear that the markets did not accept the government's bland assurances that the crisis was under control and that the UK was intact and would remain so.

Eilidh knew enough about economics to understand that these figures alone meant that the Government had to get a grip of the situation immediately. If the State of Emergency was seen not to be working then there was only one other way forward: Westminster would have to back-track and negotiate with Rodric and his advisers and find a face-saving formula to end the crisis for the good of all. Eilidh wondered when that moment would come. Perhaps it had already come. She could imagine the feverish discussions taking place at the heart of government.

When Eilidh woke on the tenth day of the State of Emergency and switched on the news she felt that this could be the critical day. It would be the financial markets that would determine the outcome of the crisis not politics. The cost of keeping the United Kingdom unified was becoming unsustainably high and the Government could not pay what seemed to be an ever-increasing price without end. The Bond market had made this abundantly clear with interest rates soaring to levels that were provoking deep disquiet. Simply put, the interest payments on Government debt were so high as to undermine finances and destroy the budget, hence the plummeting Pound and the inevitability of interest rate increases. Whispers suggested that interest rates would need to rise from two to nine percent to staunch the capital outflow and protect the Pound.

Eilidh listened closely to each BBC news broadcast waiting to hear for the gentle massaging of public opinion before government policy changed. That would be followed shortly later – probably in a matter of hours – with an announcement of a policy *volte face*. The markets would then respond accordingly and stability would be restored with a soaring of the markets – for markets tend to over-react in both directions. Wise investors knew this would happen as night followed day. They had dumped their investments in many cases as long ago as three months previously. As the constitutional and the resultant economic crises gained momentum and indices started dropping sharply. Investors watched and waited for the bottom of the market and bought just as the Government was in maximum pain. Timing markets was never easy but this seemed a rather easier bet than most. Hedge fund managers were delighted and swelled the Tory coffers accordingly.

Chapter Sixteen

ON THE ELEVENTH MORNING AFTER breakfast Eilidh walked down to the shore with Megan cheerfully wagging her tail. The views over towards the Cuillins always evoked a deep sense of the spiritual in her. This was the landscape of the poet with the pressing grandeur of nature: its mountains, lochs and seascapes.

Towards the end of her walk she saw another solitary figure walking in the distance towards her with a rucksack on his back. It was the first time she had seen anyone walking along this part of the beach. As they got closer Eilidh began to think that she recognised the gait. After another twenty yards she knew who it was: Murdo.

'What kept you?' she shouted as they each sped up to running pace with wide smiles on their faces, 'What bloody kept you?'

They hugged and Murdo kissed Eilidh on both cheeks but then, as he pulled away from her, their eyes met and they both knew what the other was thinking and feeling. The next kiss was of a different kind altogether.

'I thought I would never see you again,' Murdo said.

'I thought the same,' replied Eilidh taking his hand, 'How did you know where to come?'

'Mhairi and I guessed you would try and come home if only to see your grandfather. It would be a safe place for you, at least as safe as anywhere is at the moment. After going back to Lachie and Mhairi's farm I went to stay with Calum for a few days until things quietened down. Calum lent me his motorbike to come here. I guessed that with all the security cameras which have number recognition I would have been caught in no time on my own bike. I got to Armadale and asked where your family's farm was. Mhairi said it was at the Isleoronsay. Easy really.

'I met Ian your brother who seemed to be expecting me. He greeted me and brought me to the croft. He told me you would probably be walking on the beach at this time of day. So here I am.'

'Any news of Rodric and Lachie? Do you know exactly what happened to them? What do you think is really going on at the moment? Is Westminster getting the upper hand?' Eilidh's questions came thick and fast. There was so much she wanted to know. Somehow in those first few minutes of their relationship, a relationship that had remained dormant for so long, other pressing priorities intruded.

Murdo answered her questions as best he could.

They made their way back hand in hand, catching up with each other's news, in deep contentment that the feelings they had resisted for so long had finally won through. They got back to the croft and at long last expressed their deepest feelings for one another. They stayed in for the rest of the morning making love and talking, talking, talking. Everything they had never said to each other was now said. Lost time was made up.

'Why were you so distant with me at first?' Murdo asked.

'I could see you for what you were. I suspected your motives. I think those suspicions were justified – don't you? I could never sleep with the enemy. Rodric, too, had his suspicions about you. You were never let into his inner-most thoughts, you know. I suppose he thought he could use you for his own ends by feeding you disinformation.'

'I came to guess as much.'

'But in the end you turned your back on all that and swung over to us. I have often wondered what triggered that. What was the tipping point?'

'It was a gradual build-up of a number of things none particularly significant in itself. Each one added to the other. Ultimately I couldn't betray Rodric or you or the tens of thousands of activists who were giving their all. I suppose I realised that I am a Scot first and foremost and that is where my loyalty lies – not to a flawed union dominated by Westminister. My conscience rebelled. I couldn't let you all down even if my life depended on it.'

He told her about Emma, about her family, about the dinner party when he felt demeaned by the comments made and the laughter that the remarks about Scots and Scotland had provoked.

'Scotland is Westminster's last colonial problem, even if many Scots don't see it that way.'

'You went native, in other words,' said Eilidh looking at him intently, this new love of her life.

'Yes, I suppose you could say that. I never realised that this cause could resonate so deeply in me.'

'You're beginning to sound serious,' said Eilidh half teasingly. 'So what happened to Emma?'

'We began to drift apart. We saw each other less and less. Her life is in London. She has a good job in PR and her friendship networks are all there. We were engaged at one point but time slipped by and there were no serious plans being made for the wedding. There came a point when we both recognised the inevitable and decided to separate. There was no bitterness or rancour. I suppose it is what was meant to be. She could never be part of this, of me. She couldn't share who I have become.'

'So when exactly did you realise you had feelings for me?'

'Mmm, quite early on after I first met you. You seemed so aloof and discouraging as though you really disliked me.'

'I suppose I did then. I was always suspicious of you although I must say I did like your smile and your attempts to make me laugh even if I didn't respond. It is amusing in retrospect. It could have been okay but I didn't trust you.'

'So when did you finally tell yourself that you fancied the pants off me metaphorically and literally?'

'Not sure I do even yet, you are too full of yourself.'

'Oh aye?'

'Well, I suppose if I'm entirely honest, it was quite early on. You always seemed a pleasant easy-going person and a good listener. I liked that. What you represented was another matter altogether. It was when I arrived at Lachie's farm and saw what you had done to save Rodric that I realised you were one of us after all. That's when my earlier reservations about you melted away.'

'Now you tell me!'

'So what do we do now?'

Murdo smiled, 'Let's stay a bit longer.'

Chapter Seventeen

CREYKE MET MCLEISH IN A pub in the West of Glasgow. It had been over thirty-five years since they worked together in Northern Ireland at the time of the Troubles. Creyke had been McLeish's handler. There was little love lost between the two men but the one needed the other. It was the flow of information both ways that oiled the relationship, that and money and drink.

Crekye disliked the hardnosed, physically intimidating McLeish. There was a constant air of menace about him. He didn't need to ask McLeish questions. The file on him was voluminous. It had taken an evening to read. Crekye would leak names, details of Republicans to McLeish knowing that he was in effect signing their death warrants. McLeish would pass information from his people to the Brits. It was all part of the Dirty War that both sides were engaged in. These had been dangerous times with many lives lost, all too often the lives of innocents. The government had employed whatever methods necessary to end the conflict. High-profile attacks on the UK mainland meant the gloves were off. It was difficult to know who needed whom the most.

The two men had worked together for eighteen months when one day McLeish using the emergency contact code demanded an urgent meeting within a couple of hours. Crekye went to the chosen rendez-vous expecting a major tip-off. Instead, McLeish demanded to be pulled out immediately and taken out of the Province. He wanted a new identity and a new life. That had always been the deal. If McLeish wanted out he was to be evacuated.

McLeish was an Ulster Scot. His father was a Scot and his mother was from Ulster. He had spent time in both places with the result that his accent could switch from Ulsterman to Glaswegian, not a mean feat. Crekye didn't need to ask why he wanted pulled out so urgently, he knew.

That night McLeish was flown out of Ulster to a safe house in the UK where he remained under close guard. Some time later he went to live in Glasgow and merged easily into the unionist circles and the sub-culture of the Orange Order with its ready made support system.

He remained an asset on the books of the security state. He was one stage removed from any part of the state apparatus yet if he was needed he could always be summoned up. There was always freelance work for the likes of McLeish in that grey area between the state and its agencies and the unofficial, arms length distance of *ad hoc* agents who could be commissioned for wet disposals.

It was in this context that Creyke had called him for a meeting. The pub was remarkably busy for the time of the day.

'I have a job for you,' said Crekye watching McLeish's reaction carefully.

'Oh aye. How the fuck did you know where to find me?' McLeish asked with ill-concealed aggression.

'No one is ever lost completely,' Creyke replied.

'I wish I could say I'm pleased to see ye but I am not. Whit dae ye want?'

'Let me buy you a drink first before we talk.'

'Mine's a double malt.'

'The usual one?'

'Aye, so you remember?'

'Yes, I do. Not many of our people were drinking malts at 10am.'

'Sometimes there is a lot to forget.'

'I'm sure there is.'

Crekye went to the bar to get the drinks. He felt uncomfortable. The drinkers recognised that he was not one of them and their ill-concealed looks of contempt hit Crekye like a steel door. He could imagine what they were thinking.

A woman of no uncertain occupation entered the pub and made her way over to the bar. She stood beside Crekye – too closely – and looked him over. He felt embarrassed.

'Hey, I'll nae bite ye,' she smiled. She then lent closer to him.

'I wis going tae offer ye a fuck but the pound isn't worth it anymore!' she said loudly.

The customers nearby roared in laughter.

'Aye, the pound is dropping through the flair. I wid be better being paid in deep-fried Mars bars and cans of Irn Bru.'

The raucous laughter continued.

To Crekye's relief the barman approached.

'Whit dae ye want, pal?' he asked in an unfriendly, almost challenging tone. Crekye knew from over the years that people like this could smell a security man. Everything about him from his clothes to his demeanour and speech gave him away. It reminded him of when he had once gone into a republican pub in Derry. You could have heard a pin drop. He exited swiftly without a drink.

'I don't like being seen wi' the likes of you,' McLeish said.

'I can imagine.'

McLeish threw back the malt.

'Get tae the point.'

'We need a wet disposal. There is someone we need dealt with.'

'Oh aye? And who wid that be? Those days are over for me. I'm clean noo.'

'Let's just say a double operator. One might say a traitor.'

'There are plenty of them aboot. Make no mistake. One of these non-attributable jobs?'

'Yes. We can't be seen to get our hands dirty, you know the sort of stuff.'

McLeish knew only too well.

'Suppose I said I've had enough of that and that I want a quiet life and a clear conscience. Suppose I told you I am an upstanding member of the community and the past is the past.'

'It was a risk I was prepared to take.'

'What's the contract worth?'

'Twenty k.'

'You must be wanting to make a powerful point with that money behind it.'

'Yes, you could say that. It's to encourage the others who may have a similar flight of fancy.'

'Well the cash wid be welcome, nae doot aboot that.'

'So you'll consider it?'

'I might do. I might not. I left all that stuff behind. I dinnae want tae go back tae it. I'm a family man, ye ken. I dinnae want tae have a sabbatical in Barlinnie.'

'Make it twenty five k.'

'Ach, ye wee deil. I'll think aboot it. I'll let ye know by the weekend. I'll text ye. Now get outta here before my reputation is ruined.'

Creyke finished his half-pint and took an abrupt farewell.

'Bye, derling,' the woman shouted at him as Crekye walked quickly to the door, 'Anytime for the likes of you security yins. Special rate!'

Guffaws of laughter pursued Crekye.

'Looks like ye're keeping bad company there, Mac,' the barman said.

'Aye, that's why I sent him aff with a flea in his ear. Ye won't be seeing him in here again.'

'Guid. Ye can smell these people.'

By the weekend Creyke had the call he wanted. He knew that McLeish needed the money and had pitched it perfectly. They met again the following day in a car park. A third of the cash was paid upfront with the rest to follow on completion.

'You can decide how to do this. Ideally no fingerprints, no traces,' said Creyke.

'Ye have nae telt me aboot the target.'

Crekye handed over a photograph of Murdo.

'He looks awfu young. How dae I know where tae find him?'

'We aren't sure where he is yet. He has dropped off the radar. Once we find him I'll contact you. We want the job carried out within forty eight hours of that. He rides a motorbike. You're a biker too, aren't you? Still ride?'

'Aye, I still dae that.'

'What are you riding these days?'

'Whit's it tae you?'

'Bikers seem to have a lot of accidents – don't they?'

'Fuck off.'

'No funny business – got that? Remember, you weren't hard to find.'

'Ye bastards. What has yon jimmie done to upset yous?'

'You don't need to know that.'

McLeish left Creyke without a backward glance or farewell. One side of him was glad to be back at the centre of the action even if he had nothing but contempt for the likes of Creyke and his ilk. The money would be welcome though. He had built up a few debts he needed to pay off and soon. He almost felt sympathy for his target.

Of course, he guessed that the wet disposal was linked to the State of Emergency. All these acts were carried out off stage by private contractors like himself.

'We want no finger prints on this one,' were Creyke's last words to him. McLeish knew he meant this literally and metaphorically.

An accident on the motorbike? Made sense. He had always prided his riding skills and pitting them against another rider had a certain appeal. He had done enough riding throughout Scotland to know the roads well and to ride them at the very edge of his skills. That is what kept the adrenalin pumping, that is what gave him a purpose, a sense of worth.

Chapter Eighteen

TWO WEEKS AFTER THE STATE of Emergency had been declared unrest was still simmering. Everyone knew that Direct Rule was untenable.

Sutton was on the way to his weekly joust at Prime Minister's Questions and was scanning his papers yet again to remind himself of the issues he would have to defend. The State of Emergency and the NHS were sure to top the bill, then the refugee and immigration crises were a certainty too. He had been batting questions on these issues with ease for some months now. Somehow despite all his pumped up indignation, John Black, the leader of the Opposition rarely seemed to land a punch successfully, much to the chagrin of his backbenchers. The PM had little to fear on that score. Not for nothing had he been awarded a First.

His mobile buzzed.

'Yes?' he answered with a brusque tone. Usually he switched off his phone on the way to the Commons to give himself some few minutes of calm before the storm but somehow today he had forgotten. His attention had been diverted at the last moment as they were about to walk out of Number Ten to the waiting car.

'I am really sorry to be phoning you at such a time Prime Minister but I have some bad news that you need to know immediately,' said Bennett.

'And what is that?' asked the PM testily.

'Rodric Fraser is dead.'

'What do you mean dead? How? When did this happen?'

'He was found about fifty minutes ago lying under a tree in the exercise area where he is being held.'

'Cause of death?'

'Not sure at the moment. On the face of it it looks as though he committed suicide.'

'Fuck, fuck, fuck. The bastard has probably martyred himself for the cause. God, you can imagine how this one is going to play out? I want a full report on my desk about the circumstances of his death as soon as possible. Have the press got hold of this one yet?'

'Not to my knowledge Prime Minister. It is only a matter of time before this leaks out. We must retain control of the agenda on this one. I recommend you say something in the Commons. You know the sort of thing, *it is with great sadness I have to report that a great Scot has died today*, and then praise Fraser.'

'Yes. I shall seize the moment before this goes viral. Fuck, fuck.'

The news had taken him completely by surprise. He would have to work out the political consequences of Fraser's death. It would all hinge on the manner of death. Of course there would always be those who believed that Fraser was killed by the British state no matter what the coroner's findings. On the very few occasions the two men had met relations had been cordial if a little frosty. He regarded Fraser as a mischief-maker whose intent was to destroy the United Kingdom to which he, as Prime Minister, was totally committed.

It was with some trepidation that he entered the Commons. As he walked swiftly through the Lobby to take his seat members of his party smiled at him and shook his hand. There were the usual few who were trying to ingratiate themselves in the hope they would receive preferment in the next reshuffle which was rumoured to be within weeks. The PM never quite knew whether to feel sorry for them or contempt at their chutzpah. Probably it was the latter.

He took his seat on the front bench. The Chamber seemed fuller than usual. He looked across at the Opposition benches and his eyes fixed on John Black. He usually eyeballed him to see if he could detect any hint of what might be coming. Black seemed to have a slight smile playing on his face – had he already heard about Fraser's death? He scanned the opposition benches to see if word was going round but there seemed to be little more than the usual hubbub.

The Speaker called for the Leader of the Opposition's first question. Black rose slowly to his feet, almost as though he was savouring what he was about to unleash.

'Could the Prime Minister tell us if it is true that Rodric Fraser has been found dead?'

Silence fell like a shroud. The opposition MPs obviously had had no indication of the breaking-news but somehow, someone had informed Black.

The Prime Minister scrambled to his feet.

'It is with very great regret that I must tell you that this is correct. I was informed in the car on the way from Downing Street. I would like to express my sincere regrets that Rodric Fraser, a man most of the Members in this House did not agree with, was found dead a short while ago. Our thoughts and prayers are with his family at this difficult time. I am unable to tell the House of the exact circumstances of his death at the moment but I can say that a major police inquiry is underway. They will report back to me as soon as possible.'

The MPs on both sides sat in stunned silence digesting the news. Minds were racing as to the possible political consequences both in Scotland and in the UK as a whole.

'Rodric Fraser was a great Scot, a true patriot to that country. Our differences were profound and I cannot hide that but I can say I admired his commitment to his cause, no matter how misguided I felt it to be. There is little doubt that he was deeply loved by many of his fellow countrymen who will feel a deep sense of loss today. I urge them to react with dignity to this saddest of news. I shall be in contact with his family as soon as I leave the Chamber. I would ask, Mr Speaker, that we stand for a minute's silence in honour of this great Scot.'

The MPs rose as one and a minute's silence was observed. Meanwhile the media had gone into overdrive as the news of Fraser's death spread like a virus across the land. Tributes were soon flowing in and even Fraser's enemies seemed to be praising his single-mindedness. Political pundits were pontificating on the possible consequences. Social media platforms spiked as the information leaked out.

The remainder of PM's Questions were muted. He was going through the motions. MPs felt it inappropriate to try and score political points on this occasion. Once out of the Chamber the noise level soared as MPs chatted amongst themselves about the news and shouted into their mobiles. The sub-text of all the conversations was rooted in the likely consequences politically, for individual MPs and for the fate of the UK, that increasingly fragile union.

The PM asked Stewart Wyndham to accompany him back in the car to Downing Street.

'I have a horrible feeling that Fraser has sought martyrdom to further his cause. I have to say I never liked the man. In fact I always found him a bit of a shit.'

Stewart knew only too well what the PM's views of Fraser were and didn't disagree.

'What we need to work out now is what the consequences of this will be. What do you think Stewart?'

'This will pour oil on the flames, Prime Minister. We can expect a massive upsurge in civil unrest – not necessarily immediately as everyone will be stunned. We need to get to the bottom of what has happened as quickly as possible. It was suicide wasn't it?'

There was an awkward silence before the PM replied.

'Yes, that is the initial view but the forensic people are working on it now and two of the top pathologists in Scotland are involved too. We can't get this one wrong. There's too much at stake.'

'It couldn't have been murder could it?'

'Most unlikely. Most unlikely. Who would want Fraser killed?' the PM asked rhetorically.

Stewart didn't answer but he could think of quite a few people. He wasn't sure if he detected irony in the PM's answer. Fraser's death would throw the 'Yes' movement into disarray. It would be leaderless. There was no other figure in the 'Yes' movement who commanded as much respect or admiration as Fraser. But there were many individuals and vested interests that wanted him removed forever. Stewart decided to keep these thoughts to himself.

By the time the car swept into Downing Street a meeting of COBRA had been called for later that morning. The full apparatus of the British state had been cranked up to full pitch to deal with what was potentially another threat to its existence. The PM demanded a detailed report surrounding the circumstances of Fraser's death on his table asap so he could present the findings to COBRA.

Five hours later, Bennett brought the preliminary report to the PM.

'I am not quite sure what to say about this, Prime Minister,' warned Bennett, wary at what he was going to reveal.

'So what does it say, Crispin, for God's sake?' the PM asked testily. Bennett took his tone as a sign of stress, signs that had all been too evident in the last few weeks.

'Apparently, Fraser committed suicide.'

'Apparently? What do you mean apparently? You mean we are not sure?' The PM's tone was peremptory.

'Well, there are some strange aspects to his death.'

'And they are? Do get on with it Crispin.'

'The police say that it is a straight case of suicide. The pathologist on the other hand says that he couldn't have done it himself.'

'Give me the report,' the PM said wearily. 'I had better read the whole thing myself.'

'The pathologist has written ten pages and the toxicologist has made some preliminary findings, Prime Minister.'

'This has to take top priority for the next few hours, Crispin. Cancel all appointments in the interim. Tell the press office a full statement will be made later – hopefully in time for news bulletins this evening. We must not be on the back foot on this one.'

When the pathologist's full report arrived a few hours later it did not make for easy reading. One of the experts stated it was suicide but one of the pathologists stated unambiguously that Fraser could not have killed himself. It simply wasn't possible.

'Haemorrhage ... an incisive wound to his left wrist (the ulnar artery) ... advanced heart disease ... an ingestion of pain-killers ...' That all seemed nicely straight-forward and utterly plausible. However, the loss of blood was not commensurate with death. Fraser would have needed to have lost at least five pints of blood yet there was little sign of such a loss either on his clothes or the ground around where the body was found. Three packs of pain-killers were found beside the body with all the pills bar one missing. The pathologist said that such an ingestion would have been unlikely to have killed him. More intriguingly only three pills were actually found in Fraser's stomach. The police report also raised some difficult questions: there were no finger prints on the knife which Fraser supposedly used for the act. The small bottle of mineral water had no finger prints on it either.

This was going to require even more careful handling than the PM had thought necessary at first. The last thing he wanted was any doubt about what had happened. It was a most regrettable suicide. Anything to quietly smear Fraser in the coming days in the media would be helpful. A few well-placed stories about imagined proclivities would raise enough questions in the mind of the country. Perhaps a degree of mental instability could be hinted at – who, after all, would commit suicide? Sutton remembered that Manningtree had managed to get Fraser's medical records some months ago which suggested that for all his bluster and bonhomie, he suffered from intermittent depression even if he hid it well.

It began to sound horribly familiar to Sutton. He could see that this explanation would be severely tested in the courts and the media. He would await a fuller report which the police and intelligence services would provide. Sutton knew enough to realise that sometimes things happened in the sensitive crevasses of the state that would never be explained and that it was not too advisable to search thoroughly for the truth. Obfuscation was the best policy until the matter died down through lack of interest or the sheer exhaustion of the public. Things would eventually move on – they always did. The issues being played out were of such magnitude that sometimes it was essential to look the other way and not to ask too many questions. This was beginning to look like one such issue.

Sutton had been in politics long enough to know that there is a well-trodden path for getting out of difficulties: first, establish a Committee of Inquiry under a carefully chosen Judge, secondly, spin out proceedings for as long as possible until some years later everyone who was remotely interested in it would have more or less forgotten about it. Yes, there would be a few articles in the press, some even hostile. There would be the odd current affairs programme designed to create a fuss but, sooner or later, the dust would settle and the caravan would move on. That was the way of the world. That was the way of Westminster politics.

The only thought that made Sutton slightly queasy was that Scotland was not easily taken in by this great charade. The Scots for some reason that totally escaped him seemed to have long political memories – or at least a substantial proportion of them did.

In his more morose moments that day the PM wondered whether he would be swallowed up by events. His first act, however, was to phone Shona, Fraser's wife to offer his sincere condolences. This was not an easy thing to do. Fraser's family would be aware of the deep animosity between the two men.

Murdo and Eilidh were having a frugal lunch when they heard the news of Rodric's death on BBC Scotland.

'I suspected this would happen, I bloody knew it. They have killed him!' said Eilidh, tears of rage and sorrow glistening on her cheeks.

'There is no way that Rodric would have killed himself. No way. No way at all. The bastards. They won't get away with this one,' said Murdo.

Eilidh sobbed in Murdo's arms. Murdo, too, choked emotionally. Gradually as the emotion subsided they began to ask the questions that were beginning to be asked in the media.

They listened to the Prime Minister's tribute in the Commons.

'Bastard,' said Murdo, 'He doesn't believe a word of what he was saying. The deep state wanted rid of Rodric and were prepared to ride out the ensuing storm. He had become too much of a problem for them. He isn't the first to go this way. This is another Willie MacRae.'

'Surely not. You don't really believe that they would do that, do you?'

It was difficult to accept that the state would sanction a killing in this way.

Murdo was uncertain.

'I honestly don't know. There have been things like this in the past which have raised suspicions. It wouldn't be the state directly. It would be a freelancer several times removed. That's what happens in dirty wars. It has happened in Latin America, Eastern Europe and Northern Ireland. It is always a possibilty that Rodric had become such a liability to their aims that he was better disposed of, despite the questions his death would raise,' Murdo responded.

'It really is hard to believe but then the alternative of suicide is equally hard to accept. But these things happen. Remember the Willie MacRae murder has still to be solved. That was initially reported as suicide – a gunshot wound was found above his right ear. Why would someone whose car has come off the road then shoot himself?

'Aye, I know what you are talking about there. It has been a *cause celebre* ever since and we still haven't had all the answers,' responded Eilidh.

The murder of Willie MacRae, a lawyer and political activist, in 1985 on a quiet road in the Highlands had never been solved. MacRae was a controversial personality who had taken on the Nuclear Industry. There were too many inconsistencies in the evidence about the nature of his death. The fact that there had never been a Fatal Accident Inquiry nor the release of the post mortem data caused concern amongst many. Evidence that he was allegedly under surveillance from Special Branch and MI5 and from an ex-detective who was working as a private investigator all led to yet more unease.

The position of the Smith and Wesson pistol that had shot him, found twenty yards away from his car, was another anomaly. The briefcase which MacRae always kept with him because of burglaries at his home and office and which contained vital information about the Nuclear Industry was never found. The suspicions that it had been a wet disposal for political reasons had never gone away.

There was another silence as both thought about their own situation and the implications and possible consequences of Rodric's death.

'God, how is this going to go down in Scotland?' asked Eilidh eventually.

'I suspect all the correct formalities will be observed. You can expect the establishment to fall into line. The media will describe Rodric as a great if misguided Scot but he will be given full honours. That is the way the state deflates tension. Easier to do that than anything else. We can probably expect a royal pronouncement of deep sorrow by the end of the day.'

They sat in silence for a while, each lost in their own thoughts.

'I refuse to believe that he killed himself. He is not the sort of person to do that. Nothing I know of him suggests he was capable of such an act. It just isn't Rodric,' Eilidh said quietly. She was grappling with the realities of what had happened.

'Perhaps he was under tremendous mental strain. We know nothing about the circumstances in which he was held. Nothing at all. If he was in isolation who knows how he would have reacted. There are all sorts of ways in which a person can be ground down psychologically without torture being used. They dismantle your personality and belief system bit by bit until in the end you have lost your identity. It is all done with great subtlety,' said Murdo.

'You think that is possible?'

'Yes, but I have to say another scenario is playing in my mind: that he committed suicide to be a marytr to his beliefs and to the cause. He knew that the consequences politically for Westminster would be like an incendiary going off. For him independence was everything. He was prepared to give his life for it.'

'Difficult to believe but not impossible.'

'Not impossible at all.'

'No. I would struggle to accept that though. For me it is more likely that he was murdered.'

For the rest of the day they watched the BBC to see how it was being reported by the various pundits spouting forth their views. The mood in Scotland was predictably mixed but even Fraser's political enemies grudgingly paid their respects. 'A great but misguided Scot' was indeed the line that came across. Questions about the nature of his death were quickly brushed aside and few questioned the official line of suicide – at least not those being interviewed. A significant body of people began to ask questions.

The social media storm took off and conspiracy theories began to emerge in all shades from the utterly improbable to the theoretically possible. It was noticeable that no one from Rodric's family was interviewed. Eilidh and Murdo wondered what was going through their minds. The fact that the family did not even put a spokesperson forward was troubling.

#Fraser roared into cyberspace leaving a viral trail behind it. Internet providers noted spikes in the hours after the news was made public. It then tailed off only to pick up again as the conspiracy theorists began to get to grips with what might have happened. It was to last until long after Fraser had been buried and never entirely spluttered out.

Soon a crowd gathered outside Fraser's home in Cupar. Flowers were laid. Dignity was preserved. The overwhelming grief of so many was clear. Some from more distant parts of the country travelled to gather in silence outside his house. Others came together in George Square in Glasgow, Saltires flying at half-mast. In Edinburgh things were more muted. In Dundee the grief could have been cut with a knife.

All over Scotland groups of people came together to mourn the loss of this redoubtable man. Some compared him to William

Wallace while others quickly pointed out he had not suffered quite the same fate as that national hero.

Yes, there was pain and it was visceral. Those who had little truck with Fraser kept silent and watched the national mood with a measure of disbelief. 'How could so many have been taken in by the man?' they asked.

Chapter Nineteen

O N THE DAY OF THE funeral at St Giles' Cathedral, that temple of grey gloom, tens of thousands of Scots lined the route of the cortege. As the procession passed, spontaneous applause rippled along the road. Many realised they were saying farewell to a great Scot, regardless of their political and personal views. If ever there was a State Funeral this was one, in all but name. The media said as much.

The service was sombre but celebrated Fraser's life. Political friends and allies came together with his foes to admit that he was indeed a man who had the country's best interests at heart no matter if you thought he was wrong. The PM and the leader of the Opposition remained absent. Tributes flowed.

The Moderator's tone was measured. Only God could judge us, not our fellow man, was his message. He chose his words carefully, paying tribute to Fraser while touching on the frailties of humanity. His words caught the spirit of the occasion with a deft touch.

But it was above all the Gaelic Psalm singing that caught the mood: a mournful lament with such emotion as to still the nation as it was relayed by BBC Scotland.

There was some levity too to lift the proceedings. Political opponents and allies alike could all tell at least one funny story about Rodric. The Moderator's final words were that Scotland would never be the same without Fraser. Few disputed that.

The cortege then took Fraser's body on its last journey moving at a stately pace out of Edinburgh, over the Queensferry Crossing, the new road bridge over the Forth, and into Fife. It drove along the coastal route to St Andrews, passing through the fishing villages of the East Neuk, so beloved by Fraser. Small knots of people gathered along the route to pay their respects to one of their own. The route cut inland after Crail to the Howe of Fife, through Cupar and then across to Ceres and eventually to the cemetery on the outskirts of St Andrews. The mood in the town was solemn and subdued that day. A cruel cold wind hurled itself down from the Arctic and in from the grey of the North Sea. The *dreichne*ss of the day caught the spirit of most in the country as they laid to rest one of their greatest champions and sons. Love or loathe him Fraser would not be a footnote in the nation's history.

The interment was low-key. Only family and close friends attended. A piper played *The Flowers of the Forest* a short distance away. The media maintained a respectful distance. The Minister said the final words.

'Go forth unto your journey from this world, dear child of God, into the hands of the Father who made you ... we have entrusted our brother, Rodric to God's merciful keeping ... we now commit his body...'

Rodric's family stood, heads bowed, arms round each other. Sobs were muffled and the coffin was lowered into the ground. Shona, Rodric's wife, picked up a handful of earth and threw it on the coffin.

Rodric's children did the same. The wider family stood heads bowed too. It was one of those moments when time stands still, when the real seems unreal. It was as though they were all staring in at an event of which they were not a part. But it was all too real.

The country soon returned to its everyday comings and goings and yet politically everyone knew that there was now a gaping absence in the life of Scotland: the irreplaceable spirit of Fraser. Some secretly rejoiced at that new-found silence while others knew that there was unfinished business.

It is curious that in death we are so loved, thought Eilidh who had watched the proceedings on BBC television. She sat quiet, wishing she could have been there but fearful of arrest. Murdo, too, was subdued.

As they watched the cortege drive along Princes Street and then up to the Royal Mile they noticed the Union Jacks which fluttered from the Castle and buildings like the Bank of Scotland were at half-mast. The irony was not lost on many of the mourners. There were, of course, those who believed that Fraser had led the country to its greatest calamity. Secretly with close friends, they drank a toast of celebration to the man's passing but this they did in the privacy of their homes and clubs. The nation's nerve was raw, too raw for many.

'We should have gone,' Murdo said eventually as the proceedings came to an end.

'Yes, we should have done just that. I think I shall always regret it.' Eilidh had wept as the Gaelic Psalm singing in the service gripped her heart for it spoke of a nation in mourning in a way that nothing else could.

Three days after Fraser's funeral a Judicial Inquiry was set up under Lord Melksham, a man of fearsome integrity, it was rumoured in the media. Melksham was chosen for his care with words and his meticulous, albeit painfully slow, method of getting to the truth were major reasons for choosing him. The PM realised it was not so much what was revealed as the truth but more the way it would be presented and nuanced.

Murdo in his cynicism regarded this as part of the smoke-screen that was already being moved into place. He was not alone in this view.

'I have asked Lord Melksham to report back to Parliament within eighteen months,' the PM announced with a measure of pride and relief that the issue of Fraser's death was kicked so far down the road that events would have moved on. By that time he would be a mere footnote in history.

'As Members will be aware this is an extremely complex case and it will take time to get to the bottom of what has happened. I expect the final report when it is published to be beyond reproach.'

A few audible sighs were heard from the Opposition benches. To many, especially those with a strong interest in getting to the truth as quickly as possible, it was clear that the issue was being politically neutralised. The PM was aware that most of the UK's constituents had little real interest in the case. Of course he realised that a large section of the Scottish population would not accept the findings whatever they were. Sutton realised even as he announced the Committee that it would take more than eighteen months. Ideally, he wanted it stretched out for at least three years. The Maxwellisation ploy had its uses, after all.

The PM's Party smirked their approval at his handling of the delicate matter of Fraser's death. He was slapped on the back by both the Chancellor and Home Secretary while MPs on the bench behind lent forward to congratulate him. The PM was no stranger to sycophancy.

The media and commentariat was broadly supportive of the PM's announcement. It seemed as though the Government had successfully weathered the gathering storm or, at the least, delayed it.

Chapter Twenty

IN HER GRIEF EILIDH BECAME aware of a spirit moving within her. It was as though both Rodric and Rab were pointing her in a particular direction. She felt a burden of expectation placed on her shoulders. As she walked along the beach and looked towards the Cullins it became clear what she had to do. Her mission in life was to pick up the torch that they had set down and to carry it that final mile. There was little doubt that she would do it, even if it meant giving her life.

When Eilidh spoke to Murdo about her thoughts and her sense of mission he wasn't surprised.

'You must do all it takes,' he said. 'I'll support you all the way.'

'I didn't think you would do anything else, you PJ,' mocked Eilidh with a wide grin on her face. 'Anyway you have no choice, do you?'

'I suppose not,' he responded with a wry smile. 'The monstrous regiment of women is upon us.'

'Aye, we are that, PJ.'

Murdo understood the weight of responsibility that Eilidh bore. It was almost as though her fate had been predetermined. It seemed uncanny to him but he knew that in life some things were just so. Freewill had been cast aside for fate. It was her destiny.

Eilidh spoke in such terms too, not knowing what roads she would be led down or what lay ahead for her. She wasn't even confident that it was not all just a delusion. Yet soon her doubts subsided. This was her path. Whether or not she would reach her destination was entirely another matter. She simply knew that she had to pick up the torch and carry it forward with all the strength she could muster.

A while later, Eilidh discussed this with her mother. Fiona smiled. 'You are doing what is expected of you, Eilidh, and something tells me you will not fail.' Eilidh often felt that her mother had *an da shealladh:* literally two sights or more commonly second sight, although she never made any claim to that gift of insight. It was said to be a gift that some islanders had.

In later years Eilidh was to reflect on that conversation with her mother. Sometimes the hand of history reached out and picked us up whether we liked it or not. That was Murdo's view.

'You realise that we are HVIs as our transatlantic cousins would say?'

'What are HVIs?'

'High-value individuals,' Murdo replied. 'They won't stop until they find us. I suppose in a way it is just a matter of time before that happens. I'm not sure we should stay here. It isn't safe. We have to keep moving, perhaps leave the country altogether. For the authorities it's all about the three Fs: find, fix and finish. That could be what happened to Rodric. It could be what happens to us.'

'You mean we could simply be disposed of?'

'Yes, if that is what they want. Accidents, suicide ... these things happen. There is, of course, a big *stooshie* initially in the media but then the world moves on. Some remember these things though. We know the technology that the Surveillance State has at its disposal. It is virtually impossible to live outside its boundaries. They probably know where we are now anyway but have simply chosen not to arrest us.'

Eilidh and Murdo spent the next hour discussing what they should do. From media reports it was clear that by now most of the top tier activists had been interned. What was less clear was how many had gone into hiding.

'Let's face it. Sooner or later the door of the croft will be battered down and we'll be arrested and then God alone knows what will happen,' Murdo said.

'Yes, I can see that but where do we go? Moving around the country with road blocks and all the surveillance technology with its high-definition capability and computers make it almost impossible.'

'*Almost* impossible, not completely impossible.'

'I have a few friends here on Skye who would shelter me but I would need to keep moving around. I honestly think that's my best bet and probably yours too,' said Eilidh.

'Perhaps we should split up,' Murdo ventured.

'What would be the point? Where would you go? We wouldn't be able to contact each other. Probably we won't see each other again. We must assume that most or even all of our friends and fellow activists have either been arrested or gone to ground.'

When Ian delivered food later in the day he was brought into the discussion. He agreed that they weren't safe to stay indefinitely in the croft but equally he was uncertain that anywhere else would be any safer.

'Moving around at the moment is nae easy. Roadblocks and checkpoints are being set up at random. There is nae telling where they'll be. Whit aboot leaving the country altogether? A friend, runs a trawler out of Portree. He's sympathetic tae the cause. I'm sure he could take you tae the Faroes, Norway or even Ireland before the winter storms break.'

Murdo had read the exploits of the Shetland Bus during the Second World War and favoured Norway. Eilidh was less certain. She wanted to stay in Scotland.

'I have no intention of fleeing from my own country,' she said eventually and with finality. 'I know enough people in Skye who will help us and look after us.'

'You're right,' said Ian finally. 'We'll do it somehow.'

'I've got to get the motorcycle back to Calum as soon as possible,' Murdo said.

'How will you get back here?'

'I'm sure Calum will help, somehow.'

'Can you be sure of him? Is he one of us?'

'No, he's an agnostic. He will put friendship above all else.'

'Really?'

'Yes, really. He's that sort of person.'

'Okay. Take the bike back whenever you want. How long will it take you to get across to Fife?'

'A few hours. I'll overnight with him and his wife and make my way back as soon as I can.'

'Fine. Do it but I don't think it is worth the risk.'

Chapter Twenty-one

THREE DAYS LATER BEFORE DAWN Murdo left the farmhouse and pointed the bike towards the Skye Bridge. He had worked out his route: Invergarry, Fort William, Glencoe, Crainlarich, Killin, Aberfeldy then skirting Perth to Newburgh where Calum lived.

The weather was set fair: one of those magnificent autumnal days when the western highlands looked their most awesome.

McLeish received the text from Creyke he had been waiting for. 'Contact restored. Stand by'. Eilidh and Murdo were not to know that their presence at the croft had been reported some days ago and they were now under constant surveillance.

Later another text arrived. 'Wait in Fort William for meeting.'

McLeish didn't need to think what this meant. Two days later he was heading north to Fort William on his Fireblade.

The next text read simply 'Tomorrow morning. Route A82. Join procession on outskirts of FW. Will txt ETA on outskirts of FW.'

McLeish checked in at a B&B, fuelled up the Fireblade and went to get a fish supper. He was careful not to drink that evening. He needed a clear head and a sharp mind for the chase. He had to be at the top of his game on the Blade. There was no room for error or misjudgment. It was entirely possible that his target was a better rider than he was. It was also possible that he was riding a more powerful bike, although very few could outpace the Blade.

If his target was heading south he would take the A82 up Glencoe and then drop down to Bridge of Orchy. It was a route he knew well. Just outside Achallader there is a sharp right-hander which could test the most experienced rider especially if he was riding on the edge. If he failed to unsettle his target there he would have to wait until the next serious bend outside Tyndrum. Once the bikes entered Glencoe the road was a fast one. He expected to be riding at high speeds.

McLeish's plan was to follow his target at a discreet distance out of Fort William and then as he entered Glencoe apply pressure by closing in – just enough to make his target nervous that he was being followed. He knew his adversary would be suspicious given that he was on the wanted list.

He texted Crekye. 'Would help to know bike.'

'Will tell you tomorrow,' came the reply.

At 7.30 McLeish was up, showered and breakfasted when the text he was waiting for came through. 'ETA at FW 10.30ish. S1000RR.'

'Shit, shit, shit,' cursed McLeish. The BMW S1000RR was legendary for speed and handling. His target went up in his estimation. Here was a man to be reckoned with. Instinctively, he knew that it was going to be a nerve-wracking, difficult day. Riding at high speeds was dangerous.

It was only when Murdo entered Glencoe with its glowering mountains and its heavy atmosphere that he noticed a biker in his rear-view mirror. He dropped his speed in case it was an unmarked police motorcycle. The biker behind also dropped speed so that the distance between them remained roughly the same.

It was not difficult for Murdo to feel a degree of paranoia. He tried to set this to the back of his mind and enjoy the ride across this most glorious of routes. He did, however, keep a watchful eye on the biker behind him.

By the time Murdo had reached the top of the Glen his thoughts focussed on the bike behind him. Suddenly it seemed to accelerate rapidly to catch up with him. It was a fight-or-flight moment. Murdo instinctively opened the throttle and the bike surged forward rapidly. He had not thought of any other course of action.

At first the bike behind him fell back as Murdo accelerated, but that only seemed to last seconds. The rider behind now accelerated too and the distance between them shortened. Murdo's mind spun into over-drive. Was this someone just wanting a burn-up or was it something more sinister, more dangerous? If it was the police they would surely radio ahead and he would be stopped at a road-block. He reckoned he had at least a hundred mile range left.

Once out of the Glen the road opened out with long straight stretches, sweeping corners and vistas. He decided to make a run for it and take his chances. He knew he was riding on the edge of his capabilities when any minor miscalculation in cornering or road-positioning would be fatal. The cars he overtook seemed to be standing still.

The biker behind was still gaining on him – not significantly – but gaining nonetheless. As the road started to drop down towards Achallader Murdo noticed that his pursuer had accelerated rapidly and was now only a matter of metres behind.

Murdo was decelerating to enter the sharp bend. He was being pursued aggressively: it was his skill against his opponent's. It was as though his opponent was trying to force him off the road. Adrenalin hit his system like a hammer: this was about survival.

As the sharp bend approached the Blade was close on his tail without touching his bike. Murdo knew if he could hold him off until the apex of the sharp bend his acceleration out of the curve on the RR would be almost impossible to hold in speed. He just had to get to that apex first.

Suddenly, it all slowed down, as though he was living through a slow motion movie. Time seemed to stand still. The bike behind him was now level with him as the apex of the bend approached. He touched the brakes to steady the RR as it hit the apex but his pursuer edged ahead in that vital millisecond.

Murdo knew he had nowhere to go. He had run out of tarmac.

McLeish looked back in his rear-view mirror and saw Murdo lose control and tumble as the bike failed to take the corner. McLeish knew Murdo's chances of survival with a fall at that speed were minimal. He accelerated.

At Tyndrum he stopped to pick up fuel and to send a text to Creyke. 'All well. Heading home'.

'Good. Pleased,' was the reply.

McLeish felt satisfied. He was back in business and could still put it together. His mind re-played what had happened over and over again as he made his way back to Glasgow at a leisurely speed. Only now did he wonder what his victim had done and who he had upset so seriously. He told himself that was no business of his. These things happen and someone has to do them. He was good at his job and knew it.

What McLeish hadn't realised was that a drone had been following the pursuit in high definition. Someone somewhere in a command centre had just had the vicarious thrill of watching. He knew his boss would be satisfied.

Eilidh heard of the death of a biker later that day on BBC Scotland. Although Murdo's name wasn't mentioned she knew it was him. She felt physically sick. Their relationship was only days old when it happened. She struggled to believe it. The time they had together was just a dream. She wondered if it had even happened.

BBC Scotland reported later that evening that a witness had seen what had happened. One biker seemed to be in pursuit of the other. Eilidh now understood exactly what had happened. It was no accident.

Waves of grief crashed over her like an Atlantic storm making landfall. First Rab, then Rodric and now Murdo – all in such a short time. It was impossible for her to take it in. She thought of their few days together. They had made love only hours before. She had surprised herself with Murdo to find that such happiness could exist, that two such different people could be as one. She felt utterly empty. She sobbed in Fiona's arms.

Nothing seemed to matter. She was moved from croft to croft almost on a daily basis under cover of dark. Drones were now being deployed and it was impossible for her to go out freely.

Alister, Fiona and Ian rallied round her and wrapped her in their love and support. Megan stayed with her during her moves from one place to the next. The dog seemed to have a sense of Eilidh's deep sadness and withdrawal into herself and was increasingly attentive.

In the long hours alone and indoors, Eilidh could only read, listen and watch the media. The story they told suggested that the 'Yes' campaign had been totally destroyed and declared illegal. Her whole raison d'etre seemed to have been snatched from her. It was not hard to sink into a slough of depression. The wind and the rain that assailed Skye during those few days were in keeping with her dark mood.

Chapter Twenty-two

THAT SUNDAY EMMA WENT ACROSS to Hampstead for lunch with her family. Will suggested that they go for a walk up through Hampstead village and onto the Heath towards Parliament Hill. It was something they always enjoyed.

It was a sharp, autumnal day: crystal clear blue skies, swirling brown and russet leaves in the October wind. Winter was knocking on the door. Children and dogs ran about, kites soared, huge passenger jets lumbered across the sky on the way to Heathrow – the final few minutes of a flight that had started from anywhere from Vancouver to Singapore.

'Have you been in touch with Murdo recently?' Will asked.

'I've tried several times but his phone has been dead. To be honest, dad, I've given up.'

'Things were finished between you weren't they?'

Emma paused for a moment.

'Yes, I suppose they were.'

'You don't sound that convinced.'

'Well, he is special. We got on so well and, frankly, I haven't met anyone else like him.'

'If you don't mind me asking – why did it end?'

'I am not entirely sure. A long-distance relationship is never easy. Then even when we were together latterly he didn't seem to be with me in spirit. He seemed somewhere else mentally and emotionally. I wondered if he had met someone else but I was afraid to ask. We ended it by mutual agreement a few months ago. There were no recriminations. We said we would remain friends. For a while we did phone each other but then the intervals between calls became longer. What did you and mum think of him? You never really said.'

'We liked him a lot. We thought you were good for each other. I liked his intellect and his sense of humour.'

Will suddenly stopped as though in mid-flow.

'Emma, there is something I have to tell you. You have probably not seen this in the news – it was a short item in one of the Scottish dailies that I read online. A biker was killed on the A82 yesterday.'

Emma stopped and looked into her father's eyes. 'Why are you telling me this? It could have been anyone. What makes you think it was Murdo?'

Will took a deep breath. 'The thought crossed my mind when I saw the news item. I phoned a friend who knows about what is going on and was told that it was Murdo. Of course, it's just another accident of no particular significance to the media here and so is unlikely to be reported.'

Will put his arms and held Emma tightly in a vain attempt to absorb her pain. She started to sob quietly. It was then that Will knew the truth. that she still loved Murdo.

They stood for a few minutes as he rocked her back and forth in his arms. Gradually she regained her composure.

'Do you know anything else about the accident? How did it happen?'

'The news item quoted an eyewitness as saying that there were two bikes travelling at great speed as one was either chasing the other or racing it. The second bike seemed to be gaining on the first when they went into a series of bends and the first biker lost control on a corner. He must have been riding beyond his limit. I am sure that he was being chased.'

'Why in God's name would anyone chase him? What has been going on?'

'Emma, you have been following events in Scotland, and know what has been happening. Murdo was sent north for a purpose – you must know that. At a guess, I would say that he went native. He has probably upset some important people.'

'What happened to the other biker?'

'According to the eyewitness he continued riding and didn't stop. That's what makes me believe it was a chase. If they were friends racing each other the second biker would have certainly stopped.'

'I had my suspicions. I sensed for a while before we split up that he was going through some sort of inner conflict – that must have been it. His country – Scotland – came first in the end.'

There was a silence as Emma digested the news.

'Yes, you're probably right. I don't know whether to admire him for that or regard him as a gullible fool.'

They walked on for a few minutes until they reached the top of Parliament Hill.

'I think I admire him more for it. To have that degree of belief in something is inspiring. Of course, I always knew he cared about the country – all Scots do whatever their political views. Sometimes I envy just how much they care for it. I can almost begin to understand the emotional journey that he took to bring him to that point.'

'Yes. I agree with you. In my sad world mammon is God. Nothing else seems to matter at all. Beliefs are tossed to one side in the worship of money. Depressing really.'

'I want to walk by myself, dad, if you don't mind,' Emma said.

'I understand. Try and be back for tea later.'

Emma walked and walked, her mind going over every little detail of her relationship with Murdo ... how they met ... the happiness they shared ...the fun they had ... their sheer joy in a shared life in those early stages. There were times when she wasn't quite sure which one of them had ended the relationship first. The more she thought about it, it became clear that it had petered out because Murdo wanted it to. Maybe he had wanted to shield her from what was going to happen. Maybe he knew about the crisis that was going to unfold. Yes, that is what had happened she decided.

After two hours she made her way home. She needed to talk now. She wondered about Murdo's parents. She couldn't begin to imagine the grief that would be engulfing them. She wondered whether to phone them but decided to wait until the news was official.

Three days later Emma received a phonecall from Murdo's mother.

'Yes. It was an accident apparently. An eye-witness said it seemed he was being chased by another biker – someone who didn't stop once the accident had happened. Of course, you probably know by now what he had been doing.'

'Yes, I guessed although he never said anything.' Emma replied.

'We were sorry when the two of you drifted apart. I want you to know that. We aren't completely sure in our own minds what Murdo had been going through, what his views were. Of course, we knew his work up there was important but we never knew its exact nature but then something obviously changed. We are certain of that. He never spoke to any of the family about it.'

Emma expressed her sadness and spoke of her sense of loss.

'I wish it had all been different. Now that I look back on it all, I feel I should have made a greater effort for him and our relationship. I was too wrapped up in my career and life here in London.'

'You mustn't feel like that,' said Murdo's mother. 'We should meet up after the funeral.'

'Yes. Definitely. I would like that.'

Two days after Murdo's accident Eilidh was standing in the kitchen when she saw a couple walking up the track towards the croft. They were not dressed as walkers and didn't look like plain clothes police. They were in city clothes. She wondered what to do. If she exited by the back the chances were they would see her and call after her. She didn't want to appear as though she was acting suspiciously so decided to remain put. As the couple got closer to the croft Eilidh's heart started to race and her stomach churned. She felt trapped.

They approached the front door and knocked loudly. She decided not to answer. The knocking became more aggressive.

'Eilidh,' a woman shouted, 'We know you are in there. We want to talk to you – urgently. We are not here to harm you.'

Eilidh wondered if it was a ruse.

'We're not leaving until we have spoken to you.'

Eilidh walked across the hallway to open the door. She was confronted by a smartly dressed man and woman both in their mid-forties.

'You had better come in,' Eilidh murmured, unsure of what to expect next. 'Who are you? How did you know where I was?'

The man spoke. He seemed just a little too sure of himself. He spoke with a cultivated Scottish accent.

'Can we sit down?'

Eilidh pointed to the chairs.

'What exactly do you want?'

'We represent people who want to remain anonymous.'

'First, tell me how you knew where to find me.?' Eilidh's mind was racing. She was still trying to work out how she had been found.

'It was relatively easy,' the man answered quietly.

'You haven't answered my question. This conversation is not going anywhere until I know how you found me and who you represent.'

They were hesitant for a moment.

'We represent several business people and land-owners.'

'And how you found me?'

'There are good people on Skye who care for you and also care for Scotland. You are held in very high regard here, you know. The people I represent in Edinburgh have always kept a close eye on the party and its personalities. It has been in their interests to do so. You have always been regarded as the leader in waiting after Rodric although no one in their wildest dreams anticipated these circumstances.'

'And?' Eilidh was uncertain about her feelings towards the couple. They clearly represented powerful vested interests – not something that was likely to endear them to her.

'There is a nation out there waiting to be led out of this crisis. We think you are that person and we are not alone in that view.'

Eilidh had never thought of herself in those terms. Yes, at times she had fantasised about standing for leader of the party when Rodric stood down but that was not expected for many years.

'I don't know what to say.'

The woman spoke, 'We have the contacts with London that could bring about a settlement and let them off the hook. To be frank they realise they have bitten off more than they can chew. There is a growing consensus in Edinburgh and London that the PM has mis-judged the whole situation and has pursued the wrong policies towards Scotland. We are getting this from senior people in his party.'

'They want off the hook?'

'Yes. Precisely.'

'We can ensure you get a safe right of passage from here. You won't be arrested,' said the man.

'Why should I believe you?'

'Put it this way we could have had you taken in by now if we had chosen to by revealing your location.'

'I need to think. I need to talk to one or two people. I can't just take over the leadership of the party without the consent of its members.'

The woman pulled a card out of her pocket with her address and phone number.

'Here, take this. Phone me once you have thought about it. We'll ensure safe passage and a cessation of the State of Emergency as soon as we can.'

'You must understand one thing: I will never be beholden to the vested interests you represent. If by chance I do end up leading my party I shall govern for all Scots not for any particular group.'

'We thought you would say that. We are not surprised. Bridge building needs to be done both within Scotland and outside. Our concern is for the country as a whole not simply the people we represent. They expect no favours.'

Eilidh made them tea and they spoke about the events of the last few days.

'I think we may have done it, thank God,' the man said to the woman as they walked back down the track.

'God, I really hope we have. I was impressed by Eilidh. She has presence and charisma. I think she will make a good First Minister.'

'There is some way to go before we get to that point.'

It took months before most of the activists who had been interned were released on licence in dribs and drabs. Some refused licence and remained in custody to the embarrassment of the government who wanted an end to the problem.

It gradually leaked out that certain key figures in the independence movement had never been found. Whether they were in hiding in Scotland or had fled abroad was never known.

From time to time Dougie came down from the police station at Portree to carry out a half-hearted search for Eilidh. He would always phone the farm first to give notice that he would be there in the next hour or so. Alister and Fiona always welcomed him and he would come in and have a cup of tea with them. Little did Dougie know that Eilidh had already been found by the security forces.

Dougie never said openly where his sympathies lay but they were never in doubt. He always left with the words, 'If Eilidh is in touch do say that I was asking after her.' This was followed by a wink.

Chapter Twenty-three

THE NATIONAL NEWS, EVEN ALLOWING for bias, did suggest that Scotland was not returning to normality. Sporadic acts of civil disobedience continued. Transport strikes, power cuts, refusal to pay gas and electricity bills or council tax all struck at the heart of the country. Curfews were routinely ignored. Direct Rule from London proved increasingly impossible while the divisions in Scottish society were as visceral as ever.

Wyndham soon began to realise that Direct Rule was no longer a credible option. Events had moved beyond that point. Intense discussions in London and Edinburgh on policy options continued. The volatility of the markets and the withdrawal of capital by overseas investors continued relentlessly.

Five weeks after the start of the State of Emergency Wyndham was at Number Ten for the weekly Cabinet meeting. There was only one item on the agenda: Scotland. Wyndham pulled no punches when asked to report.

'Our position in unsustainable I have to say with deep regret. The depth of feeling in Scotland across a wide social and political spectrum will not accept Direct Rule. The State of Emergency has failed. We have lacked the security resources to impose it. We can no longer count on Police Scotland to act on our behalf. We have no alternative but to reach a settlement with the separatists and those unionists who have changed sides because of their anger at the way the government has imposed Direct Rule. The Scottish Parliament needs to be re-convened and we need to start negotiations as soon as possible.'

There were murmurs of agreement from around the table. The PM looked distinctly uncomfortable although he was not surprised by what Wyndham said.

'I would like to thank Stewart for everything he has tried to do in Edinburgh. I gave him a poisoned chalice and he has acquitted himself as well as can be expected in the circumstances. I suppose we under-estimated the Scots and their national pride. We have totally mishandled this. The stakes were high. We were trying to protect the territorial integrity of the UK, nothing less. I knew that. I knew also that we were following a high risk strategy that could fail and that has happened. I take full responsibility for that and I feel that it is in the best interests of the country that I stand down as soon as is possible.'

There was a stunned silence around the table as Ministers quickly calculated the consequences of Sutton's resignation. Wyndham was pleased. His chance of a leadership bid had come quicker than he had anticipated. Carol would be delighted.

It was Gavin Buckland, the Chancellor, who was the first to speak after what seemed to be a long pause as Cabinet Ministers absorbed the PM's words.

'Prime Minister, I know I can speak for everyone round this table when I say that you have provided quite remarkable leadership to this country over the last few years. I am sure we shall all be saddened by your departure.'

There were murmurs of agreement followed by spontaneous applause. Wyndham could not help the mischievous thought that they were applauding because Sutton was resigning.

The meeting then settled down to discuss how the Government should proceed with negotiations.

'Who exactly are we going to negotiate with, Stewart?' the PM asked.

'An initial approach has been made to Eilidh MacLeod who was widely regarded as Fraser's likely successor. You may remember we located her hiding place in Skye some days ago but chose not to have her interned.'

'Ah, yes. That woman.'

Lachie was released after two months in a detention centre somewhere in East Anglia: *Stalag Caledonia* the inmates christened it. At the end of a programme of 'detoxification' he was given a rail ticket back to Scotland. The prisoners had been able to follow events in the country. There were widespread celebrations when the State of Emergency and Direct Rule ended. Lachie's views had hardened, despite the 'detoxification' programme which the inmates were happy to play along with.

The Scotland they returned to was different. The Scottish Parliament was again in session and negotiations were underway with London.

Mhairi, Isla and Jennie met his train at Leuchars. There was great joy at being together again. Once the girls had gone to bed Lachie and Mhairi caught up with each other.

'And where do ye stand now, my maun?' Mhairi asked.

'More committed than ever,' Lachie answered.

'Guid. I expected nothing less.'

Chapter Twenty-four

A YEAR LATER EILIDH BECAME First Minister – a title she had wanted to keep – of an independent Scotland. It had been a tumultuous twelve months but good sense had prevailed. Wyndham, to the surprise of many but not Carol, was the new PM and had conducted the negotiations with Scotland. Negotiations had been tense and difficult but eventually a financial settlement was reached without rancor. The border remained 'soft' and Scotland acquired its own currency. Many people in England wished the new country well and friendly noises were made between the two respective governments. Yes, there was healing to be done and that would take a few years but Scotland had now been welcomed into the family of nations.

The Melksham Inquiry into the circumstances of Rodric's death still had to report its findings even if most people now thought they knew the truth. Some said that Fraser had martyred himself to the cause of independence. Others disputed this vehemently and said he had been murdered by the state or by one of its freelance agents, a so-called wet disposal as it was described. Still others said that he had been driven to it by harsh interrogation methods which included sleep deprivation, hooding and white noise. It was to remain a *cause celebre*. The commentariat had no doubts that the Inquiry would never get to the truth. Few disputed that, regardless of which interpretation they veered towards.

Relations with the remainder of the UK had been tense ever since the since the beginning of the crisis and the subsequent events but ultimately Westminster bowed to the inevitable and had the grace to send a message of good wishes to Eilidh, her government and the people of Scotland. Eilidh, on behalf of the Scots, thanked the people of the rest of the UK.

Lachie, Mhairi, Isla and Jennie secured places on the Royal Mile by arriving before dawn on the Day of Independence. Many others had the same idea. As the early streaks of dawn light crossed the sky people realised they were about to witness one of the very greatest days in the history of the country. Hearts swelled with pride. Many knew they would struggle with emotion when the moment of independence arrived.

Giles Sutton and Stewart Wyndham had accepted Eilidh's invitation to witness the celebrations. They did so with a mixture of relief, heavy hearts and a sense of personal failure. Eilidh personally welcomed them warmly despite the difficulties of the last few months.

On the stroke of midnight Scottish independence was formally declared. The esplanade in front of Edinburgh Castle was bathed in light as the ceremony took place. Pipe bands massed. The Union Jack was slowly pulled down as the Saltire was raised. When it reached the top of the flagpole, the cannon at Edinburgh Castle was fired and the crowds exploded into cheering, a cheering that echoed down the Royal Mile across to Princes Street and through the land. The international media circus was everywhere.

A thousand pipers including many from the Scottish diaspora played O *Flower of Scotland*, the anthem that some disliked but which had been overwhelmingly chosen by the people. Never did the song resonate so strongly.

Crowds gathered throughout the country to watch the celebrations on massive screens. Some wept tears of joy, others embraced. Round the globe wherever there were Scots, people watched with pride.

Others stared at their screens in disbelief and muttered 'They'll be hell to pay for this. Wait and see. And don't say I didn't warn you, Jessie.' But they were in a minority, truculent in mood and deeply sceptical of the country's new direction.

The joy was contagious. There was an outpouring of emotion from this supposedly dour nation. It was a difficult day for those who had bitterly opposed independence and the splitting up of the UK. But many had grown used to the idea. Inevitably some would never accept independence and moved South, afraid amongst other things that the new Scottish currency would decimate their wealth.

When Eilidh walked up to the dais to deliver her speech the cheering reached a new crescendo. Every Scot, separatist and unionist, knew only too well the heavy emotional and physical price she had paid to lead her country to this moment.

Now as she faced the people of an independent nation for the first time as its First Minister, she was acutely aware of her own emotions which she struggled to contain. In those few paces to the dais it was as though she was walking in slow motion. Faces flashed in front of her: Rab, Rodric and, yes, Murdo.

Once at the dais she waited for the cheering to die down as she regained her customary composure.

'It is with a great sense of history I stand before you today my fellow Scots. I am well aware there are many who set out on this journey who are not with us today, men and women for whom no sacrifice was too

great for this beloved country of ours. We shall not forget them nor their contribution. Nor shall we forget Rodric Fraser's contribution for he must rank as one of the very greatest Scots. To those who joined in that long march to reach this day I say with pride and humility, we have achieved what once seemed impossible.

'I also know that independence has fractured us as a nation and that for many this is a difficult day. I am aware, too, that these wounds run deep and may take some time to heal. We must move forward in a spirit of reconciliation.

'To those who opposed independence I would say we are all Scots, whatever our differences of opinion. Let me hold out the hand of friendship and invite you to help build a better and socially just nation. You are our brothers and sisters. We are all part of the same family. We must move forward together. In a spirit of humility we know the hurt that many of you feel, a pain which we ourselves have felt in defeat in the past. We are now one nation whatever our views.

'To those of you who sacrificed so much for this day and for the cause of independence I say that our work starts today and Scotland needs you more than ever. May God guide us in the days ahead and may we remember those who sacrificed so much for this day and who are not here with us. Their place in our hearts is secure.

'There is something more to a nation than the sum total of its peoples, its history and the magnificence of its landscapes. More too than its GDP. It is that indefinable spirit. It is almost as though the country – Scotland – has its own being, its own character. We all owe a deep sense of loyalty to that entity, whatever our differences.

'Scotland now steps out onto the world stage with good wishes from around the world. Of all the messages of goodwill those from England, Wales and Northern Ireland are the most precious. We may no longer be part of the United Kingdom as it was once constituted but we are your closest friends and your neighbours. We shall always be at your side when you need us. We shall always be your closest ally.

'We must move on from the last four years and forge a new relationship based on respect and trust and mutual understanding.

'Let us go forward in hope and set fear aside for this country of ours has much to offer the world. This day is ours. Let us go forward in pride and determination, with unbowed heads and soaring spirits.'

Throughout the UK the celebrations were watched with ambivalence. There were those who were glad to get rid of the FJs while for many others there was a sadness that what had been a great union for over three hundred years no longer existed.

The King's speech to the Scottish nation was muted and spoke of the bonds between the various parts of the kingdom which would remain. Nothing would alter that. The positive was emphasised and the difficulties of the previous months were passed over discreetly. All agreed it was a well-crafted speech which set a generous spirit of goodwill. He finished with a flourish, 'I am proud of the Scottish blood flows in my veins and I shall dedicate myself to working towards peace and harmony between the constituent parts of my kingdom.'

Even the many republicans, of whom the country seemed to have an abundance, could not fault the speech.

After the celebration in front of the castle the crowds surged down the Royal Mile to the Parliament behind the massed pipe bands. Streamers floated down. Eilidh made her way down the Royal Mile, floating on a tide of well-wishers. Lachie, Mhairi, Isla and Jennie followed Eilidh as her special guests.

The nation partied as never before: fireworks shot into the night air, car horns sounded, the police smiled at revellers, streamers floated down from buildings. A massive Saltire was emblazoned on the Castle ramparts. George Square in Glasgow, always a focal point was wild with excitement and celebration. Eilidh had made a special visit to Glasgow and to George Square on the previous day to be greeted by tens of thousands of enthusiastic supporters. She thanked the City of Glasgow for its special part in helping to achieve independence.

The following day there was the occasional hang-over.

On the 20th September Eilidh made her own personal pilgrimage to Skye. She walked along the beach where she had walked many times before with Rab. It was here she had made her decision which affected the history of her nation. She looked over to the Cuillins. Sgurr Alasdair and Sgurr Dearg were crowned in light while cloud touched the lower levels of the mountains. Megan trotted at her side, looking up at her expectantly every few paces to wait for her next words.

She felt Rab's presence in the gentle wind as though he was saying to her, 'Well done, my bonnie lass, well done.'

Tears rolled down her cheeks. She lifted her eyes up to the mountains as she had done many months before when she made the decision, a decision that led to the independence of her country: troublesome, querelous, magnificent Scotland.

'I shall lift up mine eyes to the hills from whence cometh my help.'